Seven Days to Tell You

Seven Days to Tell You

by

Ruby Soames

Hookline Books

Bookline & Thinker Ltd

Published by Hookline Books 2011
Bookline & Thinker Ltd
#231, 405 King's Road
London SW10 0BB
Tel: 0845 116 1476
www.booklinethinker.com

The right of Ruby Soames to be identified as the author of this work
has been asserted in accordance with the Copyright, Designs and
Patents Act 1988.

A CIP catalogue for this book is available from the British Library.

This book is a work of fiction. Names, characters, places and
incidents are either a product of the author's imagination or are used
fictitiously.
ISBN: 9780956517784

Cover design by Donald McColl
Printed and bound by Lightning Source UK

For Mimi and Xan

thursday night

I don't hear the key in the door when the intruder enters my home. Nor does any light show when he steps in from the hall and there is no click when he slowly releases the door handle behind him. He waits inside my flat. He sucks the air into his lungs without making a sound. The winter wind escapes from his clothes.

His pupils widen as he pans the room. Shapes, in varying shades of grey, claim his focus. The cushion on the sofa has retained a half-moon compression left from where I'd been lying in front of the TV. There is a damp towel twisted around a chair leg with a near-empty bottle of wine next to it. I was too tired to put the wine away. It ferments next to a box of chocolates left open with a card depicting a teddy bear holding up a sign saying, *Thank you!*

His eyes take in the remains of my last few hours.

The intruder treads into the room as cars project silver balloons of light over the ceiling. He touches my coat as it lies collapsed over a chair. He moves back a little, wary of my *iPhone* earphones dangling out of my pocket, they sway to the silent jig of an underground train. He moves his head from one side of the room to the other, the darkness around him is losing. A plate of half-eaten lasagne is now hard and congealed in its microwaveable carton. The street lamp illuminates the faces smiling out from my photographs. The man looks at each picture without moving from where he stands: my face, tanned and smiling from holiday destinations or miscellaneous landmarks in my life: graduation, weddings, parties; the shelf below is devoted to photographs of my nieces and nephews.

To his left is the kitchen which is separated from the main room by what the estate agent called a 'breakfast bar.' Not that I've ever had breakfast there, I use the surface of the low dividing wall to dump my keys and post, though sometimes, if I have time or people over, I'll put fruit in a large, hand-painted salad bowl that was a wedding present. He sees a bunch of flowers still wrapped in cellophane in the sink half-filled with water. The petals have been pushed uncomfortably against the frosted windows.

He holds his breath as if the air will make him lighter as he walks across the living room. Then he stops outside my bedroom. Since I was a little girl, I've always slept with the door open the width of my mother's foot. He pushes the door lightly with the tips of his fingers, wide enough so he can creep past.

The wooden-slat blinds in my bedroom almost shut out the street lights so he feels the way to my bed. I still don't hear anything, even the thud of his shoes dropping to the floor, the muffled fall of his jumper, T-shirt. He unbuttons his jeans, lets them slide down to his knees, shakes them off his feet. Even a few inches away, he must feel the heat from my body on his thighs. He bends right down to my face to peel off his socks and lower his boxer shorts.

My sleep isn't disturbed by the movement of someone undressing so close to me. Even when he sits on the edge of the bed, lifts the duvet and curls onto the mattress. And not when he slides over and touches my skin.

Not once do I wake up with the knowledge that someone is in my home and in my bed, placing a hand on my heart and holding it there.

Our heads lie on the same pillow. I turn and breathe in what you exhale.

Somewhere, deep in my unconscious, the person I was re-assembles itself, your hand on my back and I flow into you, I know that you are back, that it is you touching my hair and stroking my face, laying your mouth into my deadened hand, folding my palm around your kisses.

The coolness of your skin chases my blood under the skin's surface. You draw me into you, the capillary effect of desire - I can't resist moving into you although I fight reaching out for you - there have been too many times, too many disappointments. There was that dream once, almost as real as this, when I found you in the hospital car park curled up in the back of my grand-dad's Morris Minor. I said 'Marc, we've been looking everywhere for you! We thought you were dead...' and you said, 'Katherine, I was just sleeping,' and I said, 'Sleeping? For three years?' and you said, 'I was so tired, so tired.' We laughed. I told you everything we had done to find you, things that people said about you, the ways we tried to understand you. And it seemed all so funny...then the dream started to vanish and I couldn't get it back. I woke up. I still don't know how I got through that day. To lose you, to find you, and lose you again.

You stretch your thigh over me, hook me in its grip and pull me into you. You kiss my neck and I open my fingers to feel the ends of your hair. You nuzzle into the hollow under my collar bone, nip around my ear. You have returned.

That's what I keep saying in my head, 'He's back, he's back...' And you feel the same to me as you always did, although more bristly, perhaps your hands are a little rougher; have you put on weight or are you more muscular? But it is you. I've had these dreams before, but this is real. I don't want to notice the differences, I don't want to open my eyes or speak. I don't even try to find out whether you are still wearing your wedding ring. Hold me close and don't let the light in.

Now you draw me nearer to you, your hands knead my stomach, mould and squeeze me into a foetus which only you can feed, touch, or bring to life. You drown out the world with your heart-beat; it's all that's ever made sense for me. You. I drive my head into your solar plexus: opening my mouth for more, for all of you, for something of you.

You have come back, just as you left: with no warning; no words.

The winter sun edges through the blinds. The sound of cars becomes persistent and the bankers upstairs move around. You never met them, the American couple who arrived a year after you left, we often pass on the stairs and they laugh when I tell them they work longer hours than junior doctors. But later, later. This is still our time. There is that sweet smell behind your ears which takes me back to our first summer, I fill up on the smell of you. It's never enough. You tighten your hands around my hips, I press the soles of my feet on top of yours and you kiss the hollow curves around my eyes.

For this little while, the world can wait.

I know about waiting. In the first year after you left, I'd reach out in the night to touch you, and when my fingers padded the cold sheet next to me and there was nothing where you had been, I'd press the pillow to my mouth and scream until morning. Right in the beginning, of course, I didn't even go to bed at all. I slept on a line of cushions in front of the door, next to the phones and laptop. Usually with the television on. All night. All those nights.

After the first year I accepted that I'd be waking up alone. I had to. I kept a pillow close, clung to it as people do to a faith. A pillow, or maybe a man. And I talked to you. From that first night when you didn't return and I started calling your work, your friends, I was talking to you. I was defending myself against you when you'd return and be cross that I'd worried unnecessarily. When I had reason to worry, I begged you to come home, I bargained and pleaded. And all the time I spoke to you in my head, and now you are here and I am still talking to you.

And you are really here. So I keep my eyes closed as once again I let my hand go out on its own accord until it touches someone whose skin is more familiar to me than my own. Together again.

My alarm goes off. Your hand reaches out before mine and you press the button. Silence. It's almost as if the last three years hadn't happened. As if we will wake together, maybe make love before charging into the bathroom, shouting out the evening's plans from the shower, treading on each other's clothes, drinking each other's coffee by mistake and saying, 'I love you. See you tonight'.

Most mornings I wake before the alarm. For nearly three years, I haven't slept, not slept like people do, abandoned, untroubled. Since the day you left, there's been no release, neither peace nor cure; even when I've been asleep, I'm still looking for you. One thing about dreams is that you don't get to dream in them.

We turn together, your front against my back, you weave your arm through mine, holding the middle of me to the middle of you. The recovery position. I hesitate at first, then I bring my fingers up to trace the tattoo on your upper arm with my index finger. I touch the **K,** the **T,** the **I, N, E** at the end. Whenever I see my name printed, I wonder about those letters on your skin. Who is reading the Braille of your commitment to me? I was asked, over and over, to describe your 'distinguishing features', and I told them, he has the name 'Katherine' written on his upper, left bicep. 'Hard to lose, eh, tatts like that,' said one policeman looking at a photo of you and I on holiday, 'course there's always laser surgery but that can leave a right messy scar, some people tattoo over it but...' So here it is. Your mark. The letters that make up my name, engraved and embedded in your subcutaneous. Some things don't go away.

4

The alarm went off and you are still here. I should be getting ready for work. You lift yourself over me, your elbows taking the weight of your torso. I feel the current of air from your nose onto my face. You hold me down like a collapsed building and close my lips with your mouth. We stay like that as the minutes go by. I don't want you to move. I do not want to go back to my life. You kiss my eyes and I have to open them now to see you.

To see you again. The glare of the sky shuts them closed but your silhouette is imprinted on my lids. I look again. I can see you now that the room is as light as it will ever get today. It was the first thing about you that I ever noticed. Your blue eyes, Alpine blue eyes. Holiday eyes. You have more creases in the corners when you smile now. You drop your elbows, lift me back in your hands and make yourself into a blanket, covering me with your skin. And we laugh.

At first it sounds so canned. We laugh like a director has asked two actors to laugh. And laugh. And cut. And laugh. And then it becomes real and we laugh because we are so happy right there and then. The day is starting and all I want is my husband home and he is home: here, covering every part of me.

You are back.

We stop laughing, I draw my knuckles up to my mouth and bite hard to stop myself from crying – I learnt this the first year you left when I needed to stop the tears in supermarkets or driving the car, sometimes in mid-conversation with someone I didn't know. I'd just start melting and nothing could mop me up. I hold my breath like that, my teeth cutting into the back of my hands. You watch me. You pull my hand away, kiss where the skin's been broken and kiss my mouth again. I lick your shoulders. I can't leave you but I must.

June 6th, 2007: you left.

You didn't need to get up that morning just because I had to be at work for eight, but it was one of the rules you made for yourself when we first married, that you would always have breakfast with me if you could. You said a big love is made up of all the little things, the little acts of appreciation, and that once they stopped, people started taking each other for granted and then, what was the point?

5

I didn't always do that for you, Marc, and I was sorry for that later.

You made me coffee, brought me a couple of pain killers. I didn't have time to drink but swallowed down the pills.

We'd been to dinner with an old school friend of mine whom I'd not seen since sixth form and never liked anyway. She'd arranged the supper so I could meet a friend of hers who had returned from medical training in the US. It had been a terrible mistake to drag you out there. That night you'd said that you wanted to stay in, you had something to tell me. I said if it was important, it could wait till the weekend. I hadn't caught up on my sleep after a long shift, I was working the next day, a Tuesday, and we'd barely seen each other the week before. I was snappy, we were running late. You know I hate to be late and I was resentful about having to go out, having to wake up early the following day, having to galvanise you into doing something neither of us wanted to.

I hadn't eaten that day and the wine on an empty stomach knocked me out. I drank too much and couldn't stop apologising to you while we waited for a taxi. We'd quarrelled on the way home, something about Gina's friend flirting with me. It was all too clearly a set up on his part to meet me. I said things which hurt you, hurt you because they were true.

I've run over those last twelve hours so many times, always hoping that in the autopsy of your words, your gestures, what was unsaid, I might uncover a detail that would lead to a different ending.

And now I could ask you, was it that night? My friend and her shrill excitement, the conversations about children's schools, house prices and her fridge covered with animal-shaped certificates announcing things like, *Gold Star for Grace who smiled nicely today!* Months later, that's what I thought. It was that boring dinner party that drove you out. Their indifferent questions to you, their educational holiday plans and their tucked-up eco-friendly children. You saw a glimpse into our future and it wasn't good enough for you. I wasn't good enough for you. So after I apologised again, dressed and kissed you good-bye, I left our flat.

When I returned, you were gone.

It's policy in hospitals to let relatives have time alone with the deceased. In some hospices they give families the option to video a relative's last hours. I've always encouraged wives and husbands, even the children, to stay as long as they need to say goodbye. Since you disappeared, I've envied the grieving the chance to see those they've lost for one last time.

I've witnessed how loved ones cry over a corpse. How they bury their faces into a cold, hardened frame. How they try to warm the bodies, shake the arms out of their torpor, bringing lifeless hands up to their faces. Sometimes they'll scream at the cadaver, often they'll pat the torso, softly, gingerly, as if afraid of waking them up. How they wait for a smile to appear on lips that can't speak. Junior house doctors have asked me to help remove a family member who's fallen asleep with a dead body in their arms. Mothers sometimes believe that if a dead baby will breast feed, it'll come back to life. Some talk – saying all that was never said while the person was alive. Sometimes there's wailing, sometimes there's a low guttural croak. Often, nothing at all. A father might stand just a few seconds before leaving his child to the morgue.

And then there are the un-grieved, the unclaimed. Before I specialised in paediatric cardiology, I worked in Accident & Emergency – well, you know that, I remember you sitting on those wonky chairs trying to hold a plastic cup of scorching coffee, waiting for me to be free long enough to have a quick chat or a snog in the utilities' room. I frequently saw cases of the homeless or people who've lived on their own, who'd died with no-one but the doctor on duty to note their last breath. Since you left, I can't leave those bodies without fretting that someone needs to be notified; someone who can't sleep, who checks the missing persons' websites, whose life is devoid of meaning because that person never came home.

You close your hand over the back of my neck and then release the skin like a mother cat does her kitten. You turn, look at the ceiling. I reach my hand over your chest. It rises and falls. Your heartbeat is regular. I have my body.

We line up our profiles on the pillow, and I see half of you. I have always only ever seen half of you.

Even on this black and white late March morning, your eyes are blue. You touch my face, everyone has their touch, like a fingerprint or a snowflake, and yours is the touch I have been searching for. In all those men, I found no one who came anywhere close to touching me like you do.

friday morning

'I'm going to move into radiology,' says Mona as she makes incisions into her cheese and tomato sandwich, 'I've decided. I can't take the nights anymore, I just can't.'

She squints over her plate while carefully extracting the tomato slices with two plastic spoons. She looks up at me. 'Want it?'

'Why d'you have tomatoes in your sandwich if you don't like them?'

'Well, I thought I did, but then I remembered that I didn't. It's the nights and,' she looks around the room before divulging, 'we're trying for a baby...but don't tell anybody, will you? You know what they're like around here.'

'Sure.'

'And with Johnny being made a consultant we can afford to have one of us at home...I'm not saying I want to be like some stay-at-home mum or something, but with kids and that, you can't be rushing out the house with a weekend bag three nights a week and I don't want to give up absolutely so, if I make a change now...well, what do you think?'

'I think it'd be a good move. Marc and I always said that if we had a family I'd have to stop being on call, at least for the first few years.'

Mona nods before looking down into her food. She winces at the khaki-coloured lettuce leaves before removing them. Maybe she wonders if she'd been insensitive talking about families when I don't have a husband, or I have a husband, he just disappeared.

Disappeared that is, until last night.

Mona's one of the few friends who still asks about you. Most feel that they've put in their time supporting me over the worst bits and now they hope I've moved on and am looking forward to my new life. 'Keep focusing on the future, Kate,' they say, looking ahead with their eyes. They believe that part of encouraging me in the getting-on-with-it process is not to remind me of you – if they remind me, I'll get upset and then they'll be the cause of my distress. But Mona isn't like that. She attributes her talent as a doctor to her investigative skills and not shying away from the questions that others daren't ask. She's fascinated by my extra-curricular life of private detectives, morgues, clairvoyants, being a minor celebrity in the missing persons' world and, of course, the occasional trips abroad to check out possible sightings.

'Any news...of him?' she asks, quietly looking away.

'Funnily enough, he came back last night.'

Mona stops chewing. ' What?'

I look back at her with a straight, no-messing expression. She knows I'm not joking. Not the type.

'What?' she repeats.

I bite my bottom lip.

'Kate? Kate! What are you saying? He came back? Last night?'

'Yes'.

'What do you mean?'

'I mean, when I was sleeping he got into to bed with me.'

'Are you joking? He got into bed? With you?'

I nod.

'How did he get in?'

'With his key.'

Mona draws up her lower jaw.

'What did he say?' Her sandwich balances limp in her hands.

'Nothing.'

'Nothing?'

I nod again.

'So how do you know it was him? Maybe it was a burglar?'

'Well, he didn't take anything...and he looked very like the Marc I was married to.' My jaunty tone sinks into a whisper. 'It was him. It was Marc.'

'It was him? Him? Marc?'

'Mona, you're repeating everything I say.'

'But I can't believe it! What, he really came back? You didn't just imagine it, did you, Kate?'

'No, he was there.'

'He must have said something?'

'He didn't need to.'

'Kate. He didn't need to?'

'You're doing it again.'

'But Kate...Kate...he walks in after nearly three years and not so much as a *sorry I'm late, love, the traffic was murder?*'

Devinder from Paediatrics brings his tray over and sits down with us. He smiles while taking out an extremely red apple from his pocket and polishes it on his white coat.

'All right ladies?' He checks the shine.

'Kate's husband came back last night after three years.'

'Oh.'

'Can you believe that?' Mona asks, holding onto his sleeve to keep reality within reach.

'Oh,' he says, sinking his teeth down into his apple.

'Is that all you can say?' Mona's head swivels from Devinder to me, from me back to Devinder and back again. 'So he just got into bed with you. That's it. Fine.' She prods Devinder's white coat. 'He just got into bed with her after disappearing in 2007. I mean, is he back? Is he not? Is he...what? And Katie, what the hell are you doing here sitting with us?'

People turn to look at us.

I continue eating, not really acknowledging the food or the questions.

'Oh, I don't know,' sighs Mona. 'I don't know!' She hits the table in frustration. 'So what do you think, Devinder, huh? He just turns up out of the blue for a cuddle without any explanation and no one thinks that's odd?'

Devinder looks at me while he chews loudly.

'My mum had a cat like that.'

I often asked myself, what would I do if I found you? Of all the scenarios I came up with, going limp, rolling over and becoming mute was never the role I'd cast for myself. So Mona is right to react as she does, but I can't explain what it was like, to have you back, and just want that moment.

You turned, sat up and, after waiting a few seconds, lifted yourself off the bed and walked into the bathroom. I heard you urinating. You returned after three years to use the toilet, I thought, leaning over the side of the bed and touching your clothes. Different clothes. I picked up a T-shirt and sniffed it. I listened to see if you flushed the toilet...no, you never did. So you're still trying to conserve water.

You stood in the doorway like in a dream. You moved with a look of concentration over to my clothes' cupboard, opened it, and took out a dark green suit. It is in fact my interview suit which I'd only recently worn, but you wouldn't have known that. You bent down and picked out a pair of black boots. You opened my top drawer and touched my underwear gently, as though the tossed-in pants and bras were kittens gathering for warmth. You drew out a pair of black pants, stroked your cheek with them and then plucked out a bra. You lay the outfit on the bed, then, after consideration, added a pair of tights. The look was a little austere for me - but I let you dress me, moving your hands over my breasts, drawing the skirt over my hips, turning me over in the bed as you closed me up for the day.

You walked me to the bathroom and while I peed, you squeezed the toothpaste on my toothbrush and held it up to me. I wanted you to insist I didn't go to work today but we both knew it was the right thing to do. I took the brush – held it up as if to say, 'no, I'm not letting you do that' – and you smiled. You brushed my hair and then looked into my make-up bag. You pulled out a lipstick, 'Fuschia Fun' it was called.

You touched my lips with the colour and you were about to open the mascara but put it back. Why did you put it back, Marc, because I might cry today?

The mime continued with you sitting me down and returning with a coffee and my boots. You kissed my toes and slid them into the tights, after that my legs were shut up in the boots. I drank the coffee. I looked at you, you looked back: if you knew what I knew, you were giving nothing away. I understood that you wanted me to go to work, I knew that you had somewhere you needed to go, someone you had to see. And then you bent down, took me by the elbows firmly in your hands and levelled your eyes with mine.

'When you come back, I'll be here,' you said. 'Katherine, I will be here. I have something I want to ask you.'

I slit open a *Kit-Kat* for Mona and me. We sip our murky filtered-coffee. The three of us look out the windows at the rain.

'So where was he then?' Devinder asks.

'I don't know,' I answer. 'We didn't say anything, just slept.'

'I know the feeling,' he says.

'God you two! This is so unreal! I don't understand. You didn't say anything? I'd have...I'd have punched his bloody lights out! I'd have...I'd have... Have you told the police?'

'No. I've a lot on today...anyway, I don't know what to say.'

Mona shakes her head as she chops her chocolate into four equal pieces and lines them up.

'Well I don't know what to say either; this is very strange, too weird for me. I can't believe you didn't even ask him where he'd been...I mean, there's a time for sleeping and a time for...sorting these things out. What the bloody hell did – that's my bleeper. Shit. Gotta go. Are you going to be okay?'

Mona stands up, shakes the crumbs from her coat over my tray.

'Oh!' she says, looking at me. She shuffles over and hugs me, leaving slivers of wafer on my cheek.

'Uurgh,' winces Devinder.

'What?'

'Don't do all that lesbo stuff while I'm eating thank you.'

'It's called giving your friend support, you freak. Kate, find me if you need...I don't know, if you need anything.'

Mona's bleeper goes off again. ' Devinder, talk to her.'

She squeezes my hand and drops her two strips of chocolate on my tray. 'This is really...really...too...bloody weird.'

'Katherine, I will be here,' you said. All this morning I've been about to run out of the hospital doors and go home to you, just to see you, to see if it really, really is true, but coming to work is what saved me over the last three years, it needs to save me now.

'There are tubes and wires and drips and bits of plastic stuck all over him...and what's that going into his belly button?' asks baby Jamie's grandmother. 'It must hurt him. Doesn't it hurt him?'

'The line going into his stomach was fed in today. I know it looks a little...bulky, but it's getting all the medication directly into him. Babies' veins can't keep taking perforations so this is the most effective way of giving Jamie what he needs. We're pleased with his progress so far.'

'But you don't think he'll make it, do you, Doctor?'

'All babies are different. Jamie's a fighter, so, for the moment, there's no indication that he won't. I know how –'

'But it looks so painful, all those –'

'Jamie's had extensive heart surgery Mrs...'

'Harris.'

'Harris. At the moment, his situation appears comfortable.'

'Well, I'll tell my daughter he's "comfortable". He doesn't look very comfortable. He's her first, well, all of our first and this is just so...'

Red veins swim under her tears. She shakes them off. 'I'm here so she can have some rest.'

It's Friday afternoon now, six hours after I left you in my flat. Our flat.

'Oh, and here she is now, I said, take a rest dear, what are you doing back?'

'I couldn't sleep. Hello,' says Jamie's mother.

We all look at Jamie.

'The doctor says he's "comfortable". He's a fighter.'

The granny nods to me, urging me to lay on the reassurance.

'It'll take the next few days to see how the procedure has worked but he's as stable as can be for the moment.'

'See, "stable" the doctor said. Why didn't you sleep?'

I am just about to move onto my next patient when Mrs Harris grips my arm, 'It's just she can't touch him. She says she can't touch him, that's all. With all those tubes...'

With the help of two nurses, we manoeuvre the equipment around so that Jamie's mother can prise her fingers through a hole at the top of the clear plastic cot.

'Here,' I say, 'you can put your fingers through...just gently rub his ears. Babies like that.'

'Yes, see,' encouraged Jamie's granny, 'he hasn't got anything going into his little ears at least.'

'Thank you, Doctor,' whispers the new mother.

'If he remains stable, you might be able to feed him some of your expressed milk through this drip here later tonight. So try and get some sleep – Jamie needs you to be well and rested, the nurses are here all the time. He's in very good hands. Goodbye. Goodbye. Goodbye, Jamie.'

'Mummy, I won't be able to make this Sunday.'

'Oh darling, how disappointing. You sound terrible. Ghastly week?'

'I'm sorry, but...'

'Oh I do wish you were coming. Daddy's got his Johns Hopkins' brigade over, such bores those Americans, and such fussy eaters! And so I won't be seeing the lovely Anthony either?'

'No, no...'

'You haven't had a tiff have you? Katie, you sound a bit...like you have...'

'No, mummy, it's not that.'

'Well what? Is everything all right?'

'Marc is back.'

There's a long silence, muffled sounds and a crack. Perhaps she'd dropped the phone. Then she murmurs something like, 'Oh darling.'

'Mummy?'

'What do you mean, he's back?'

'Just that. He came back last night, actually very early this morning.'

'And...and...what happened?'

'I was asleep and...then I had to go to work.'

'Where is he now?'

'I don't know. He said we'll see each other tonight. He has something he wants to ask me.'

'Well I imagine you have a few things to ask him too!'

'Of course, but...I don't really know.'

'Know what?'

'What difference it would make.'

'Kate, you off?' asks Dr McKendrick while I unbutton my white coat and drop it into the laundry basket. 'Oh, and how did Monday go?'

'Monday? Oh, okay. They asked a lot about budgets, databases, training hospitals, local authority funding - and a little bit about whether or not I could tell the difference between a heart or a toe.'

'You did say that the heart was the one without nail varnish?'

'Now you tell me!'

I stand in front of him lifting my winter coat over my shoulders. I button up and wait like a child requiring permission to be dismissed.

'Have a good afternoon,' McKendrick nods.

'You too.' I want to smile back at him but I can't. After turning towards the door, I twist round to face him. 'You know, I minded you writing about my personal life in your report. You told them that I'd had problems.' McKendrick is about to interrupt but I go on. 'It wasn't necessary. I've never given you reason to doubt my...'

'Hold on, hold on, Kate, I had to say something. I couldn't have recommended a 31-year-old to take on a job of such responsibility without making sure they knew absolutely everything about you. So that's why I've been getting dirty looks from you all week! Look, I stressed emphatically that what you've been through has never affected your work.'

'So why mention it? Why? And you said I'd had counselling, didn't you? Made me look like a loony!'

'Don't be silly Kate. It's all credit to you. The loonies are those who don't recognise they need help...and I think we could both name a few in this department, hum?'

I went to pull my hair out of my scarf before remembering that I'd recently had it cut.

'Come on,' he says, 'if I hadn't said something, someone else would've, hum? A lot of people want that post. You can read a copy of my letter if that'd make you feel better. It's embarrassingly effusive, sycophantic even...Anyway, you wouldn't be such a remarkable doctor if you weren't such a loony.'

'I just want to know, what did you say...exactly?'

'I alluded to a bereavement of a personal nature which you'd dealt with showing strength and maturity. I said you'd availed yourself of professional help and continued working as efficiently and competently as ever. It's nothing new Kate, we all have problems - it's just a matter of how we deal with them.'

'Funnily enough, that's what the counsellor said.'

McKendrick chuckled.

'Look, I hope they give you the job, but you'll be sorely missed – I said that too if you want to know.'

I couldn't be cross at him anymore: McKendrick wasn't just my direct boss but an old friend of my father's. I lifted my arms up as far as my coat would allow and gave him a hug.

'Hurry up or I'll have to visit the counsellor myself,' he says.

I follow the strip lights until I leave the building.

'Bereaved', so that's what they call it. I open my car door. A bereavement: I had a bereavement. I repeat McKendrick's words to myself. Whenever I've had to describe my experience of losing you, that's what I've said, it's like a 'bereavement without the body'.

A better description would be 'deconstructed'. I've been completely deconstructed, slapped together in a rush job and dropped back into the world, looking normal but feeling nothing like it. As I insert my key in the ignition, I whisper, '*dextrocardia with situs inversus*,' recalling the symptoms of an anomaly where one in ten thousand babies are formed with all their major organs arranged the wrong way around. The heart beats on the right side of the chest. I lean back in my car as it starts. My heart hurts with every beat, whichever side it's on.

Bereavement, I called it. A death without a body, a coffin, a note or a reason. But now what do I call it, what do I call it now that you've come back?

friday afternoon

I always knew you were coming back.

I put my gloved hand out of the window and press my security pass against the machine. The barrier lifts. I'm out.

Mona thought I'd dreamt you up. Perhaps delusion is better than nothing. Sometimes the force of wanting you knocked out all other instincts, my ability to reason and my desire to live. I even wonder myself if the person in my bed was really there, or that my mind delivered you. Just when I thought I was getting better.

You said you would still be there, but I should never have left. If I'd lost you once, were you mine to lose twice?

I look at myself in the rear-view mirror: I look strange, preternatural. My pupils take up most of my iris, my lips are red and dry from your kisses, my face is flushed. You did this to me. But I can't see your touches, and I can't see you now.

What did you see? Me, now, over 30! A faint line in the middle of my forehead, a short, practical haircut like the one I had when we first met in France. I'm on my way to becoming a consultant now, and godmother to three children. My time is spent messing with the hearts of men, watching them cry with scientific fascination. I found my first grey hair about two years ago; I could probably identify a handful now. But I let you dress me this morning, like I'd been lobotomised, drugged or limbless.

Windows down. The frosty breeze cauterises whatever's clawing away in my chest. Someone beeps as I swing off Exhibition Road, drive parallel to the park. I wonder if we will go for walks together again, now that you are back.

This is my route home. A checklist of memories: Kensington High Street, shops where we bought things for the flat; cafes we sat in; The Coronet where you could smoke while watching films; the park where we'd often walk or picnic with friends; streets, restaurants, conversations – all landmarks in our story. There's no one else I can share my history with. So much time in my life that I keep to myself and when you left, our story was corrupted. All those memories were overwritten by irony, suspicion and hurt. And I can't forget self-pity. Sometimes I tried to remind others of you or talk about something that happened to us, but I'd be met with silence, an embarrassed smile and sympathy. Sympathy that I felt all too much for myself.

Of course, Mona was right. I should have demanded something – everything – from you, but I didn't. It wasn't answers that I wanted this morning. Just you. I wanted to be there again, just us. Just like before.

I turn off Westbourne Grove for my street. There's a space just outside the block where I live. We lived. It's rare to be able to park just outside my building. I stop. Indicate. Reverse and the car stops, the engine cools. I sit.

He's either there, or he's not.

My phone shivers inside my bag. Another call. I've avoided looking at the messages all day, but it hasn't stopped them. I take out my mobile and see Frances' name on the screen. Frances picked up the phone and was there for me three years ago, and for that, I can never let her calls go unanswered.

'Hello? Hello?'

'Yes, it's me.'

'Kate? Kate? I can't hear you very well...it's Frances. Sorry, I'm in the car, stuck in traffic. Can you hear me?'

'Yes...'

'Kate...I've got news...'

'I know...'

'What?...Kate? Are you there?'

I'm surprisingly calm when I hear of the breakthrough.

'We got some info on him this morning. I think we found him, Kate. We found Marc. Kate, can you hear me?'

'Frances, can I call you back later? '

'Of course...Kate?'

I'm sure Frances must have imagined this moment as well, for mine and for all her cases. She's found the answer to the riddle. I don't think either of us thought it would be like this.

'Yes?'

'Are you okay?'

'Yes.'

'Look, I'm here, if ever...and you've got my home number. Call. Whenever you feel ready. Or whenever.'

'Thanks, Frances.'

'Take care.'

There must be times, and it would be understandable in her line of work, when she doesn't really want it all to end.

I stretch before opening the car door and lever myself out unsteadily. Blood rushes down from my head. The bare trees prick into a filthy sky. I'm about to lean in and drag out my bag when I hear someone call my name.

You are sitting on the wall opposite our flat. You've been watching me all this time. You are smiling.

'Katherine.' You swing your legs out and jump off, then walk over as if we're in a bar and you're about to go through some chat-up lines. You slap your hand on the roof and say, 'I saved the place for you.'

You put your arm around me, or rather catch me, while picking up my bag with your other hand.

'Do you have to go back to work later?'

I shake my head.

'Good,' you say. 'I've made lunch.'

You take my keys.

With your arm still around me we walk up the steps to the front door. You are so solid, strong. I stand back to let you push the key in. Your fingers are clean, like mine, a chef and surgeon must always have scrubbed hands. But unlike mine, yours show no sign of nerves or panic. You lean against the weight of the door and hold it open for me to pass through.

The hallway is in a half light and your shadow eclipses mine over the dusk-rose coloured carpet. I hear you behind me tugging the key out of the lock. I walk ahead so I don't notice if you see the poster of your face under the heading, *Missing*. I'll have to rip it down now. Call off the search.

I take each stair carefully as if it might give way. And I remember that bright Saturday morning when the estate agent bounced ahead of us for the first viewing of what became our flat. Do you remember? She'd been in the middle of yet another story about a dispute between her and a parking warden. We'd nicknamed her

'Hamster-Munster' but I can't remember why - we should have been more grateful to her, one of the few agents who worked on a Saturday morning and didn't scoff at our paltry budget. Still jabbering, she turned the key, pushed the door open and coughed at the dust.

We knew then and there that it was for us. It was the plane trees through the double windows, the light coming in from both sides, the nearby Central Line and the wooden floors. Two bedrooms. Original fireplace. Neither of us listened to Hamster-Munster as she listed all the problems of its dilapidated state. We defended the property and I didn't need to check with you when I said, 'We'll make an offer.'

That particular memory, you and I standing at the top of these stairs and the light coming in, the daffodils in the window-boxes and the rubble on the floor, the space in front of us and Hamster-Munster saying we'd better hurry as she was double-parked: that's one of the moments I concentrate on so hard that I almost believe I can transport myself back there.

But today it is dark, the stairs are worn and when you punch the timer-switch, the light doesn't come on.

'Ssssh, shhhhh. It's okay, Katherine, it's okay now...'

friday evening

The policeman slid me the Missing Persons' Report Form. I took out a pen, tugged off the lid and began writing the answers to questions about you. I thought I knew you so well: Name, Address, Date of birth, Time last seen...

'Excuse me. Could you...?' He gestured for me to move over for the next complainant.

'Sorry,' I said, taking the paper to one side and filling in the description of my husband.

My hands were shaking. Ethnic background? Colour of eyes? Height? I pressed down on the pen, wrote in capitals. That was not the time I wanted to be picked up on having a doctor's illegible handwriting. Distinguishing features? I filled out half the page until I arrived at, 'List previous convictions'.

'My husband has been missing for two days – no one's seen him, at home, at work... I think he could be in real danger...Every minute not searching for him is vital...'

'Is it you who's been on the phone?'

'Yes. Probably. I've telephoned every hospital, police station, the Foreign Office...nobody is doing anything. You said wait 48 hours and it's been 48 hours now. I really need some help. This...this...' I said, pressing my fingers into the Missing Persons' Form, 'This is just a form...I need to talk to someone who can help. Please.'

'Madam,' he looked at the queue behind me.

'Please...this is just wasting time. I need you to do something to find my husband.'

'Madam, if someone is missing then we need their details before we can do anything - otherwise, how would we know who to look for?'

'Let me just tell you all that now, and then you can find him!'

'Excuse me,' he said, nodding at the woman behind me.

'It's just...I've been through all this on the phone a hundred times and I don't see anything being done about it.'

'Madam, all you need to do is fill that in and come back to me when it's fully completed.'

'But I'm asking –'

'Everything all right?' asked an older officer stepping in from a side door. He did a quick mental count of the room. When I arrived there were only a few people, now there were some seated, some reading notices, others tutting behind me.

'Lady's lost her husband, Sir,' said the younger officer, squeezing in a smirk.

His superior looked at me.

'Follow me, Madam,' he said, before adding, 'with the form.'

I was still glaring at the young policeman who was taking down the details of a stolen bicycle. He pretended not to see me but as I was led off, he piped up cheerily, 'Thanks, Sergeant!'

Behind the counter there was a side door which opened into a grubby corridor. I followed him into the third room from the left. I looked around, noticing everything so I could tell you all about it later.

It was no larger than a changing room cubicle really. The sergeant landed on his chair, faced me, slapped the desk.

'Detective Sergeant Brian Wells.'

I saw too late that he had put out his hand. He pointed at the chair and said, 'Take a seat.'

And I did, facing a landscape of plastic coffee cups, forms and files. There was a column of papers in a work tray piled so high that it towered over a shrivelled African Violet; a gift from a woman I supposed, was it to thank him for retrieving her husband? Behind him there was an aluminium blind at half-mast being slowly strangled by loops of knotted cord, the dust on the twisted slats looked like rats' fur hovering over rows of folders with sun-faded, peeling labels. That was what happened to the forms people filled in. There was a nest of wires trailing out from under his desk which housed two blackened, unplugged computer monitors.

'I have to ask some routine questions...' He glanced at my form. 'I see, you're a doctor.'

'A specialist registrar. Cardiology. At University College Hospital.'

'Ah, cardiology, that's heart, isn't it? My wife's always going on about mine...' He patted his chest, 'Too many Indian takeaways. So, you still work all those long hours we read about, junior doctors...?'

'Yes, unfortunately coronaries don't work 9 to 5.'

He laughed. My breathing relaxed into something more regular now that I'd found an ally.

'Same with this lark, eh? Criminals don't take the weekends off either, or Christmas, or... so sometimes you work maybe three days and nights in a row?'

'Frequently.'

'And so Mr Venelles – that's your husband, right? - he's quite used to being left on his own for a long weekend or a week even?'

So that was where it was going. I tried to stay calm. To find you, I had to keep these people on our side.

'Yes, but we talk, all the time. All the time. He's a chef at a restaurant. He works late at night as well, they haven't seen him either. No one has seen him. He's never done this before.'

'How long have you been married?'

'Two years.'

'So when you say he's never done this before, you mean in two years?'

I swallowed into a dry throat. I thought he was a friend, but that was worse, he was tricking me, making me say things about you that weren't true.

'You haven't filled out this section, "State of mind when person was last seen?" Did you have a row, disagreement, tension between you?'

'We are very much in love.'

'Good, good, that's nice to hear. Unusual these days. Has he had problems at work, debts, conflict with management, drinking a bit too much, anything like that?'

'His state of mind was normal. Yes, we've had the usual stress about money – we've just finished doing up our flat and...but nothing serious. Please. I know you don't want to waste your time if he's just gone off in a huff or he's in bed with someone else,' the sergeant jolted a little at this, 'but I'm telling you he's disappeared. Something has happened and every minute is crucial. He could be suffering...held captive...I don't know. Please, please, can you go out and find him?'

Detective Sergeant Wells brought the heels of his hands together, the palms, and then the fingers, one by one, starting from the smallest. Finishing this exercise, he looked at me in a way that warned it would be the last time he was going to explain this to me.

'Dr Brenton. Your husband has not come home for two days. He's a grown man. It doesn't appear that he is a danger to himself or others. There's been no sign of a break in, no abduction. No-one's reported anything suspicious, you've not heard from kidnappers or been threatened yourself. I have the details.'

'That's all?'

'For the moment.'

'But he's missing and –'

'He has a right to his privacy. Your husband's French –'

'So?'

'It's very likely he suddenly had an urge to go home for a while, or maybe, we have to be realistic, he just might be with someone else. You're not there to keep an eye on things and –'

'What?'

'Dr Brenton, when husbands don't come home, I regret to say, infidelity is often the reason. Fast followed by credit card debt, but that's...'

'The last thing he said was, "A tout à l'heure" - See you later...
and...he never came back.'

'If you'd like to finish completing this, we can start the process
of tracing him.'

Detective Sergeant Wells gave me some time to collect myself
before handing me back my form. I opened my pen again, this
time my writing was faint, jagged.

'About 250,000 people are reported missing every year; most
of these turn up in the first 72 hours. I know all this admin may
appear unnecessary to you but you have to trust we're experienced
in this. That's your reference number.'

'So you're not going to do anything?'

'The thing is, Marc Venelles is probably not missing as far as
he's concerned. He knows where he is.' Detective Wells couldn't
resist chortling before he concluded, 'All we can do is make the
relevant authorities aware that you are looking for him should he
turn up.'

'I don't believe this!'

'Dr Brenton, if I were to say to you that I thought I might have
a heart condition but I had no symptoms or complaints, would you
rush for your surgical knife and open me up?'

'No.'

'There you go.'

'But I'd give you more than just a form to fill out.'

'Good. Good to know. But Mr Venelles is a consenting adult - if
he wants to go walkabout, that's his privilege. After 48 hours we
can only do as much as we are doing now.'

Detective Sergeant Wells pressed the leaflet into my hand,
wrapping the interview up.

'I've got a hunch Mr Venelles will be back very soon and he'll
have a lot of explaining to do. The next port of call for you, as it
were, is the National Missing Persons' Helpline. They'll assign you
a liaison officer and get you onto the next level of enquiries. After
72 hours, mind! Here's a card for Frances White, she does a
blinding job. But let's hope it doesn't come to that, eh?'

*

'Ssssh... Katherine, look, I've made some food.'

And you have. I can smell your homemade lasagne. We used to

joke that you, renowned for cooking the most elaborate, complex dishes, would come home and bake me a lasagne with chocolate mousse to finish off. And I can see the chocolaty glass bowl in the sink; you've replicated my favourite meal. I wonder if it could possibly taste the same.

The table is laid for two. It even has a table cloth I don't remember seeing before. The flowers I'd not bothered to put in a vase last night have been tended to. A bottle of wine uncorked and two glasses wait on either side like a shy couple. The dining area looks like an advert for an upmarket kitchen company. Even a candle! You've really cornered all the clichés.

For months after you disappeared, I couldn't eat, but I continued to shop for food, just in case when you came home you'd be hungry. The flat waited, ready for your return, full of food and wine, and then, I can't remember when, I got fed up with throwing out vegetables and fruit, glugging back the alcohol when I was alone and needed to be put to sleep.

'Drink?' you ask, opening a bottle of red.

You pour two glasses.

I just don't know how to start this. I face you, mute because two questions are fighting in my throat and I don't want to let them out because they will destroy this gift of unreality you are arranging for me. But you are here. Now we have to open our mouths and go public, and I have to ask you: why did you leave, and why did you come back?

And all the other questions in between.

*

'Oh my God, you're baking cakes. What's up?' asked Anna, walking through the door and dropping a heap of shopping bags to the floor.

'I told you, Marc's not been home for three days.'

And then I was about to be sick.

I crossed the living room, opened the window and leant out of it.

'I didn't know he did that,' she said, dropping her handbag and walking up behind me.

'Did what?'

'Disappear. Nick does it all the time.'

24

'Nick's a travel writer, Anna. That's his job. And anyway, not all men are Nick.'

'Oh, I think you'll find, baby sister, they are.'

I closed the window. My hand left an imprint of flour on the pane. An arc of white petals should you look up.

'You know a quarter of his last book was about how he was taken in by a Tanzanian village girl who believed he was a god and wouldn't let him leave until she and her sisters had satisfied him in every way. This is while I was waiting by the phone every night, pregnant, with two screaming children and the electricity about to be cut off.'

I returned to the kitchen, stirred the mixture. Anna moved around behind me, flicking through a pile of photographs of you which I'd taken out to show people.

'You know he wasn't even sorry, said I should be proud of him!'

'Sounds like you are,' I said under my breath.

'Well! He's making it all up to me – treating me to a dirty weekend at Claridge's – so now I'll be satisfied in every way! We've packed the kids off to mum and dad's. I thought we'd go to the Tate Modern tomorrow afternoon. Do you know, I've still never been there? Oh, I had lunch with Elspeth – she's practically running that publishing house – I had to make an appointment weeks ahead to see her! Is she still in your book group?'

Anna's monologue wound down when she stopped to look around the room. Most of the floor, chairs and tables were covered in papers, scribbled-on notes and lists of names. There were clusters of half-drunk cups of coffee, phones dotted around and piles of your clothes still out after I'd ransacked the flat looking for clues as to where you were. The air was stale, sick with dread; I was ashen, almost unconscious with fear. Anna realised that she hadn't just popped in on an ordinary afternoon.

'Why don't you go to the police?'

'I've done that! I've been there, they've been here. I've filled out more forms than a Stasi officer. I've rung every hospital, police station, I've called the National Missing Persons Helpline, I'm thinking about private investigators – I've done everything – where is he? Where is he!'

'Okay, okay...' she said, tuning in to the wave-length of my disaster.

Anna made a space for herself on the sofa by putting aside my medical books and trying not to look at a picture of a boy with testicles the size of a football. She resigned herself to my domestic crisis.

'Did you have a row?'

'We had dinner on Monday night with Gina Brightman. We got back late, exhausted. Tuesday morning we said that we'd both be home late that night. I went to work, when I got back about two in the morning, he wasn't home. The answering machine was already full of messages asking why he wasn't at work. I just waited, thinking any minute he'd come home. It's now Friday. All his stuff's here, everything! His wallet, credit cards, his phone...except his keys. I can't find his keys. The door was double locked. He must have locked it. I think he might have gone out and –'

I covered my face with my hands. Tears turned the flour into pellets of dough.

'Oh, Kate.' *Anna put her arms around me.*

'I went through his address book – I've called every number – nobody's seen him. I've asked the neighbours, been to all the shops around here...even stopped people on the street. I just don't know what else to do...'

'It'll be alright...'

'Not till he comes home it won't.'

I slid down the wall and dropped to my knees.

'What're you making?'

'Sponge cake, just using what I've got here, I daren't go out in case he comes back. I don't want to use the phone in case he's trying to call...'

She scoops up some mixture in her finger, puts it in her mouth.

'Yummy.'

'Anything to keep my mind off... I'll take it to work. I'm back tomorrow morning unless I can swap the hours with someone. Again. God, Anna, where is he?'

'Kate, have you any suspicion or reason to believe he was having an affair?'

Anna's expression changed. Earlier, she'd taken your disappearance as a tedious interruption to her fun day out – now, she was looking into my face, squeezing my arms, and looking like me, desperate.

'Ow! Anna, you're hurting me.'

'Sorry but...Was he seeing someone else?'

'No! You're worse than the police,' I said, moving back from her.

'Why? Do they think that?'

'I don't know if they think about him at all. I'd have more support if he were a kitten.'

'He couldn't have been unfaithful, could he, Kate? Could he?'

'Anna, something bad has happened...'

'Have you tried Eddie?'

'Yes. He's talking to people in France – I told him not to tell mum and dad.'

'Good, good, Katie, on the ball as always...'

Anna put her hands on my shoulders and brought her pale grey eyes level with mine.

'Kate, I'm sure it's just a mix up or he's...I don't know...there'll be some explanation. Come and visit us at Claridge's – have a jacuzzi and a massage, on me, well, on Nick, well, not on Nick!'

'Until Marc comes back I just can't do anything, Anna. Don't you see?'

'Yeah, sure, well, when he gets back then...'

I stood by the window. That was where I'd been spending most of my time, waiting for you to cross the road and come home. Anna was downstairs, the door closing behind her. She stopped on the doorstep, moved her bags from hand to hand. I'd siphoned all the joy out of her big weekend. Now I'd gone and reminded her that London isn't just shopping and catching up with friends, it's a place where people disappear. A place where people suffer, go out of their minds for those they love who sometimes don't make it back.

The breeze shook the tough, glossy new leaves. You were going to return any minute. There'd be an explanation, a message, a note I'd overlooked. Or, maybe a confession. I'd have been devastated, Marc, but then, to see you, I'd have forgiven anything. I understood then why Anna took Nick back time and time again.

Anna hesitated on the doorstep. A man crossed the road in front of her and caught her smile. Anna always looks as if she's smiling even if she isn't. He winked at her as if he knew that she was thinking naughty thoughts. Anna always looks like she's thinking *naughty thoughts. And often is. This time it was probably of room service, champagne, hot baths and some TV before Nick returned from his publishers.*

Only family can dish up that special brew of guilt, throwing in a handful of resentments, a spoonful of anger and a few pinches of shame covered with a light sauce of anxiety. And season with a taste of regret. Anna had her foot out - it was just about to land on the last stair out of the building - but it stayed there, stuck midway. She didn't know what to do.

I watched her. I didn't want it to be a test but I couldn't help thinking that if it were me, I would have stayed and helped. So would mum. But Anna's not like either of us.

She didn't budge from my doorstep, just stared ahead of her, deciding what to do.

*

I won't come to the table. I will not sit down, eat and drink with you. You know it too. You pull up a seat, drink the wine until your glass is empty. You refill it, drink again and bring out a packet of cigarettes from your inside pocket. They are unopened. You unravel the cellophane, scrunch it up, defiant, it springs open again on the work surface. You light a cigarette; draw in the smoke before releasing a long, grey gust between us.

I think about a woman somewhere – assuming there's just the one – who is waiting for you to return. At this point she will have rung your work, your friends. All those people who've never known you to be late or sick since you first appeared in their lives. She might have people out looking for you already, and she'll be walking from room to room before stopping at the phone. I could call her, talk to her. I've more in common with this person, my love, than I do with you.

'So, where were you?'

'Oh Katherine,' you say.

I'm disappointed too, that I can't come up with anything more original. You'd have thought I'd had enough preparation time. You look at me, weary, as if I'm returning to an argument you'd thought was long since over.

'Where were you all that time?'

'Why?'

'I want to hear you tell me.'

'Why?'

'I'm curious...' I answer.

I look over at the shelves of reports, files, folders, *missing* posters and dossiers from the 'Missing Helpline', the MPB, letters to governments, banks, charitable trusts; photos pinned up of clothing found in forests and beaches - the only physical remains left from someone. There are quotes from private detectives, tracing agencies, letters from psychics, well-wishers – people all over the world. But not one word from you.

'I'm curious Marc, curious to know which fucking square inch on this planet I didn't cover! I'm curious to know how you think you can walk back in and not have to answer for anything!'

I'm on the other side of the flat – the one devoted to your search. I pull out a folder named *Missing 2007* and throw it at your feet. Shouting, I throw another folder at you as well – *Missing 2008* - and another – you cover your head with your arms, ducking to avoid the onslaught.

'This wall chart is a timeline pinpointing where you might have been over the last three years – these lines and dates in *green* are for positive sightings, in *orange* for possible places and people you've been to...these lines in *red* are where I was taken completely down the wrong path – see! Hey Marc, now you're back, you could check it for me, give me an overall grade!'

Swinging the board in your direction, the corner cuts down into your shoulder. You clasp the sudden wound but continue to move fast and low towards me.

'Did you ever think that I'd be out of my mind worrying about you? Can you imagine? Just a little bit? What I went through? And there you were, hiding! So tell me - was it West London? Eastern Europe? Was it America...it's says here "Mexico" September 2008? Of course some men start up new families just down the road from where they were living - is that what you did? Was it that? Did I pass you every day? How far did you have to go to escape me, Marc?'

I turn the desk over, pick up a hole-puncher and hurl it at your knee. It catches you, you buckle.

'You know I even checked the lists of applicants for ESA space missions to Mars? Which galaxy Marc? Which fucking rock have you been squirming under?'

You move around the room until you are able to make a grab for my wrists. You don't even use half your strength and I'm immobilized.

When our breathing calms, you say, 'Boats.'

'Oh.'

All the hours I spent searching through names of crew on boats. Marbella. Sardinia. Monaco. Boats. Of course, boats. It's not easy hide these days, but if you're not on land, it's one way. Fish don't leave paper trails.

'You must have been under a different name.'

'Of course.'

You sit down. Light another cigarette.

'My father's.'

'Were you looking for him?'

'Who?'

'Your father?'

'No,' you laugh. 'Why would I look for someone I don't know?'

'Quite.'

And then it's my turn to laugh, an in-joke. You'd have to be me to get it.

You move closer to me, cigarette hanging out the side of your mouth. 'You're upset.'

'Don't you think I have every right to be upset?'

'Of course, Katherine, of course.'

You touch my cheek, gently. My throat.

'I cut my hair.'

'Yes, I see. It's very...*gamine*.'

'You always liked it long. I cut my hair when I thought you would never come back.'

'Katherine. You always knew I would come back. But maybe what you don't know is if you want me back.'

We both breathe hard against each other.

*

I stopped watching Anna as she equivocated on my doorstep. I didn't want to see her walk away as I predicted she would, leaving me to the naked horror of the first weekend without you.

My sister must have been thinking that surely I had friends to call on. Friends. Friends are the most important thing to Anna after her children. Everybody is Anna's friend. She's always hungry for people, she devours their stories, their passions, the secrets they unburden to her. Anna never locks her front door at night just in case someone might pass by and need to chat. But this is London, and this is my life. You were my only friend.

And I was lucky to have found you. I hadn't been looking. Anna is always looking. She seems to be the only one in our family who has a sense that there is a world outside the Brenton household.

Dad always blamed mum for 'what went wrong with Anna'. He disapproved of my mother's wild side, the woman who once got a speeding fine, who could be so cavalier as to leave the house with the washing machine on, but most of all, her latent interest in the Arts. When mum gave up nursing, she took up with an amateur poetry club which met weekly in Summertown. Dad hadn't approved of his wife reading us Plath, Keats, Dickinson and John Berryman at night; he thought it'd bring on too much melancholia. Perhaps it did. Anna's imagination became far too colourful for the hum-drum world of laboratories, disinfectants and latex gloves. She didn't even contemplate science A' Levels and, as well as reading books about wily heroines, she wanted to be one.

And now she lives the dream. She has an errant husband, three children and the messiest home in Oxfordshire. They still have no money but if ever something trickles in from Nick's books or deceased relatives, they'll blow the whole lot on an antique harp or a weekend in a London hotel. Meanwhile, the roof's still leaking, the kids run wild all over the countryside and Anna sleeps all day only to stay up all night editing Nick's manuscripts.

You adored Anna – but you were scathing about Nick's selfish lifestyle, their bohemian existence and non-exclusive relationship. And now I guess, it will be Nick's turn to sneer at you, or rather, me.

Your mobile phone started ringing. The sound startled me so much I knocked my head against the window. I dived for it as it vibrated out of my hands and across the table. Oh Marc, for a moment I thought you were back and the torture was over. But why would you call yourself? Panic blocks lateral thinking.

It was my sister.

She was saying your name.

'Anna? It's me.'

'Marc?'

'Anna. It's me! You just called Marc's phone.'

'Oh God, did I? Yes. How stupid of me. Stupid, I –'

'I told you he left everything here apart from his keys. I thought I'd said that.'

'I meant to call you.'

'But this is Marc's number – what do you want?'

'I just wanted to say...I hope that bloody cake's worth it!'

'Anna...thanks.'

'Come on. We'll find him. He must be somewhere.'

He must be somewhere. He must be somewhere. You know the frantic desperation of losing your keys just as you're about to go out the front door. How your life stops but the rest of the world speeds up - making you twice, three, four times as late. Your future existence renders down to this one test. Nothing will ever happen again until those keys are found...and they just aren't there.

They've gone. They've gone. You search through your bag, your coat, your bag, your coat, your bag. You look by the kettle, back pocket, under a hat, in pots. Ha! They're still hanging on the outside of the door. No. Did you change bags? Look through another bag and then back to the first bag you looked through. Check pockets again. You stand in the middle of the room. Twirl around. Stopping. Darting. Diving under chairs. Up again. Did you put them in the fridge? Check the fridge. The oven while you're at it.

Fingers to your temples, you re-run the last time you saw them. You re-trace your steps...

You're breathing like a dragon. You empty out all the contents of your bag on the floor, spread them out, find a lipstick you lost but didn't know you'd lost. You throw your coat down. Time is passing even faster now: your heart is beating even faster now. You scream inwardly. You shout outwardly. You check down the sides of chairs, tripping over your coat and bin and treading on the contents of both. You start kicking at things. This must be someone else's fault. The keys must be somewhere. They can't have walked off on their own – but what if they have? Try to come up with a back-up plan. But with no keys, nothing can start. Check the coat again, by the toilet, check by the kettle...under the sofa, pray to St Anthony, saint of lost things.

I'd lost my husband. Where should I check first?

friday night

We are sitting on the floor, you and I, against the wall. It is dark. My head is on your thigh with your hand over it, stroking my hair. I'm coiled around you, not asleep, not awake; it's enough not having to think. Enough to imagine us as two London pigeons keeping each other warm as the world rolls from day to night, week to weekend, winter to spring. We are surrounded by islands of scattered paperwork and broken files, all the stuff I'd thrown around the room. It doesn't matter anymore.

Earlier today, you must have opened the kitchen window and now the night air has broken in and started scrambling around the back of our necks and hands. You try to stretch without moving me.

'Katherine, I'll make you a tea, uh? Then we'll eat. After, maybe see a movie or stay in. Whatever you like.'

I sit up, rub my arms and legs, bringing them back to life.

'So have you come back after two years and nine months just to entertain me?'

'*Oui ma Cherie*, whatever you like.'

'I'd like some answers.'

You sigh. 'Katherine, all these...answers. You know more about me than I do!'

'Yeah, maybe you're right, but Marc, this is what you've done to me.'

You stand up, stretch and move about picking up the papers, envelopes, the newspaper cuttings and the letters.

'It doesn't help to look for answers now.'

'I want to know why you left me.'

'I'm here now.'

You try to catch me but I feel constrained and push you away.

'But what? Marc, what? You just vanished – what the fuck is "I'm here now?" Is that all? Are you back? Are you just stopping by? And how come you don't have any questions? Eh Marc. Don't you want to know things? Like how the restaurant's been doing without you? Are my parents okay? What about your little goddaughter who still asks about you? How have I been paying the mortgage you left me with? And where are your clothes? Your CDs? How many kids does

Anna have now? Maybe, who did I fuck when you were away? Do you care about any of it or did you just walk out and give none of us a thought? And...'

You put the kettle on, with your back to me, it's less humiliating to ask, 'And...did you ever love me?'

You turn from the cupboard with a box of tea in your hand. You put it down, pour another glass of wine. 'It is, what it is.'

'And that is....what...exactly...?'

My voice cracks with frustration. You taught me to love, and you taught me to hate. I'm not sure which I feel for you right now.

You look older, sadder. When I imagined you coming home, I didn't think that in three years, you would have changed. Aged. It's the crumpled look around your eyes and the way gravity has tugged at the skin on your jaw, the grey hairs at your temples, even your hands. Maggie upstairs who has regular contact with the spirit world said that ghosts don't change from the age they die, unless they are children, then they grow up until 21, no more. So you are mortal after all. Doesn't that allow us to all make mistakes, and to be given second chances? To forgive is divine, but too bloody difficult. I want to go up and hold you but at the same time, I must give you your medicine.

'We were married. You remember? You said, in front of me, my family, our friends, you said, "forever".'

'Exactly.'

You drop a tea bag in my cup. Still the same cup I always had my tea in. You remembered.

I don't want to fight. It was better when we were quiet, just sitting in silence but now we're up, I'm back in the ring. I'm almost happy with 'exactly' but I have to keep it going for the sake of the person who for the last three years was left with nothing. What do you mean by 'exactly'? Sometimes I didn't always understand you. Sometimes you couldn't express yourself in English and the dictionaries let you down. Somehow, it never really mattered. But I wonder now if it wasn't about language, if it wasn't the words I had confused, it was the person.

I understand that you want to make me food and tea, and pour wine and clean around the sink because you feel at home in a kitchen. You look different in a kitchen than you do anywhere else. No one can attack you in a kitchen, you are invincible, always able to seduce any public.

'Here.' You bring me tea and I wonder why you didn't just pour me some wine as you did for yourself. Perhaps I drink more now than I did then, in fact, I know I do.

'You said this morning you had something to ask me?'

'I do.'

'I have so much I want to ask you, Marc, but I'm just so afraid...'

'Of what?'

'...afraid...I don't know...afraid you'll disappoint me.'

'Very probably!'

You laugh a little. But you don't think it's funny, I'm prodding where you are most raw.

I take your hands in my hands. I'm asking for intimacy. I didn't know until this moment that that is really all I've ever wanted. How do you make a question like that? You let me push back your thumbs, circle your wrists. I loved doing this when we were together. Fitting our fingers into each other, pressing into the warmth, sliding through the spaces, and just looking. All the lines, the crosses, valleys and flats, places you've been and will go.

'I know things now, about you, stuff, facts and dates. I don't know why you kept so much from me – I would have –'

I'm about to say more – there's a lot more that I could say about you - but there's no point hearing it all from me, it has to come from you.

'Katherine,' you say, as if I'm some impossible child, '*Mon amour.*'

'Yes, *mon amour.*'

'I want to ask you something.'

'What?'

'Will you give me a week?'

'A what?'

'A week. All I ask is for seven days for us to start again, to be together, see what we find. And then, after, you decide.'

'A week? Is this all you can come up with! You've been gone nearly three years! A week with you now isn't going to make up for all that time! How can you possibly imagine that after a week everything will be fine!' I'm half laughing, half crying at the idea you could insult me this much. 'And there's no such thing as "starting again" – you start or you repeat – but not both. You had your chance Marc, every day you were missing you moved further away from us ever being together like before. You left me! And now, now! When I've nothing left to give, you want everything.'

'But that's it, not *everything*. Just seven days. Then it's your choice. Huh, Katherine? You have one week to tell me.'

'Tell you what?'

'To tell me about you, me, anything. Ask for whatever you need from me. One week. Together. That's all. Seven days, and then, if you want, we'll say goodbye.' Now your fingers are over mine and you say, 'One week.'

Your palms are rougher than they were. You have a cut on your little finger. You are not wearing your wedding ring. Nor am I. But I've a diamond ring on the third finger of my left hand.

You place little kisses on my face like you are decorating the top of a cake with utmost care. Your lips soothe me. Return me to that quiet state. I don't even hear what you're saying now, but the words take effect like the drain of an anaesthetic seeping into my veins...count backwards from ten...count backwards from a week...count backwards from when we met...

late friday night

The summer I met you, I'd only just qualified as a doctor. I was on holiday before going to live in London to start my in-house training at University College Hospital. And Dave was my boyfriend. My first boyfriend. Ever. Also a medic. We'd been going out since Michaelmas in the fourth year, and by undergraduate standards, we were 'together-together'. Dave wasn't following me to London but staying on at the Clinical School in Cambridge. This was the beginning of my first grown-up holiday: abroad without my parents, with a boy, paid for with money that I'd earned and staying with people who were my friends - friends who happened to have a château on the Côte d'Azur.

The airport in Nice, eight years ago. Tatyana waving across the Arrivals lounge. She streamed towards me like a spot of sunlight while travellers turned to her probably thinking, 'Now that's exactly how I want to look on holiday'. She was blonder than when I'd last seen her in London or maybe that was just the contrast of her caramel skin and the dazzle of her azure eyes.

36

Cigarettes and an oversized box of household matches in one hand and her car keys in the other, she shuffled over in those Moroccan babouche slippers she'd worn every day at Cambridge whatever the weather. She put out her arms and folded them around my neck. Tatyana's hair was warm and smelt of swimming-pool water. She reeked of holiday. And she was late. But her excuse, made in that low-rev of an expensive, powerful engine of a voice, was that she'd been reading on her lilo all morning and had lost all track of time. And that was fine, that was precisely what we'd left England for.

Dave did not think it was fine. He said people like Tatyana always let everyone down and, confident that he knew her character inside out without even having met her, had gone off to find a bus timetable and a hostel.

'So where's the boyfriend?' asked Tatyana.

I looked around for him.

'Over there.'

I flicked my wrist in Dave's direction. It wasn't difficult to pick him out from the hairdos and crisp white shirts. He was in his grey combat trousers, muddied trainers and a Linkin Park T-shirt, fingering leaflets advertising cheap rental cars. He turned around, nodded to us and put the bumph back exactly how he'd found it.

Keeping her eyes on the approaching Dave, Tatyana said, 'He's taller than I expected. Kate, you said he was a geek, he's really sexy.'

Dave swaggered over, conscious that we were talking about him.

'Tatyana, hello, David Wheeler.'

'Hello,' said Tatyana, smiling back at my boyfriend. She extended her hand, rested it on his biceps and kissed each of his cheeks in a way I suspected she'd copied from someone she'd admired.

'I'm Tatty. Welcome to the Riviera!'

Dave, not expecting the kisses nor that Tatyana would slide in between us and put an arm around each of our waists, gulped for air.

'Kind of you to fetch us,' boomed Dave as he lifted our cases. He waved us towards the glass doors, 'I believe the exit's this way.'

'Oh God, that's my car. Whoops!'

Tatyana pointed to a white Renault 4 parked on the curb which *was surrounded by police.*

She wheedled in between the trolleys and on-coming traffic to where three gendarmes were circling her car. There was a line of waiting drivers behind her, one hooted as he saw us coming.

'Je suis vraiment désolée,' she sang, waving her arms, gazing at the uniformed men, her lips pulling back like a wave over those little white teeth. The police put away their ticket books, rested their hands on their guns and motioned her to hurry up. The younger of the three paced by the boot of the car, helping us with our rucksacks, the other two looked on, kicking themselves for not having had the initiative to ingratiate themselves with the blonde in the skimpy top. One came over to Dave and said something crossly that neither of us understood, though the gist was clear. Dave squared up to the policeman, tried to find the words to reply, but nothing came. He tugged at the door and climbed through to the back seat.

Tatyana jumped in and was about to turn on the ignition when we saw the policeman's face in the window. She wound the handle round until his head was almost in the car.

'Oui?'

'Bonnes vacances!'

'Merci, c'est trop gentil. Bon après-midi à vous!'

She looked to me as she winked in the wing mirror.

'Should have asked him to come back with us, n'est-ce pas?'

Dave was upset at being subject to a chastisement from the police when it wasn't his fault. It would be another mark against my friend I'd have to try to defend, along with her being late. And titled. And a smoker. And hilariously beautiful.

We'd planned a three week tour around the South of France after our finals and Dave was not happy when I told him that Tatyana had invited us to stay with her for the first few days. He was outraged that she'd sabotaged what he'd planned to be my introduction to France. As my family usually took the same caravan in South Wales every holiday, he felt it necessary to broaden my cultural experiences. So I was about to decline Tatyana's offer when he changed his mind on the grounds it would save us a few nights' hotel money.

I knew that Dave didn't admire Tatyana as I did. The 'Sebastian Flyte brigade', he called her and her entourage. He couldn't understand why I'd be friends with her, why I'd chosen to do acting with her when I could have been in the Medical Society production of Whose Life is it Anyway? with him instead. He'd never spent any time with Tatyana and her friends but despised them on principle. They were public school 'toffs' who'd no right to be taking up university places when much worthier students needed them.

'But Dave, she got the A' Level grades, the university took her on the same merits as you.'

'Kate, even if we agree it wasn't nepotism that got her into Cambridge in the first place, she went to one of those selective, exclusive, extremely expensive hot-house schools – she'd have to have been a moron not to get in – and then all she does is flounce around drunk in an all-year tan wearing practically nothing. Hopefully she'll overdose soon and then we can all have some peace at night.'

'You know, her life hasn't been all that easy,' I said.

'Why's that?'

'For most of her childhood her mother was in rehab for alcoholism.'

'Kate, what happens to working-class alcoholics?'

'What?'

'They die. Right? So don't give me Four Star Michelin guide hospitals, overstaffed with private nurses pampering Tory-voting, Daily-Mail-reading, fox-hunting dipsomaniacs like your friend's mother. That's not a bad childhood, Kate, that's a bespoke holiday.'

At this point I reminded Dave that unlike him, I'd also been to a private school. This would shut him up temporarily until he'd argue that it was different, my father and mother worked hard to pay for my education.

'But Tatyana's mother worked, she was a model,' I retorted, turning him apoplectic.

The car was very hot. Once inside Tatyana twisted up her hair in a chignon kept together by an old pencil she'd found in the glove compartment. She wiggled her skirt down so that the tops of her thighs didn't stick to the seat.

My host lit a cigarette, handed it to me. I waved it away.

'David?'

'Cheers,' he said.

I was about to express my surprise because I'd never seen Dave smoke before, but let it go as he took the lighter from Tatyana's fingers.

'There's the Negresco Hotel,' said Tatyana, 'Look, billionaire Russians. Up there, that's where Grace Kelly died.'

Early summer. La Promenade des Anglais. I turned to Dave who was using the sun's glare as an excuse to ignore me.

'So blue!' I said.

'Yeah...no one knows why the sky in Provence is this colour. Some say it's the reflection from the Alps, or the salt, others think it's the algae. It's cool, hein?'

I smiled at the way Tatyana intoned her phrases with a French lilt. I agreed, still trying to catch Dave's eye. He held a view on palm trees and blue skies. Palm trees, he said, looked far too much like pineapples, and blue skies only reminded you they wouldn't stay like that for long.

As we headed towards Cannes, Tatyana pointed out spots of local interest though her commentary was vague, she was better on the subject of herself and her London life. She curled the car around a number of treacherous corners on steep hills until we reached a plateau where there were no other houses in sight. A quarter of an hour later she took a turning through two stone pillars.

I actually gasped when I saw Tatyana's family home, or rather, one of them. Knowing it was called a 'château' I'd been expecting a British-style castle - a grey, crenulated building erupting from the earth like a decayed molar, with maybe a moat, even a Beefeater or two, but this house was beyond all my imaginings.

Le Château de la Gravière stood at the end of a three-minute drive lined with cyprus trees and flanked by acres of overgrown grass, a lake, olive groves and two old tennis courts. It was grand, but welcoming and unpretentious. With the sun dropping to the west of its ochre walls, it glowed. Through the vines and wisteria were rows of bottle-green shutters equally placed into the warm stone. Right in the middle of the building were large, open double doors leading into the main hall.

'Cool,' said Dave, as Tatyana swerved up to a line of parked cars.

'Oh!' she yawned, stretching her arms wide and then taking my hand, 'Let's get everything off and jump in!'

By the time I closed the boot and passed Dave's rucksack to him, Tatyana was already naked and walking through the castle doors.

*

I'm lying on the floor, face down, you are pressing your hands down my back, over my buttocks, around the top of my thighs, I move my hips up to you, your fingers flicker around my pubic bone and travel up again. Every time your hands come a little nearer to where I want them to go, you leave me wanting more. You stroke the sides of my breasts. Your touch controls my breathing: all that I am is just a response to you. You tease me, you take your time. The telephone rings.

I cover my eyes with my hands, this could be Anthony. I have a few seconds to decide whether I pick up, speak to him or risk both of us listening to his 'Goodnight-sleep-well' call.

'You okay?' you ask, feeling me tense under your hands.

'Sure.'

It's the first time since you left that I've not rushed to the phone.

The answering machine clicks on.

My mother's voice.

I listen to her forcing an up-tempo and carefree 'just-checking-in' message, but her heart's not in it, every few words she's stuttering, trying too hard to deflect her concern, aware that I might not be alone when we listen to her.

'Your leaving tore my family apart.'

Mum closes with, 'Daddy and I love you very much darling, you come home if you need to, we're here. Bye-Bye...Bye...'

I look at your face but see no change in expression – no guilt. I wonder if that's what I'm looking for at the end of the week. For you to take back everything you did when you went away.

'I'll run you a bath,' you say jumping up as if you'd been remiss not to think of it before.

'I'd like lots of bubbles.'

'And me?'

'Yes, lots of you.'

While you're in the bathroom, I find my mobile phone and quickly run through the missed calls. He's been ringing all evening. It won't be long.

I call out to you over the gush of water, 'Shall we put candles all around the tub?'

I can afford to be cheerful right now. That was a near miss.

*

The entrance opened out into a hall furnished with a pool table at one end and a piano at the other, apart from that, just ashtrays filled with cigarette butts and burnt-out roaches, empty wine bottles and a pair of red, crocodile high-heeled shoes on the mantelpiece above the walk-in fireplace. Dave and I followed Tatyana past the front staircase through to the garden which sprawled out in various directions. We took the path leading to the swimming pool.

'Hey you fuckers!' called Tatyana to her house-guests.

'There you are!' called Max Penrose, a notorious heart breaker and orator, chair of the university debating team and hot-listed to be Prime Minister one day.

'Ah, did you miss me?' asked Tatyana, testing the water with her toe.

'No, but you took the only matches.'

'That's what they say, you can't start a fire without Tatty. You all know my cousin Kate, don't you?'

Tatyana often called me her 'cousin' but she was, in fact, a cousin of Nick's, my sister's husband. It was through Anna, whom Tatyana idolised, that we'd become friends.

'Course,' waved Max. 'Good trip?'

'Yeah, fine.' I answered. 'And this is Dave.'

'Hi,' said Max.

He turned from Dave to Tatyana who slowly immersed herself in the water with a long groan of pleasure.

'Hello, David Wheeler. Weren't you on the rowing team for Christ's College? I believe we won against you last year?'

Max looked at Dave and shook his head.

'We lost?'

'Fraid so, you stood in for Mike Batton.'

'God, yes! I remember. You know Neil crossed me off the team after that, little shit!'

'Kate, do you know everyone else?' asked Tatyana as she treaded the water.

'You know me,' said Chris looking up from his backgammon, 'Remember? I came to see you and Tatty in that play, we had dinner after.'

'Yes, of course,' I said, wilting under the weight of my bag.

'I'm having a little pre-prandial Spritzer, fancy one?'

'Thanks,' I said, unsure what I'd agreed to.

I turned to ask if Dave wanted anything from the pool bar but he was laughing loudly at something Max was saying while sliding his focus over Tatyana's body.

'Kate! Jump in. Aren't you boiling in that jumper?' asked Tatyana.

I was unable to explain why I just didn't feel up to stripping off and leaping into the water. And as for leaping out again...

It seemed ludicrous that someone who was training to be a doctor should be embarrassed by a friend's unabashed nudity, but I was. It dawned on me that I probably knew more about the insides of the human body than the outsides. Over the last five years I'd drawn, dissected and read about every part of it but I'd no idea what it was like to touch or to be touched, or how a body could shimmer in the fading Provençal light. Tatyana certainly didn't look like the cadavers we'd cut up in the science labs. I tried to picture her spleen, her femur or gallstones, perhaps they were hideous, but what glided under the surface of her pool was nothing less than gorgeous.

'Want some?' Chris asked, offering me a joint.

'No thanks,' I said.

I was not beautiful, not like Tatyana or my sister, women who could alter people's moods with a smile. My dress sense, before I met you, had been designed for entirely practical purposes and the idea of adorning myself seemed laughable. I'd always had girlfriends, good friends, but most of them were like me, switched off where boys and fashion were concerned, although there were a few who, for some bizarre reason, handed me the role of agony aunt, which seemed highly ironic seeing as the only advice I could offer was purely theoretical.

'I'm going to have a last splash of the day. You?' asked Chris.

'No, I'm...fine.'

Despite the setting sun, it was still very hot and I didn't entirely understand what prevented me from joining the others in the pool although I suspected that it was because only three nights before

I'd had sex for the first time.

It had become an issue I couldn't dodge. After having turned 22, I couldn't say I was too young, and being an atheist discredited me on moral grounds - I had no reasons for wanting to put 'it' off but that I simply didn't want to. But Dave had been patient long enough, my sister kept reminding me she'd had two children by my age, so a few nights before our holiday, I stayed over at Dave's parents' house while they visited his granny. The opportunity only pointed in one direction. Dave took me to his bed, tried to relax me as much as possible by running over the names of Coventry's football team players before setting off to do what humans are fundamentally made for. I hadn't expected it to be so painful. Afterwards he said that the first time with anybody was always a bit of a let-down. I believed him. I hadn't yet met you.

'Fantastic! The doctors are here!'

Out from the house a platinum blonde emerged, all smiles and curves. Behind her a large, older woman followed, carrying a tray of cocktails.

Tatyana called out, 'Francoise! Mon ange! Merci!'

'Kate, I'm Georgie – Tatty's told us all about you, how you're so brainy and everyone wants you in their plays and you're really nice too. Made us all sick! That's Josh over there. We think he's dead.'

It was only then I saw someone lying in the grass wearing a velvet jacket and a pair of cycling shorts.

'Is he unconscious?'

'Well, we're not sure,' Georgie mused, crunching on an ice cube. 'That's why we need a professional opinion.'

'Have you checked his pupils?' asked Dave taking a drag of the joint and inhaling studiously.

'No... Where are they?'

We gathered around Josh while Tatyana swam slowly up and down the pool. Dave took his pulse, pulled on his eye lids and looked up at us.

'What's he taken?' he asked Georgie.

'Oh, he had a few beers, some dope...'

'Two bottles of port, Ketamine,' added Chris.

'And some ecstasy.'

'And cocaine,' yawned Max.

44

'Oh, don't offer me any!' said Georgie kicking Max.

'Nembutal, Vitamin C, some red wine at lunch.'

'We thought it best not to touch him. Was that right?'

Dave looked up. 'He's in a PVS.'

'I know, those awful shorts.'

'No, a Persistent Vegetative State.'

'Oh, so nothing unusual then,' said Georgie arching her back and lifting her breasts to the last of the sun.

Dave opened Josh's mouth, felt for his tongue and prised open his eyelids again. 'His pupils are responding to the light...he's dreaming.'

'So he's alive?'

'Oh yes,' said Dave.

'Bloody sod giving us a scare like that!' said Chris.

Then he and Georgie looked to each other. They winked at Dave and three of them lifted Josh by his limbs and carried him over to the pool.

'One. Two. Three!' and on three, Josh was hurled into the water.

He woke in the water with a start, screaming and kicking, splashing Tatyana as she passed.

'Oh Josh! I preferred you dead,' she laughed.

*

You always called it making love, I think you're probably the last man left who does. It isn't your lack of vocabulary, but that is what you do, and that is what we do after my bath, from the bathroom to the bedroom and later, watching TV and eating ice-cream.

'Did you sleep with many women when you are away?'

'You're my wife.'

'Is that a yes or a no?'

'You're my wife, I promised you I'd always be monogamous.'

'Marc, sorry, but...husband and wives live together, that's the point. I don't mean to be facetious but... you've broken every agreement, every pact, every idea of what husbands and wives are.'

'Maybe.'

'Do you want to know about me?'

'It doesn't matter to me.'

'You were the second man I've ever had, but my first love, first time...you know, that was...nice. And now, I've probably lost count

45

how many men I've been with.'

I study your eyes. You look at the TV, you don't turn to me when you say, 'Why's that?'

'Because, because it was just a little bit like being with you.'

'I see.'

'And because I was angry. Raging. Murderously furious. At you. And you weren't there, and they were, so, I fucked them. "Making hate" you'd probably call it. Some men might even have said I raped them.'

This makes you chuckle.

'You couldn't rape anybody Katherine.'

'That's not the point.'

'What's the point?'

'The point is, when you first loved me I was innocent, I saw the good in everyone...I was stupid enough to believe everything you said. And now I'm a slut, soiled goods. And a rapist to boot.'

'You are what you are, you did those things then, you are a different person now, today, with me.'

'Have you been on some Adult Education Elementary Philosophy course for the last three years?'

You laugh. How can you still have light in your eyes when mine has gone forever?

'Show me Katherine, show me what you did with those men, eh? Come on, rape me. Hey, I promise I'll put up a fight, oh! Oh no!'

*

'It's beautiful here, isn't it?' I said, watching the moonlight reflected in the trees outside our windows.

Dave and I had finally gone to bed after a long dinner and several sessions of 'Truth or Dare'. I could still hear voices downstairs and someone splashing about in the pool.

'Kate, you don't need to gush so much.'

'Gush?'

'Gush, about the food, the view, the house...people like Tatyana don't know anything else, you've just got to act like you expect it all, rather than some third-world child at the Queen's garden party.'

I thought about what he'd said. I hadn't been at all aware of being effusive but yes, I had admired the house, the garden,

Francoise's cooking, the view, the paintings – maybe a bit too much. I'd remember to be cool the following day.

'You've just got to know how to treat people like that. Goodnight my darling girl,' he said, turning over and falling asleep.

saturday morning

This time last night you came back to me. I watch you while you sleep, trying to catch your dreams with the rise and fall of your chest and the flicker of your eyes under your lids. Now the tide has taken you into a slow-wave sleep and I follow the progress of your dim, distant pulse. I count six grey hairs around your temple. Your lips move just a little, but your face is calm, not a ripple. Between our legs, what was a few hours ago wet is drying into a salty film. Your breath is now almost undetectable and, when I'm satisfied that you won't be woken, I slip out of bed.

I'm perched over the side of the bath, running warm water over myself but it won't clean away the question which has been itching away at me since yesterday.

Tying my bathrobe around me and flexing my feet on the cold wooden floor, I stand in the living room. With the light behind me, I can see the outline of your trousers over the back of the sofa. My heart speeds up as I move over to the pile of your clothes. I pick up your trousers and slide my fingers into your pockets. There is no reason, I tell myself, to feel like a thief. Empty pockets. You had a jacket. I spin around in search of your jacket – I was sure I saw a brown suede jacket. When did I see it? You bought the shopping, with what? You must have a wallet, things, in your jacket. Where are your things?

Now I remember dropping my coat over your jacket when we came in. I lift up my coat, careful not to make a noise. The suede jacket is underneath. I feel the smooth, cool hide in my fingers; still holding the heaviness of my coat over my other arm I fumble in the inside pockets.

'Katherine.'

Your voice startles me because it is so quiet. I can only see your silhouette in the doorway.

'Where are your things?' I speak my thoughts, not meaning to.

'My things?' you ask.

'How did you pay for the shopping?'

'There was £20 there on the table. You see, the change. And receipt.'

I'd left the money for my cleaner last week and now there are a few coins scattered by the flowers, and yes, there's a receipt.

'Is that why you came back? Because you ran out of money?'

'Don't be stupid.'

'But where are your things?'

'Come to bed. It's cold.'

'But you don't have any clothes, a toothbrush, a passport? Everybody has things.'

'Come on, let's sleep.'

'Where are your things? I can't sleep until you tell me.'

'Come on, Katherine.'

'How do I know you'll be here in the morning? Don't you see? I can't trust you Marc and the fact you refuse to tell me anything just makes it impossible. I always thought that once I found you, dead or alive, I'd understand, but this is...this is worse.'

'Because you don't understand something?'

You walk over to me, try to put your arms over me and lead me back into the bedroom. I use my weight against you and stay with my hand in your empty jacket pocket.

'Calm down,' you say.

You take the coats from me like a brave policeman might prise away a gun from a madman. You rest them over the back of the chair. You speak slowly, trying to reason with me.

'It's morning already. I'm here. Later, too, I'll be here, with you, I'll be right next to you.'

'Marc, I'm even questioning whether you really are here?'

'I'm here. I'm freezing.'

I allow you to walk me back to bed. We both lay side by side absorbing the darkness. The central heating, which is set to come on at 6 a.m., clicks before I hear the rush of the boiler's flame. I nestle into you.

'I thought I saw you once, last year, on the Northern Line. You got off the tube in Barnet. I followed you. You were walking fast, it was about five in the afternoon, you were wearing a grey coat with a long scarf. There were so many people all coming the other direction and I had to run to catch you up. Then you crossed the road and a bus came in front of me and I lost you...was it you?'

'No.'

'I went back to the tube station every day for the next week at the same time to see if you'd come again, but you didn't. It wasn't you then?'

'No.'

'Definitely wasn't you?'

'I've never been to Barnet.'

'Right.'

We fit perfectly together. You've never crushed or jabbed me, never been too heavy or light. I've never had to complain of sharp elbows in my ribs, scratchy toe nails or limbs giving me a dead leg.

'Why don't you have any things?'

'I only have you.'

saturday, midday

I know Maggie's little tap, kept light so that it doesn't wake you, and I open the door before it becomes a knock.

'Oh sorry! Stupid me, have I...?'

'It's okay, I was awake.'

'Two things. I've just come back from a trip to *Sainsbury's* – dashed out early before the hordes descended – I know, I should get them to deliver and this is the last time I'm going to throw myself into the fray – I'm going to have to learn how to order it all on the internet like you do – even the most steadfast Luddite needs to have their toilet paper brought direct I fear – but! I'm parked miles away and I noticed your car's just outside – could we change parking spots just now while I unload? I'm so sorry to be such a nuisance.'

'Sure.'

'Second point,' Maggie continues talking while I go in search of my car keys, 'There's this TV chef – God, what's his name? – the Italian, with an accent...anyway, he does a programme where you buy the ingredients beforehand and then cook it in real time with him giving instructions, I doubled up just in case we could do it together?...Thursday nights, nine o'clock – are you...?'

Her mouth stops working when you stand by my side. She tries to recover herself as she hears me say, 'Maggie, this is Marc.'

'I know.'

I look to you to see what she is staring at.

You are like a planet, Marc, a vital force that draws us all around you. Even standing there, in my dressing gown, you have us in your pull. You put an arm around me, covering my shoulder in your hand. Maggie doesn't see me anymore, she sees us. A Couple. That two-headed being.

'I remember the little dog,' you say.

'Walter,' she whispers, thrilled that you remembered her pet.

'Walter, yes. He's okay?'

'Oh yes, well, we had rather a scare...' She looks at me... 'Kate saved his life a while back...he's on fighting form now. Thanks to her.'

'Good,' you say, looking to me. 'Here, I'll re-park the car. I'll get dressed, just a second.'

You turn back into the flat. I'm left at the door. Maggie seems to be wobbling, staring at the space where you were standing.

'Does he know?'

'Know what?'

Maggie's face twitches and tics away in different directions as her neurons run back and forth trying to think exactly what Marc might want to know first. Maggie and I have been close these last two years, but now you have returned, there's a dividing line between us.

'That...he's...missing?'

'I think so.'

'When did he come back?'

'Thursday night.'

'Nice that he remembered Walter. I suppose you won't want the recipe now?'

'The what?'

And then her voice is louder, friendlier and I can tell that you are behind me. 'When you have a moment Katie, I'd be so grateful if you could just set me up on the *Sainsbury's* site and get me going.'

'Sure.'

You toss my car keys in your hand up and down and kiss me good bye with, '*A bientôt ma chérie.*'

*

I'll take you back to when I first met Maggie, that way I wasn't always so alone. She also gave me my first lead to you.

I was woken at six in the morning by frantic knocking at the door. My first thought was that there was news of you. Even in my sleep, I was prepared for that moment and without even opening my eyes I was sliding the door chain.

In front of me stood a middle-aged woman with mascara streaking down her cheeks. Her face was red and her lips quivered. She was holding a little white dog in her hands.

'Oh no, I've woken you up. I'm so sorry, I'm so sorry...I've been waiting for a good time to speak to you all night and look, I've woken you...sorry. I'm Maggie, from upstairs. We've passed each other a few times and,' she stops to sniff loudly, 'this is Walter, my dog.'

I'd seen her before and had certainly heard the dog yapping when his owner was out during the day, often when I'd been trying to sleep off a night-shift.

'Is everything all right?'

'No,' the woman nodded, 'No, not at all.' Her eyes welled with tears. She held the dog up to me, 'I think he's dying.'

The dog did look sick. I took him in my hands. His nose was hot, his stomach convulsing.

'Is he passing blood?'

'Yes. It's like strawberry jam...it's ruined my carpets. He hasn't eaten for two days and no water either. He must be very dehydrated.'

It takes Maggie all her strength to keep her composure to give me the right information.

'Have you rung the vet?'

'The surgery's closed until eight. I've left messages but no one's got back to me! I'm so sorry to have woken you - I see your post on the landing sometimes...Dr Brenton. You're a doctor, aren't you?'

'Yes, but for people, not for dogs. Sorry. Do you want to come in?'

'Thank you.'

Maggie stepped into the flat as I bundled up the quivering dog in a tea-towel and handed him back to his owner.

'I thought doctors had to train as vets first...'

'No, it's the other way around,' I answer, switching on the coffee maker. 'Coffee?'

My neighbour nodded her head, 'Two sugars, please.'

'Usually the first two years of medical training are taken with students who will go on to being vets so I've a vague idea of how many diseases cows get and how to handle a terrapin...Walter's a Westie, isn't he?' Maggie nods, her trust affirmed.

'My parents had one of these, we called her Star. Hum? Walter, you'd have liked Star.'

Maggie chewed her bottom lip.

'Would you just look at Walter, please? You're one of those people who I would completely trust him with. I can tell by your face.'

That made me laugh.

'I wish it were so.'

By that time I was completely awake.

'Well, let's have a look at you Walter.'

Walter rolled over, paws in the air, surrendering to my general prodding. He looked up at me and yelped a little where he was particularly tender.

'My guess – and it's just a guess – is that he's got the doggy equivalent of gastro-enteritis, see, it's enflamed here, that's his colon, sssh, sssh, that's it little one. Can you see that this part is in spasm, that's what's aggravating the lining of his lower intestines...causing the bleeding.'

'Can you give him something?'

'No, I'm afraid not. Drugs for humans don't quite work on dogs, but he seems to like being massaged, here...'

The dog flattened his ears and let me smooth out his hair.

'I knew you'd have magic fingers. This is the calmest he's been. He's not going to...'

She gulped several times before I answered, 'No, no, he'll be all right. Has he been drinking from ponds or been near bird faeces?'

'I don't think - Yes! Yes! We went for a walk in the Serpentine and he went in chasing the geese.'

'That might be it. The vet will give you something to calm the activity down and some antibiotics. He should be all right by tonight.'

'Thank you so much, I had such a scare. You don't really know how much you love them until the thought of...' Maggie doesn't continue.

The sky is ordering itself into a tricolour of red, white and blue outside my window. I have to be at work for 8:30.

'Real coffee! What a treat, thank you.'

'My husband always insisted on real coffee...' I looked into the cup. 'It's quite a palaver but...'

'That's him, isn't it?' she asked looking at a photograph of you. It was one of my favourite photographs of you in Barcelona reading a newspaper outside a café.

'Yes, that's Marc. My husband.'

'I heard what happened...and I see all the posters. There's one I pass everyday outside the police station. Funny enough, the secretaries at work were talking about him the other day. They were saying if they found him it'd be hard to give him back!'

We looked at your picture. Maggie screwed up her eyes.

'They were only joking...I hope that doesn't sound insensitive. I'm so sorry for you...really...it must be awful...you've no idea where he could be?'

'No idea at all.'

Those days, I was scared of my own company, terrified to be alone, but around other people, I felt asphyxiated. All the while I was talking to someone, my mind was plotting how to escape them. My patients were the easiest people to deal with, people who had no right or interest in asking about my private life. As for the rest, all day long people said things about you that they immediately regretted. The worst was dealing with their embarrassment and quasi-spiritual aphorisms such as "it's all in God's plan" or "perhaps he wasn't the right one anyway." No one could say anything remotely helpful but at the same time, they couldn't leave it alone. It was difficult to remember a time when a simple question wasn't a brutal attack.

'It's just that he really was – I mean – is, quite a dish. I used to pass him on the stairs. He was always polite and friendly. And smelt so heavenly! Sometimes he'd say hello and stroke Walter... such a gentleman, I used to think that he was the perfect man.'

'Yes, I thought so too.'

'It must be coming up to a year now.'

'Yes, nearly.'

Maggie looked at my desk in the corner of the living room.

'I see you're still busy with the search...'

'The Thames Valley Police are producing a new report about missing people, I'm trying to pass on some of my experiences of how Marc's disappearance was handled.'

'Have they been good, the police?'

'They haven't found him, but yes, I suppose.'

'I had a policeman come to my door, asking about you and him. What was he like? When had I last seen him? Did you row together? I so wanted to help, so wanted to say something which would make a difference but all I could tell him was that I'd see you both in the supermarket or on the street, always holding hands, laughing, kissing...Oh please don't think I am nosey neighbour, it's just that in London you can go days without recognising anyone and well, I did train as a psychologist, I find it hard to take my work hat off. I told him that you both seemed so much in love.'

I continued patting the dog while she spoke.

'Everyone living in this building was so shocked and sorry. We talked about starting up a collection for you, give you something to show how concerned we were but ...we couldn't think what to call it, it's not like a death or a divorce –'

'That's very kind.'

The time on my DVD player was 7.35. Would I get away with a shower or would it be a case of grabbing my clothes and rushing out?

'Look we'll be running. Thank you so much for seeing Walter and being here to chat to.'

'Any time, even at night. I don't sleep much these days so if you see my light on and fancy a night cap or a natter, just knock.'

I handed the dog back to Maggie at the door.

'Thanks again,' she said, stepping into the corridor to look at me. I could see in her eyes she was having second thoughts about saying something.

'There was something I thought about later. I didn't ring the police because it didn't seem important but maybe...' Maggie hesitated.

'What's that?'

'There was a woman.'

My breath stopped mid-flow and my muscles locked up.

'It must have been about two weeks before he disappeared, I saw a woman. It's probably nothing, but she was often around the building. Sometimes I saw her looking up at your flat. She was small, very...very...elegant, rich looking. She had red hair – she reminded me of a mermaid in a way. Does that mean anything to you?'

'No.'

'I didn't connect the two until I remembered her talking to a taxi driver one time and I heard her accent. She was French, definitely. I thought she might be a cousin or friend of Marc's from home...anyway, it was just a thought. I hope I haven't made you late.'

✻

You put the car keys down, 'Come back to bed,' you say.

I'm supposed to be at my parents, you're supposed to be missing, but we go back to bed. And maybe because you are back and the story is coming to an end, I am re-opening those first memories of us, looking through them, sorting, re-filing and tossing some of them out forever.

✻

The next morning in France, I woke alone with the sun making its way over the tops of the trees. Dave's watch was propped up by the bed like a centurion overseeing his belongings. I waited for him to return, but over twenty minutes passed. I wondered if he'd gone downstairs to make me a coffee and I was afraid of bodging up a tender gesture by going down myself, but maybe everyone had got up early and gone out without waking me. Anxiety got the better of me, so I wandered along corridors and down the stone stairs, through to the kitchen and outside terrace where the table was already being laid for breakfast.

Tatyana was arguing with someone in the kitchen while carrying out a fresh pot of coffee. She was so involved in her conversation that she didn't see me. She was wearing only a long white lace robe, her pale hair was piled on top of her head, matching her golden feet which danced over the tiles. Close behind her shuffled Dave with a basket of croissants. He was raising his voice at her while chewing on a piece of pain au raisin.

'So then explain then how America has less social mobility than anywhere else in the Western world?'

I stood by the kitchen door watching them coming in and out while they set the table, or rather, a stage, for their debate. Dave must have been for a run already that morning, his bare torso shone in the light, his hair stood up around his head like black

56

shredded satin. They made an attractive couple.

Even when I sat down and helped myself to orange juice, Dave didn't acknowledge me. He was waving his fists at the sky in mock fury at something Tatyana had said but I'd not heard.

Max came out on the porch. 'Bit bloody early for Milton Freidman, isn't it?' he said with a yawn, focusing on the pot of coffee as if he expected it to pour itself into his cup.

Tatyana perched herself on her chair and lit a cigarette. She waved a spent match in the air, exhaled and looked at me as if exasperated. She was about to say something but was interrupted by a shriek from one of the overhead bedrooms. It was followed by giggling and the unmistakable sound of a hand slapping against bare buttocks.

We looked up at Georgie and Josh's bedroom window. The spanking session was now underway in regular sequences, interspersed by yelps, suppressed laughter and groaning.

Max cleared his throat. 'Don't tell me that's my sister?' He helped himself to a croissant.

'Care for some cake, Marie Antoinette?' asked Dave, waving a brioche at Tatyana. Tatyana laughed, taking a bite out of the bread while Dave held it.

'I thought you were doing the bacon and eggs?' asked Tatyana.

'Consider it done, Your Majesty!'

With that, Dave put a hand on my shoulder, kissed my head and left for the kitchen.

Leonie came in reading a leather-bound collection of Swinbourne's poetry as the next set of spanks started up again in multiples of three followed by a voice saying sternly 'naughty, naughty girl'. Chris lowered his voice, 'Is that...?' He pointed to the room upstairs as they heard Georgie Penrose's voice begging, 'No! no!' before another whack was sent from their window.

Chris looked up at the group with a mischievous grin as Tatyana whispered, 'Don't laugh, please. All of you...behave.'

As breakfast was being cleared, Josh and Georgie emerged refreshed and rosy cheeked declaring that they were ravenous. The rest of the day was spent swaying in hammocks or by the pool, interrupted only by Francoise bringing trays of things to eat.

For our second day an excursion was planned to some nearby waterfalls. It had been a gorgeous day, we'd swum, picnicked and drunk a lot. As we were leaving, Dave suggested that I drive Chris *and Leonie back while he went with Tatyana, Georgie and Josh. The parties were split that way because, he explained, he and I were the most sober.*

Our car reached the house first and, as it was Francoise's day off, we started making supper for the others. By the time it was dark we heard the second car pull up, I watched from the kitchen window as Tatyana and Dave fell out of the car, doubled over laughing. They were both completely naked.

Still laughing, they burst into the house, covering their bodies with their damp clothes.

'We couldn't bear to put our wet clothes on, so we drove back like this! Can you imagine the looks we got at the péage!'

I tried to laugh along with the joke, but I felt my stomach turn. But of course, if their clothes had been wet, well, it was very sensible to take them off rather than sit in them and risk getting haemorrhoids.

'Where are Georgie and Josh?'

'Oh, dropped them off in Cannes, they wanted a dinner à deux. What's for supper?'

Late that night, I woke alone in the bedroom. It was completely dark, no moon, no birds. The bed was hot. I waited for Dave to return from the bathroom but couldn't hear anything. After dozing for about half an hour, I whispered his name, there was no answer. And then I worried about him, I don't know why, but he had been very drunk, maybe he'd decided on a late night swim or to jump off the roof, or simply got lost in the château, there were still floors we'd never been to. Spending time in A & E departments teaches one to fear even the most seemingly harmless activities.

The day's heat was being expunged from the old stone walls, even the floor tiles were body temperature. Through the windows the garden lights cast a silver sheen on the front lawn. Dave wasn't in the kitchen, or the hall or the drawing room, but hearing a match being struck led me to the library.

As soon as I saw him, I knew something was terribly wrong. From the distance of the threshold, he sat like a poorly slapped together sculpture. He seemed to be waiting for someone in the dark, in the corner of the living room, smoking a cigarette and staring into the floor.

'Dave?'

He didn't answer me. I touched his clammy shoulder.

'Are you alright?'

He continued staring at the space on the floor. I squatted down in front of him.

'Do you want a glass of water?'

He didn't answer me, so I went to the kitchen and brought over some ice and water. He didn't acknowledge me or the drink.

'Dave? Say something.'

I rocked his knees. He didn't even turn to look at me. I stayed by him a little longer and then he took my hand. He brought it to his mouth and kissed it.

'Sorry,' he croaked.

'Sorry for what?'

'Sorry.'

I stayed an hour, then too tired to stifle my yawns, went back to bed.

Dave didn't come down for breakfast, and I didn't see him all that morning. There was no sign from him at lunchtime or later that afternoon.

'Have you had a row?' Tatyana asked softly as we swam lengths together.

'I don't think so...'

'You don't think so?' Tatyana laughed.

'Well, we went to bed...he was himself...then he got up in the middle of the night and wouldn't speak to me...'

'Men,' concluded Tatyana, 'he's probably jealous.'

'Why?'

'Chris...he's absolutely mad about you.'

'But we're supposed to be leaving tomorrow, I'm just a bit –'

'Oh don't be silly, stay, stay here, really, we all want you to stay.'

Around the time Francoise was bringing in our afternoon tea someone noticed that Dave had moved himself to an attic room on the top floor. We looked up and saw him sitting by the window, watching us.

After the afternoon's volley ball tournament, Chris and Max took the opportunity to go on, what they called, 'a peace mission' and invite him to play, but they returned saying he'd refused to speak to them.

At supper I took him some food, chatted about the day and tried to get him to eat something. He only looked at me once, and it was a look of hostility. He said 'No thank you' to the food and requested some whisky and more cigarettes.

I reported this back to the rest of the group. No-one knew what to make of it.

I slept alone that night, hoping Dave would relent and find his way to our room, but he didn't.

The following morning, the house party carried on as usual. In the afternoon Leonie and I went to the shops to buy Dave his nicotine and alcohol provisions. I returned to him in the evening, he'd barely changed positions since midday.

The nocturnal party games lost their appeal, Dave's invisible presence hung over us. I was the first to go to bed, lying there wondering at what point I should call his parents.

The next day was the day Dave had programmed for us to be leaving for the Pyrenees – we should have been half way through our tour of the South of France but we hadn't even started it, nor did he look like he was going anywhere. Before breakfast I went up to ask him if he were ready to leave, assuming that he'd recover himself now that we needed to move on. He was gaunt, with a stubble and yellow nicotine-stained fingers. I lost my patience with him, said we had to go whether he liked it or not, Tatyana had more guests coming, he was being rude, I threatened to call his parents. All I got back was a thick, slow, 'You go then!'

Going down the stairs, I overheard what I understood in French to be Francoise berating Tatyana for not calling a doctor. Tatyana replied, 'But he is a doctor.'

'Any closer to finding out what Dave's crise is all about?' asked Tatyana applying some sun scream to her shoulders.

'No...no idea at all. Do you think I ought to ring his parents or...someone?'

'He'll snap out of it...'

I wondered what form this 'snap' would take.

Dave's dinner tray that night was left untouched. He did, however, find enough energy to snatch a packet of cigarettes out of my hands when I'd come to remove it. Later on Max took him up some wine after saying he was determined to find out what the problem *was. He came down scratching his head.*

'Well?' we asked.

Max took in a deep breath and announced dramatically, 'He has spoken.'

'And what has he spoken?' they chanted, encouraged by the breakthrough.

'He said he wants to speak to Tatyana, and only Tatty.'

We all looked to Tatyana who raised her eyebrows in surprise.

'Okay,' she said, getting up from the table.

'Shouldn't I come with you?' offered Chris.

'I think I can manage, but if I scream, don't just open another bottle of wine, eh?'

The group clustered around Tatyana as she mounted the stairs, they wished her luck as though she were about to steal a sacred pearl from a sea monster's lair.

We pretended to carry on as normal. Georgie tried to engage me in a backgammon game while we bantered about topics far removed from our curiosity. All ears were trained on the staircase, waiting to hear Tatyana's light tread returning to us with the mystery solved.

Before midnight, while I rocked in the hammock staring up at Dave's light, Tatyana emerged from the house carrying a tumbler of Cognac for each of us. She lay next to me and sighed.

'Hey,' she said, swinging her hand out to catch mine. She squeezed my fingers.

'So?' I asked.

'Oh God, Kate,' Tatyana moaned.

'What Tatyana? Tell me?'

'Finally, I know what is the matter with Dave,' she said.

I took a moment to prepare myself. She sighed, then sighed again.

'I wish he'd tell you himself, but he won't. He's really confused...really, you know,' she waved her hand around her head, 'really mixed up. Out there.'

'Why, what did he say?'

'Oh, you know. Life. Parents, money, career, girls...love. And stuff. He thinks he's in love.'

I lay back watching the sky swinging above me.

'I think I love him too...' I said quietly.

She leant over, brought the glass to her lips, shook her head, put the glass back on the ground.

'Yes, but...Katie, he thinks he's in love with me,' said Tatyana.

'You?'

'Ever since he saw me come for my interview apparently - four years ago.'

'Are you sure he said that?'

'It's what he told me. He wants me to go up to him, at midnight, and if I don't, he's going to kill himself.'

'Kill himself?'

'Kate, he's serious.'

'So am I! What did he say – exactly?'

'He wants me to go to him or...'

'But you won't...will you?'

'I can't say. I can't say, and least of all to you...'

She closed her eyes as if the memory of his words swept over her like a moving piece of music.

'Do you love him?'

'David is so...so...passionate, strong, romantic...he said inside of him is this nucleic fusion of love and tenderness - he says I'm the only person who can dismantle him or he'll explode...you know?'

'No. I don't know. I've never heard such nonsense in all my life. You make your decision Tatyana. I'm obviously nothing to do with this.'

'But that's it, Katie. Listen, nobody's ever understood him, not his parents, his teachers... or you...'

Tatyana tried to catch up with me as I stomped towards the house.

'But you do?' I said swinging around to her.

'I want to try...'

'Well go ahead then – "explode" together!'

I anticipated that she'd run after me, but she didn't.

In the darkness of my room, I shoved my stuff into my rucksack. At midnight, while I was rechecking my passport and ticket home, I heard Tatyana's little feet padding their way up to Dave's room.

In the morning, Dave came into 'our' room to collect his things. He found me sitting on the bed, waiting for him. He appeared surprised to see me, perhaps he had thought I'd already left the house but more likely, he'd forgotten about me altogether.

He grunted while I continued to stare at him as he swung out his arms to scoop t-shirts and his camera from the floor like a lethargic orang-utan.

'What's going on?'

'Uh?' he said, picking up a pair of boxer shorts and unconsciously smelling them.

'Dave, we're supposed to be travelling around France together. Aren't we?'

He opened both his hands and scraped his belongings into his rucksack.

'No one's stopping you...'

His ruck-sack over one shoulder, he tapped the doorframe as if inspecting the timber, jumped up and swung himself into the hall.

saturday afternoon

'Do you think about when we first met?'

This is what I ask you when you return from re-parking the car.

'No,' you answer.

'When you were gone, I used to think, one day with you was better than my whole life put together.'

'Why are you crying?'

'Because it's only now that you have returned, that I can really feel what it was like to have lost you.'

So I have my husband all Saturday – it's how I think of it, "I'm having him," like I've heard men say, "I had her." I've never felt a need to take over someone's body and person as well, but this morning, I won't let you go until I've finished with you, that missing man, Marc Venelles. Every time I touch you is for all the times I craved you. One for the team. Your body is there for the taking and in those seconds when the world fades out and I arrive at a place where nothing exists but the sensation of you, I'm not searching anymore.

Then I come back and you are still here. And you listen to me. I lay back on the bed and talk, whatever comes into my head. You say little, you prompt me, restart me, but most of all, you listen.

'I missed going to the park with you. It's something you can't really do on your own, without a dog, I mean, unless you're

schizophrenic or training for a marathon.'
  'We'll go to the park if you like.'
  'I'm scared.'
  'I'm here, don't be afraid.'
  'Oh yes, I've got five days left...'
  'It's for you to decide Katherine.'
  'To decide what?'

*

I thought I was prepared for what I'd find at the NMPs' Helpline offices, but arriving at the call centre, seeing the rows of volunteers on the phones, the whiteboards listing names, details and updates, the walls covered in snapshots of faces, it was a different world. That's all I can say, Marc, a different place altogether. You left for somewhere, and I ended up there, where I didn't want to be at all.

One face snapped into life from behind the phone.

'Kate? Hi I'm Frances.'

I'd liked her voice when I'd first heard it a few days before and I liked it then. Frances moved towards me, and I was warmed by the smile, the colourful wooden beads jangling on her chest, the plump handshake.

'Thanks for coming in.'

It was kind of her to welcome me like this, as it had been me who'd insisted I see her in person. When Detective Wells gave me her card I'd instilled hope in it. Even when she said that really, there was little she could do to help, I couldn't shake the belief that this person was going to lead me to you. So I just thought if she actually met me, I wouldn't be just another woman enquiring after a wayward partner.

'There's a room at the back which is quieter.'

She was my guide in that new world: what was strange and terrifying to me was just another day's work for her. Walking behind her, I tried to take in everything I saw, the post-it notes, dates of sightings, of deaths, case numbers.

'You alright, darling?'

'So many...'

'So many. You're right there.'

We stopped and looked around us at the gallery of ruptured lives. She put her hand on my shoulder.

'Sometimes I wonder if there's anyone not missing to someone somewhere, if you get my drift. The last two years there've been some high profile cases, it's brought a lot of people out of the woodwork, so to speak, we've had to move offices twice, double our staff...our oldest unsolved case is from 1893.'

She led me into what I can describe as a little stable, separate but still overlooking the floor. As she manoeuvred herself round to her desk she picked up a box of tissues and put them in front of me.

'Did you manage to get some of the stuff I asked for?'

'Yes. This is his wallet, bus pass, video card, credit and current account card. Here's his passport, his driving licence, cheque book...NHS card...'

'Birth certificate?'

'No, I don't have that.'

'Huh.'

'French ID card?'

'No. And a recent photo of him.'

She fingered the belongings as I laid them out. She looked into them as if they'd rearrange themselves back into you. Her eyes rested on your photo, asking questions of that face. She moved the pieces around, as if contemplating a puzzle. She was contemplating a puzzle.

'Honey, with what's here, I see two pictures. Okay? He's out there, taking some time out, it's very likely someone's looking after him...I mean, where's he gonna go, eat, sleep without his chequebook, credit card, passport, you know? The other is less likely. He's switched identities. This takes planning, though – since 9/11 even more so – and to some extent, it's illegal – you can't go around on a false identity – you can only go on-the-run so long like that these days. But sweetheart, in both of these scenarios, he won't want to be found.'

'Could anyone have taken him, harmed him...?'

'It's unlikely...'

She pushed the tissue box nearer me and placed Marc's things next to each other.

'There's no reason he would have wanted to disappear unless something was very wrong.'

'Yes. Yes, something's wrong, Kate, there's no denying it – he's left you without any warning and he's left his stuff. His details are up on the Missing Persons' site, they've done routine *checks...you've filed your report. This must be hell for you, I totally appreciate that. But it's a waiting game from here on. We're a few weeks in and...even if you were a blood relative, we couldn't do much more.'*

'You'd do the posters –'

'Social network sites are better –'

'What about appeals, TV announcements.'

'If you could get a family member to report him, as I said on the phone, yeah, that. It would also open the links with France. But you say he hasn't any family...any? And you say you know nothing of his life before he met you...'

She blew over your things, a curled buss pass trembled on the table. 'As I said, sweetie, our charity only provides for blood relatives.'

'Mrs White, I'm desperate. What can I do?'

'If you don't have one already, I recommend you invest in a fast, powerful computer with high-speed connection and then, all I can say is, wait. Wait.'

*

The telephone rings in octaves up and down the solipsistic cavern we've made for ourselves.

'Take his call, Katherine.'

I can't look at you.

The answering machine clicks on but the person rings off. I can't hide my relief that we've been spared the discomfort of someone talking out loud to me with you in the room – more precisely, of Anthony talking to me, in front of my husband.

You move into the kitchen, open the fridge and take out possibilities for a late lunch. My mobile phone leaps into a jolly tune from inside the lining of my pocket. You watch me as I move quickly to pull it out. Despite being muffled, the tune becomes increasingly loud until I hold the phone in my hand. I see Anthony's face on the screen, his name, number. I switch off the phone, Anthony's picture dissolves. I don't feel relief, this respite is temporary.

You stand behind me. Then you say something which I find hilariously funny.

'Don't let me get in the way of your life.'

The coffee machine put-puts.

'I'm getting married,' I say it out loud. For you, and for me.

*

I didn't sleep at all that last night at the château. I'd been kept awake by the late night swimming session which seemed to involve, from what I heard, a naked diving contest and Dave, shouting out novel ideas for things to do as if he'd been elected in-château game-show host. All this was followed by the love-making session between him and Tatyana which continued until Francoise arrived to prepare the breakfast. At one point, Chris had stopped off at my room. When I asked him what he was doing tugging at my sheets, he mumbled something about looking for the loo.

'I am not a toilet, Chris. Go to bed.'

Making sure he did exactly that, I led him onto one of the landings. Returning to my room, I caught sight of Dave coming up the back-stairs carrying a cup of herbal tea for Tatyana. He stopped when he saw me. He looked like he wanted to say something but changed his mind and moved on.

At breakfast the group made a noticeable fuss of me, particularly Chris, who insisted I have the last croissant, refilled my coffee cup after every few mouthfuls. Whatever I said, all eyes turned to me with concern, especially when Dave came down and prepared a tray to take back up for himself and Tatyana. I wondered if the way I felt was similar to when invalids returned home after an accident. I tried to accept their kindness and not let humility slump into humiliation.

The plan was to go to Aix-en-Provence for a late lunch. I was to drive with Leonie, Josh, Georgie and Chris - Dave and Tatyana had sent a message through Leonie that they would be staying in that day. As we were five in the car, Max would zoom ahead on his bike as the 'advance party,' as he called it. His job was to book a table for lunch and scout around for drugs, which they were fast running out of.

As we left, I discreetly lifted my case into the boot of the car.

Approaching Aix, while I was thinking how to change my flight, my throat contracting with sadness and flicking a tear off my cheek as I would a greenfly, I noticed that we were driving through the scene of a serious road accident. It was Leonie who saw Max's body being carried into the ambulance.

*

'If we can't talk about the past or the future, I guess feeding ducks is a good way to spend an afternoon.'

We watch a pair of eiders floating through a swirl of goose excrement.

'Sometimes I really wanted to talk about you, just to tell a story or repeat something you said...I don't know, I wanted to include you, I guess, but I couldn't – it was too awkward and embarrassing for other people - apart from Mimi and Bruno - they used to want to talk about Uncle Marc...I was probably happiest with them. When you left you took my future but also my past. All those memories, just kept to myself, and after a while, I didn't know whether they were real or not.'

Your eyes have taken on the shades of the pond.

'But memories aren't real, are they? Just stories.'

'They're something, when the person isn't there...you want to know that once they were...'

'But you can't really re-make how it was, only how you see it after, you fit the picture to what you want. That's why Katherine, I don't like to tell stories about me. It's not important and more than that, I would be lying to you. I don't want to lie to you.'

'Do you think I'm so gullible, such a fool? Do you think I take everything at face value – even you? Especially you? Maybe once, maybe... But not now. Not after what you've done to me.'

The cold air grazes my throat and I'm aware of a nearby family looking at me and calling their children away from the pond's edge.

'I live in the same world as you, Marc, I know that most relationships are based on approximations, probability and a whole lot of blind trust. That's all I had to go by when I married you, but I took that chance. I got you wrong though, didn't I? And I've paid for it.'

'Yes. So don't keep paying by asking all these questions. Take what's good, leave what's bad.'

'But which is which?'

'Ah!' And you smile. I flop against you, my eyelids half closed because I'm smiling too, warm and soft, looking up at you. And we go back into something which is us. There's so much that goes on between two people that you can never explain to anyone, even if you did understand it yourself.

The ducks waddle away from us at great speed. You put your arm around me and lead me back to the bench where we'd been sitting. You take a cigarette out and jab it on your thigh. I put out my hand for a cigarette too. You raise your eyebrows and light both of them. It's too cold to be sitting in a park, even for two refugees like us.

You ask, 'Shall we?'

*

Georgie paced outside the main entrance of Aix hospital as Chris and Leonie relayed between us and the A&E doctors who were seeing Max. I went in search of refreshments.

Once in the hospital vicinity, I started to feel like myself for the first time that holiday. Although it was more like a business hotel compared to where I'd be working, everything about the A & E part of the hospital was familiar to me: the signs leading to the departments, the porters' slippers, the information listed on the monitors.

I'd forgotten about the next three years of training ahead of me. Thinking about the salary I'd finally be receiving and the badge with the title "Dr" on it made me excited for my future, even when I saw the yawning junior doctors walking as fast as they could without running down the corridors. I didn't understand the words which passed between the nurses, but I could probably give a good translation.

I was reminded of Anna saying that there was nothing better than walking past a screaming baby when it wasn't yours; it was like that for me, being there and not on duty, not having to deal with it.

I found a drinks' dispenser by the maternity ward. While I tried to decipher the meaning of 'noisette', 'longue', 'court', 'café crème' and negotiating the amount of money in my purse, I was aware of someone standing beside me.

'Sorry, go ahead,' I said, counting through my coins. And then, realising that I'd spoken in English, I looked up at the man.

'Pardon. Allez-vous devant moi...' I said, hoping that meant something.

The man was staring at me. Really, really staring as if he had suddenly stumbled on a creature so rare and so nervous even a blink might frighten it away. I must have seemed that way in those days, to you.

The look in your eyes struck me in the chest. That's when he became 'you'. I couldn't catch my breath for long enough to rationalise what exactly had hit me. You didn't break your stare, but you smiled and when you smiled at me, I was weightless, giddy. Free. You controlled me from the inside.

I never had any choice.

'What would you like?' you asked.

Your voice was so deep, relaxed, as if you were just waking from a daytime sleep by the sea, as if we'd always known each other. It was your voice I loved first, your accent, the reverberation, the safety it promised – I heard something then, Marc, on a sonar level, that showed me the way home.

You were looking at the change in my hand and then into my eyes. When you smiled your blue eyes reflected the sunlight, emitting white sparks of light against your skin.

I brought my fingers up to my face, took a deep breath and laughed at my light-headedness. I regained my equilibrium by inhaling the familiar scent of disinfected floors and not looking up at the stranger.

'I'm getting three coffees and I can't remember how my friends wanted them...so do go ahead.'

I looked up, right into your eyes. 'Merci,' I added.

'English?' you asked, not moving.

'Yes, I'm here on holiday.'

'I didn't know the hospital was a tourist attraction.'

'No, I'm not visiting the hospital,' I laughed. 'My friend was in a motor bike accident.'

'Oh. He is okay?'

'Yes, he's got a fractured tibia and a few broken ribs and clavicle – the usual.'

I noticed you were frowning. 'Sorry, a leg break, and his...' I tapped my collar bone.

'Driving in the heat, it's dangerous.'

You shrugged and I had the urge to rest my head on your shoulders and just stay there till old age took me off. I looked at the buttons on your denim shirt and back to the machine.

'The collar bone'll take him a good few months to recover, though.'

'I'm sorry?'

'This part,' I said, touching my shoulder and noticing that his eyes were running over my hand. 'It's an uncomfortable break.'

'Aie, I imagine.'

'And this is such a wonderful hospital, not like where I work in England, this is just...'

I put my arms out in appreciation of the white walls and open courtyards. I'd never really said so much to anyone who I'd not been formally introduced to before.

Anna chats to everyone but I don't. I don't know why I wanted to talk to you; it was the shock of the morning and the longing for an ally after so many days feeling alone with people who were supposed to be my friends.

'You're a doctor?' you asked, incredulous. I shook my head. 'But you are so young!'

'Oh I'm still in training, five years down another eight or so to go!'

The coffee machine gurgled.

'Sorry, do go ahead.'

When you put your finger up to the screen to punch in the number of your order, you turned to me again.

'What would you like?'

I rubbed the back of my head, spilling change on the ground, 'That's so kind...urm...hot chocolate would be...reviving!'

And again, you smiled at me. I had this feeling that I had so much I wanted to tell you, to talk to you about. It was from that moment that I started planning what I'm writing to you now, Marc, it started then, this letter to an alien.

You faced the machine. Your back was wide, strong. As you bent to see the drink being poured, I noticed cigarettes in your pocket. You wore a silver chain around your neck and carried a leather wallet. All these things that belonged to you made me feel secure, like being with relatives, we were all joined together as parts of you.

'Are you from London?' you asked as the flow of drink came to a few last drops.

'I'm from Oxford, originally, that's where my parents live, but in September I'll be living in London. Have you been there?'

'Oh yes, many times.'

Stop right there. Why didn't I stop right there? Instead of picking up these clues which would have solved you, I hobbled around the floor picking up coins that I'd dropped instead.

'One hot chocolate for Mademoiselle...'

I brought my fingers up to yours and, as they touched, the feel of you went through me. The temperature in my body soared.

You were about to say something when I heard, 'Kate! There you are!'

Leonie rushed towards me panting. 'There you are!' she repeated, catching her breath and letting her feet slide over the linoleum floor. I looked at her, wishing her away.

'Max's ready to leave now. What do you want to do? We could all squeeze in and go back together but...or we could come back for you or you could...'

Leonie looked up at you and then back to me.

She knew my stay at the château was over but she didn't want to be the one to say it.

'I'm fine, I'll make my own way, really. I'll get my suitcase out of the car.'

'Well, are you sure?' asked Leonie, relieved I was sparing them a complicated exit. I turned to the Frenchman.

'Bye.'

I wanted to say more but couldn't think of anything else.

'Goodbye. Enjoy the rest of your holiday,' you said.

'Yes, you too.'

The words 'you too' came out simultaneously with the realisation of how crass they were. You weren't on holiday, and I'd never asked what you were doing there in the hospital.

As Leonie and I reached the exit, my cheeks were still burning as if I'd pressed myself up to a lamp.

Max was levered into the car with his head on Georgie's lap as she perched herself over one of Josh's knees, the other was pressed into the back of Chris's seat which was set as forward into the car as it could go without crushing him into the dashboard.

'Thank God I was driving pissed or I think I'd have died,' surmised Max. 'Have you seen the drugs they've given me? Chris, have you?'

'Shut up!'

'Can we just get something to drink?' Georgie said.

Leonie started the car, it staggered out of the hospital car park. Chris was the only one to call out. 'Bon Voyage, Kate! Aix is that way!'

I took a deep but unfulfilling breath of hot air and made an attempt to shuffle forward. Yes, I did regret bringing my Oxford Handbook of Clinical Medicine and no, I had no idea what to do next. The only part of that whole holiday I'd enjoyed was the last two hours in the hospital, so I turned around and walked back through the electronic doors.

I sat on a chair at the entrance under an air conditioning vent watching people as they moved in and out the main doors. I opened my case and brought out the plastic wallet which held my passport, flight information and Tatyana's email giving the directions to the château. I looked at the print out of my ticket marked for Saturday and knew that I just wasn't up to sightseeing. I wanted to go home. Collecting all my change together I called the airline about changing my flight. I finally managed to get through and booked a seat leaving for Gatwick that night. There was an extra cost of a hundred and fifty pounds. I gave her my card number, trembling at the price of immediate freedom. I had set aside contingency money in case of emergencies and as I looked at the glaring heat, I decreed that this was an emergency.

With the last bit of remaining change, I tapped in my home number. It felt pathetic, at 22 years old, to suddenly want my mum.

✲

We walk in silence in front of the white stucco houses leading to our home. You stop and tuck me into you like a scarf, when we breathe out, ghosts dance between us.

You say, 'Tell me.'

I press my lips together to stop what I don't want to say coming out.

'Do you want me to go? I can go. I can go and come back whenever you want. Maybe it was a bad idea, staying all this time together, maybe you need a chance to think about it all...Katherine, I can go, *hein*? I can –'

'I don't want you to go. But...'

'But what, what is it?'

I look around, everywhere but your questioning eyes. You have asked the question, 'But what?' and I'm going to answer it.

'You're here. With me. You're right here and you've come back...'

'Yes, I've come back...for you...for always...if you like. I'm here, Katherine, touch me.'

You place my cold hands up to your cheek...

'So why do I still miss you?'

We walk up to our building, both carrying bags of clothes and stuff we picked out for you. Now you have 'things' – some clothes, a toothbrush, razor and foam, bits and pieces to get you through the week.

When we stop at the door, Tom is coming out. He sees us and looks as if he might scuttle back in again but you move fast to catch the door while it's open. There is a wordless exchange between you, two men holding open that damned heavy door.

'Marc, this is Tom. He lives in flat 1.'

'We met once...long time ago...' says Tom staring at you rather too intently.

'I think so, yes. Long time.'

You put out your hand towards him, Tom takes it, it's a quaint gesture he's not used to.

'Cold, isn't it?' says Tom kneading a fist into the palm of the other. He looks up into the sky as if he were reciting the opening lines of a sixth-form play.

You say, 'Yes, it is,' and then turn to me.

'Maybe we should buy some food now...eh?'

'Sure.'

You let the door close and come back to me.

'Have a good one,' hails Tom, as he shoots off down the street.

I want to go after Tom, hug him tightly. Only I could know just how brave he'd been just then.

We head for a small supermarket nearby. I say nothing about Tom but wonder if I'm being more conspicuous by my silence. You walk around the supermarket filling the trolley with enough food for the next few days, neither of us question if we should plan after that.

'*Ça va, ma chérie?*' you ask as we stand by the counter.

'Tom's been a real friend to me, since...'

'Tom?'

'The boy, in Flat 1.'

'Ah.'

'What, "ah".'

'Ah. That explains it.'

'Explains what?'

'He said to me, "If you hurt her again, I'll fucking kill you." Nice friend, Katherine.'

Coming home to the flat is such a different experience with you than it is alone. Compared with how my life has been, it's like stepping into someone's 21st birthday party. Lights go on, the oven's lit, there's running water; you play music, we move about, light candles, change out of and into clothes, people bob up and down on the TV screen, fridge opens and closes, cupboards open and close as you put food away. I'd forgotten what a difference in energy two people are compared to one. I've been so quiet here. It's been almost a game for me sometimes, to exist without disturbing anything, without leaving a trace. I think, Marc, a part of me wanted to live as though I too had disappeared.

We lie on the sofa eating cashew nuts and drinking a bottle of white wine you've opened.

'What are you thinking?' you ask.

'About my work.'

'It's the weekend.'

'No, not like that. I was just thinking that I repair people.'

'The human body mechanic.'

'That's right – open the bonnet, tinker around, try to fix what's gone wrong. That's all. I can never make them like they were before the accident, or illness.'

I yawn into your chest.

'No one expects you to. Sleepy?'

'Yes. But I don't want to close my eyes in case I open them and you're not here.'

'Lie in my arms, I won't go anywhere.'

'And talk to me; keep talking to me, so I can hear your voice. Did I ever tell you that it was your voice I first fell in love with?'

'Come here.'

'Talk to me in French, will you?'

'*Bien sûr, ma petite.*'

You enclose me in your arms and in the vibrations of your voice I drift around in time and place, anchored to nothing but the rhythm of your speech.

*

I recognised Frances' voice immediately when she telephoned, even though it had been a year since we met at the NMPs' Helpline. She suggested we had a chat and without asking why, I arranged to have coffee with her after my shift.

'*Last time I saw you, you told me to join Facebook and wait.*'

'*Did I? Good advice.*'

'*Advice but not much help.*'

'*Right...so, how are you getting on with your search?*'

'*I'm still searching. Every time a child goes missing and they drain the lakes or take apart some serial killer's basement, I wonder if they'll find Marc's remains. I've been down to the morgue to identify bodies – nothing yet – I've made up posters and I've followed up some sightings, but I haven't found him if that's what you mean. I haven't come close.*'

'*Look Kate, the reason I called is because I've left the NMPH – a difficult decision but...well it was expanding in size, costs and...that's great, but everything got bigger except for the budget – if you know what I mean – my life was drowning in admin: getting in donations, fundraising, meeting targets and making deadlines. Okay, you know the feeling. One day I thought, I used to look for people, and now I just look for money! I remembered a time when I wanted to help, particularly those in the Afro-Caribbean community who are often under-represented in the media and police searches. Those were my original aims and I'd come a long way from that. So I decided to set up on my own. A Detective Agency. Sounds all very raincoats and camera-spy pens but I'm basically tracing people, people like your husband. Do any of these names mean anything to you?*'

She showed me a page on a note pad with a list of five men's names: Marc Rocher, Xavier Venelles, Momo El-Jahiz, Xavier Rocher and Marc Venelles.

'*Only this name. That's Marc.*'

'Oh, sweetie, they're all the same person.'

She took a sip of her coffee and let me stare at the page. The first time I'd heard of Frances I'd had the feeling that she was the person who could guide me out of my despair, and here she was, offering me five new leads.

'See Kate, I did what I could for you within the confines of where I was working but there are avenues I'd like to go down in terms of looking for' – she tapped the page of names – 'your hubby. Two things: I don't believe someone doesn't have any family or contacts, secondly, I don't believe people change: they can modify their behaviour, sure, but not change. If I had a detailed character profile of him – really detailed Kate – I mean everything – that would take me beyond just names and numbers. When we look for people, we follow what we call "magnets": places, people and things that our targets are inevitably drawn to – that's how they come into our range.'

The coffee sours my tongue. Did I want to be guided out of my despair? I was only just getting the hang of it.

'Presuming I still want to know where he is.'

'Presuming that, Miss Doctor, yes. Cards on the table: I rarely get thanked for finding someone. Draw your own conclusions, but the way I see it, and I have seen it over and over, people very often lose more in the search than they ever gain at the end of it. If you've walked away from it all, go girlfriend.'

'So why do you do it?'

'I won't lie – we've all got to make a living and I'm good at it. Darling, I just came to say that if you need help I'm here – I felt bad turning you away that day when you came to our offices. I know how hard it can be when the track goes cold.'

'You've lost someone, haven't you?'

'That's right, honey.'

But she doesn't want to talk about it.

'I think you contacting me was a sign. You know, this'll be my second Christmas without him. Last year I bought his presents, wrapped them up and actually got excited about giving them to him. I'm not going to this year, but it doesn't stop me looking at things in shops and wondering if he'd like them. When do we start?'

'I'm expensive Kate.'

'I don't doubt it.'

I looked up and saw Tom standing in front of me, bending down to kiss my mouth.

'Frances, this is Tom, my friend.'

'Tom, Frances. Hi.'

'Hi,' he says, biting into my chocolate fudge cake. 'If you wanna see the film, we better mosey.'

'Oh, what are you two going to see?'

'The new Woody Allen.'

'It's great, good one. I've got to go too. Kate, I've got your address, I'll pop that stuff into the post. Enjoy the rest of your evening. Nice meeting you, Tom.'

We watched Frances merge into the Tottenham Court Road crowd. Tom finished the food on both our plates as I wrapped up for the cold night.

'She seemed nice.'

'I think she is.'

'Is she a nurse?'

'No. She's a private detective.'

'Cool. What she want?'

'Work.'

saturday evening

'Darling! You wouldn't believe they've just had to call off Wimbledon because of the rain. Daddy came home especially for the match and now he's off to the garden centre. Don't tell me it's gorgeous where you are! Have you met your friend, the titled one?'

'Mum...there's been a change of plan.'

'A what?'

I fed in my last coin which gave me another 30 seconds.

'My money's running out...'

'What on earth are you doing on a pay phone?'

'I can't phone abroad on my mobile – look, I'll be back tonight. Will you be able to pick me up from the airport? Gatwick. I know it's far – but, please mummy. It's the BA flight, coming in 22.35. I'm so sorry but...please, could you?'

After four consecutive beeps, she asked, 'Katie, is David with you?'

'Look, I've got to go – can you collect me?'

'Well, of course! But are you all right?'

'Please, tonight. Can you?'

The beeps interrupt us: the connection ended.

I put the phone down and picture mum standing in our hall, our dog, Biscuit, lying asleep on the landing, dad plodding down the aisles of the garden centre with the rain tapping on the glass roof. Gradually the sharpness of my picture dulled and I dragged my case outside where the sun seared my skin. I took a few steps before I felt a hand on my shoulder.

'Let me.'

Your voice. I have a religious aunt who says God speaks through people, and right then, I understood what she meant. Without waiting for my consent, you took my case and gave me a bottle of cold water.

I walked beside you, unable to think of anything to say. My cerebrum was hard-boiled and polite conversation went up in smoke. We walked down a small hill together and over a main road. On the other side, we stopped and shared the water.

I looked up at the stranger again, but you didn't look at me, just straight ahead. It gave me a little time to admire you. And I did. *He's so handsome!* I thought, wishing I had some knowledge of how to deal with people like you: desirable, confident, adventurous – people you feel alive with, who you don't want to let out of your sight. Then you looked at me, raised your eyebrows, and we continued walking. I wondered if we should be talking, if I were being unappreciative by not asking about the population density of Provence or the annual rainfall in Aix, but then, I thought, you weren't saying anything either.

'This is just...' I said, stopping to look at the doors and facades... 'Are you from here?'

'I'm from...all over.'

The dimples on either side of your lips gave the effect of a smile, but twice over.

The Town Hall's clock shifted into position, 1.45pm. Men were spraying down the cobbled streets to wash away remnants of that morning's market.

'Do you mind if I sit for a moment? Sorry, I'm being pathetic. Not used to this heat.'

We sat on the edge of yet another little fountain as the spray hit our backs.

'Your friends left?'

'Yes'.

'Have you eaten?'

'No, no, I haven't.'

'Come, I know a restaurant you would like.'

I didn't know how to respond to this proposition. I'd followed a strange man into town, surely it wouldn't be right to accept lunch with him? But I didn't want to leave you, even then. Wherever you were, that's where I wanted to be. I wanted to keep looking at you and hearing your voice, I was already addicted to those moments when the heat made us lose our balance and we brushed our bodies against each other. But wasn't the vertiginous thrill a warning that there would be a deep drop down?

I was a little afraid of you. I've always been. The sensible part of me kept reminding myself that I was being shepherded around a new place by a man whose name I didn't even know: surely this was a potentially dangerous situation. I could see myself in court being cross-examined, "And you just followed this man, this complete stranger, into an unknown town and had lunch with him?" "Yes, Your Honour. He had such beautiful eyes."

But a new voice was emerging in my mind. I asked myself, how well did I really know Dave after all those months together? And Tatyana? And anyone? This man, I thought, sneaking a look at your strong shoulders and the smile lines around his eyes, this man was a kind man. He was a good man. He was here to look after me. Always. And I knew this for a fact.

'You know, that's really kind of you but I think I should be –'

'As you like.'

'No, I'd like to but –"

I tried to keep the squeak out of my voice and come up with a reasonable argument against having a meal with someone I'd only just met.

'It's not far.'

With that settled, we reached a shaded alley where you led me into a lively restaurant. I watched your hand rest on the door as you pushed it open. Then you turned to me.

'Look, before we go in, tell me your name?'

'Katherine Brenton. Kate.'

'Marc.'

You walked right to the middle of the restaurant where you were greeted by the waiters and someone who seemed to be the owner. We were seated and handed a menu each. I looked at mine – the prices rather than the dishes. None of it made any sense and without asking, you closed my menu and winked.

'Let me decide for you,' you said, 'and I am inviting you.'

I was to come to that restaurant a few years later, and I was to meet with the owner again, but it was to answer all the questions that I should have asked there and then.

*

'Would we be doing this if you hadn't left three years ago?'

'Of course, why not?'

I look at you from the furrow of your shoulder.

'Because we'd probably have bought a house – outside the centre of London where we could afford a garden and a few bedrooms – we'd have had to stay inside because of gun crime and teenage vandals - we'd have had a child – probably two – we'd be working, looking after kids, tired a lot of the time, spending afternoons in playgrounds trying to prevent our children from harming themselves or others, not able to afford babysitters, resenting the other person if they seemed to be doing anything but making money or looking after the children – Sally said that every time she looks at Paul all she thinks about are the odd jobs in the house he could be doing – so how could it be like this? I see it all the time, once you have children, you can't just grab a bottle of wine and go to bed for a few hours.'

'So we wouldn't be able to make love in the afternoon, but children, it doesn't have to be too terrible, if so, people wouldn't have them. I have an idea.'

'What?'

'Why don't we meet again, like a first time?'

'Um-hum...'

'Get out your sexiest dress, your heels, lipstick and wear your hair up – let's go dancing! It's Saturday night! Shall we meet again in a few hours?'

'What about *The Nadir*?'

'Okay. I'm gonna pick you up, at the bar, midnight. You don't know me.'

'You're right there, Marc. I don't know you.'

'Let's meet for the first time,' you said.

Sally believes that marriages should be on seven-year renewable contracts. She said that as we change so much over the years, why spend most of our life trying to force an ever angular square peg into a round hole. If it fits, it fits, but checks have to done. For quality assurance purposes.

And we've asked the question, if we met again, as we are now, would we still want to spend the rest of our lives together?

I know more about you than I'm letting on. I didn't play games with you in the beginning, but I am now.

What did I know about you that lunch, in Aix? Nothing! And because you talked honestly, I thought you were being honest. I thought you were telling me all about you: that you'd no family, you lived to cook, you were ambitious. Your life was arranged around the seasons, you loved Eastern food, mimosas in February and jazz. You'd travelled everywhere. You'd trained in London, learnt English from Beatles songs and Spanish from a year working in Granada. Life was for enjoying, you said, and that was a new one for me. I was so impressed. You were unlike anyone I'd ever met. Exactly. So it didn't occur to me that you were, essentially, telling me nothing by telling me what I wanted to hear.

And I was unlike anyone you'd ever met. You said so, in your way.

'This is the first time I've ever spoken to a professional person, you know. Like a doctor. Except, when I visit a doctor, of course.'

You seemed fascinated by me, asking questions, getting me to repeat things like you were cramming for an exam on me. You couldn't have had any idea what it was like to be me, to come from a family of protestant, academic people whose notion of a racy evening was eating in the living room in front of *Inspector Morse*. It must have taken you seconds to see the young doctor with the short sensible haircut was a gentle girl, studious and calming for your prismatic brain. That her heart had four distinct chambers: one for family, one for work, one for friends and another which was empty. It was empty, waiting for you. And now that I'd met you, the vacuum inside ached to be filled.

When the lunch ended and you lit a cigarette, you asked if I'd like to go to a secret cove in the *Calanques*. I had to say no, I was heading home. I told you about my changed flight. You were quiet, and then said it was a shame, you had so much you wanted to show me. Neither of us hid our disappointment. You asked, 'Tell me, if you hadn't changed your flight, would you have come with me now?'

I didn't hesitate. 'Yes.'

You put your hand over mine.

We spent the rest of the afternoon together until it was time for me to leave for the airport. You wanted to come all the way with me but I insisted that I wanted to remember you in Aix, that afternoon, the day we had.

The coach station was just a large road with bus stops along it. We arrived late. The bus headed for the airport was already filling up.

'Katherine,' you said, after I bought my ticket and came back to you.

'I don't want to go now...' I said.

You stroked my cheek and held my face in one hand while the other circled my waist. The coach driver flicked his cigarette to the ground and twisted it into the pavement with his foot.

'Thank you for lunch, the coffees, the ice-cream...for showing me around. Everything. I've loved today,' I said struggling with the sadness that it was soon going to be over and I might never see you again. I added, meaning every word, 'After today, this has been the best holiday ever!'

As the last of the passengers climbed on, you asked, 'Would you like me to kiss you?'

I wanted more than anything to have you kiss me, to touch you and have our friendship confirmed, to know that you wanted me and to move into something private, romantic, memorable. I wanted it more than the embarrassment of answering, 'Yes. I would like you to kiss me.'

You held me, looked into my face as a couple of elderly, breathless British women flagged down the driver and jumped onto the bus.

I was still waiting for my kiss. You moved your fingers over my lips, brought your mouth to my ear and whispered.

'No, Katherine. You are not ready for me to kiss you. I will come for you when it is the right time. *Et tu seras ma femme.*'

I blinked into the light. I knew enough French to translate *femme* as meaning either woman or wife. I didn't understand what had happened. The coach's engine started up. I could see the driver looking into his rear view mirror, preparing to pull out.

'Goodbye, *au revoir*,' you said, releasing your hold, your lips in a smile, your eyes soft, regretful.

I stepped onto the bus, found my seat, looked to see you, but you were gone.

When we pulled away, the air conditioning started up and the coach rolled onto the motorway away from Aix, and you. I strained my neck round to see you once more, to reassure myself it was all real, my modern day highwayman, the man who nearly made me beg for his kiss and who decided at the last minute, that no, I wasn't quite ready.

But the coach and the plane, my family and my work, were like quicksand, covering up those hours, the heat, and the moment you robbed me of.

*

'*Don't look now...Don't look now...Who's the brunette right behind you? Tall, thin, all in black...wait...wait...Okay, look now!*'

'*Gideon,*' whispered Anna, '*that's my sister, Kate.*'

'*Good God! I thought you had a "little" sister...*'

'*She is a "little" sister, she's only 28. She's a doctor.*'

'*Hummmm, certainly all grown up now...*'

I'm thinking back to October 2007, the night of Nick's book launch, five months after you'd gone. Although it was evening, it was still warm as well as bright. The sun had squeezed out the last bit of chrome yellow left in the tube and spread it over Hyde Park. Nick and Anna looked out at the full cast of their lives: the major roles – parents from both sides: hers all the way from their 1930s semi-detached in Oxford, and Nick's – a short taxi ride from Mayfair. All their closest friends were placed like expensive chocolates in an assorted mix dotted around two hired rooms in the Royal Geographical Society building. And maybe it was the weather or the guest list or genuine interest in Nick's travels to Vanuatu, but the gathering was sprouting a surprising capacity for carefree fun and daring that they had thought the years had long since concreted over. You can still enjoy yourself in your forties, they affirmed to themselves.

My family used Nick's literary bashes as a tidemark to measure where Anna and Nick's life had risen. His first book had stimulated envy. Straight out of Oxford, Nick was already published and married when most of his peers were anxious to find jobs and uncomplicated sex. His second book arrived along with their friends' first weddings and an increase in London's property prices. After a five-year hiatus he wrote his third book about his year in a Nicaraguan rainforest. This coincided with the second crop of babies and first grey hairs sprouting from the heavier bodies of distracted parents. 'Crap sales' figures,' Anna told us over Sunday lunch. His fourth and most successful book was received by fewer friends: business trips, flaky baby-sitters, fatigue, were the usual excuses. By then there'd been deaths, divorces, chemotherapy as well as awards, promotions and extra-marital affairs. And tonight? They'd made it. Anna could tick off names of celebrities amongst their friends, editors, politicians, CEOs, faces from TV - there were fewer couples, but what many had lost in their personal lives, they had gained professionally. Did their friends really look like the middle-aged people they were becoming? Anna had asked me earlier. I said, no, not at all, some of them looked just as they always had - although it cost more and took them longer. Anna had said that this launch was marked by a renewed interest in travel, philosophy, culture. And love. Imagine, all that again. For the first time since college the women were looking – and acting – really quite sexy – was it for the men or the other women? Who cared? It wasn't just thanks to the smattering of divorces and cosmetic surgery. This was, Anna had said, the last chance saloon for anyone who wanted to make a last grab at making something of their lives.

'You see, Katie,' she said slurring a little. 'People go on about the mid-life crisis being about getting old – but it's not – it's absolutely not - it's suddenly realising you are young – we've only got a finite number of heartbeats per lifetime, only so many Springs left in which to fall in love!'

Talk about the future terrified me. I was taking it minute by minute.

'So does little sister have some hulking surgeon around who'll slice me up with a scalpel if I try to arrange a full examination?'

'It's complicated,' I overheard Anna say.

'Tell all.'

'Her husband just upped and left this summer. Not a word.'

'Ouch.'

Anna and Gideon must have had a little too much champagne as they didn't seem to realise I could hear every word. I could feel them looking at me, their heads dropping to their shoulders, as if I were a painting in a gallery that they needed to extract intelligent meaning out of.

'My baby sister's been through hell.'

I was standing in front of one of Nick's photographs, a ruined Persian palace where a tribe of herdsman had built a make-shift village. I wondered if you were amongst the men in headscarves and sticks, far away from my efforts to track you down.

You were getting away, interest in finding you was waning; new missing people had knocked you off your spot. The police no longer hid the fact that they thought I was naïve to the point of delusional. Gone were the smirks, the familiarity, even the irritation. They were not returning my calls. They had proper jobs to do, like looking for people who wanted to be found.

'Katie, this is Gideon. He's an Art's critic. Gideon this is Kate, my sister. Kate's a heart surgeon. I've just got to say hello to...'

'So you mend broken hearts do you?' asked Gideon. I finished my champagne. 'Sorry, bad joke. You probably get that all the time. What made you specialise in the ol' ticker?'

'When I was little my father showed me a cross section of a heart diagram to copy from and I copied it over and over again. It was the only thing I could draw, so I stuck to that.'

'Gosh, I only ever drew pictures of boys pissing...what do you think that makes me?'

'A piss-artist?'

I made an attempt to move on.

'Course,' he continued, 'my heart's never been the same since your sister married Nick. Devastated I was, and the worst thing is, she's even more beautiful now, the post-birth babushka look's given her an earthy, raw sexuality...hum...'

He appraised Anna laughing with some girlfriends, 'She's always been the love of my life. And you're her little sister! Well, I would never have known that...not that you're not – I mean, it's just that...'

I hear someone call my name.

Heads whirled like turbines to follow Tatyana across the room. She was still as beautiful as she had been five years ago when I last saw her in the South of France. She kissed me, turning to Gideon.

'Hi, I'm Tatyana Davenport,' she said, as if that explained everything.

'Tatyana, I'm Gideon Bradshaw. We've actually met a few –'

'I haven't seen Kate for so many years - I've been longing to catch up with her. Do you mind?'

And with that she led me away from Gideon, sat me down and took me by the hands.

'Katie, I really hoped you were here...I never come out to these sorts of things, I'm virtually a recluse these days. I only just got off the plane from LA a few hours ago but I had to see you. I even dreamt about you last night.'

Tatyana said all this while keeping one hand on me and lighting a cigarette with the other.

'You've been so on my mind...Anna told me about your husband...'

A security guard came over and said that if she wanted to smoke, she'd have to go outside.

The night had brought in the indifferent winter chill, and I found it so hard to accept that the season was changing without you. Tatyana's voice took me back to that last night in France. There had been a time before you. Hearing her again was like opening a book and seeing notes in the margin, at some point it must have been important but I'd long forgotten it was there.

'From next week I'm going to change my life completely. I'm doing this deep spiritual cleansing course in Sante Fe and my personal guide recommended that I mend as many rifts as I could before I start, and you were one of the people on my list.'

'Tatty, I don't have any bad feeling towards you. I never did. Nor towards Dave.'

'You know he went completely mad – he began stalking me and threatening me – my family had to get a restraint order against him, it was awful! But I deserved it because I'd done a terrible thing to you!'

'Don't be silly, it was just one of those things.'

'Friends!' she called out, throwing her arms around my neck. 'Now Katie, what about you?'

Even Tatyana, whose life was made up of extraordinary events couldn't match this one. She listened, her eyes wide with incredulity.

'Oh Kate...' she whispered. 'Oh Kate...that must be...'

'You can't imagine...'

'No, no...I can't. Listen, come with me to Sante Fe - it's a retreat run by white witches, shamen, wizards – I know it sounds a bit Harry Potter - but it's not! They're scientists – they've developed a software program that can read your DNA memory and karmic imprint – they can overwrite your destiny from this lifetime and the next – oh, do come.'

'It sounds very interesting but my job is all that's keeping me going at the moment.'

'Is there anything I can do?' asked Tatyana.

'There is actually. I've got hundreds of posters, numbers, leaflets, pictures of Marc – when you go to the States, could you post them up for me?'

'Consider it done.'

Tatyana followed me to my car where I gave her as many flyers about you as she could fit in her designer handbag. And then she asked, 'And Katie, something for me?'

'What?'

'Nick's my favourite cousin. I worry so much about him...please...I can't say anymore but...will you look out for him, help him if you can?'

'Nick?'

'Kate. I can't say anymore. I love you darling. I've got to be at Quaglino's at nine. Bisous!'

So it was thanks to Tatyana that your search went transatlantic.

saturday night

I arrive at *The Nadir* before you. The club was your idea, run by your friend Johan, but what you don't know is that it's not new to me. One of the first things I did when you disappeared was to seek out all your friends, colleagues and the places you went. Because these people knew you, because they missed you too, we've become close. So when Johan sees me, it is not as great a shock as when he will see you.

'Kate! Kate! Kate, you're coming to the opening of my new club in New York – it's going to be the party of the year – right in the middle of fashion week...fly over – bring Tom – you look divine – who are you with?'

I grip Johan's arm. 'Marc.'

'Hum, darling?'

'Marc.'

'What?'

'He came back.'

Hearing this, Johan waves the voices around him down. They obey.

'He's back?' he repeats.

'A few days ago. He won't say where he was. He won't say anything, really. But he had this idea we try to start again, meet each other, like for the first time – I thought an evening out here would be a good place to start.'

'Kate.'

'What?'

'Kate. Don't let him hurt you again...'

'He's never stopped hurting me.'

'Does he know, that you know, about Yasmeen?'

'No. He won't talk, so I won't talk.'

'Oh Kate.'

'I'm going to get a drink, if you see him...'

'I'm gonna punch him, darling, he's worth breaking a nail over.'

'Don't. Let's just play this one out...Revenge is a dish...'

'Let's serve it on ice. I like it Katie. And I did just have a manicure.'

*

I stood on the corner of Exhibition Road watching the streetlights reflected against Tatyana's long, bronzed legs as she flagged down a taxi. I wondered if you could've ever walked out on her one morning and never come back.

There, I'd come to the end of my first party without you. This was the part I was dreading. Going home alone. We would have gone to dinner, or maybe walked back through the park. What was I supposed to do with myself now? Turning back to say my goodbyes, I saw Nick huddled in the doorway.

As I passed him I heard him say, 'Look...trying to see you all day, didn't you...my messages? No, I can't get away...I've got this bloody book thing. Please, just wait for me...I'll only be a minute. I've got to see you...please! Okay, okay...'

'All right?' Nick asked me as I kissed my parents goodbye.

'Yes...you?'

I moved sharply, throwing his hand from my shoulder.

'Have I signed you a copy, Kate?'

'No. It's okay.'

'Here, let me. Might be worth a fortune in a few years, eh?' He laughed, taking one of his books off a nearby pile. "To Kate" - he wrote, and then stopped. He didn't know whether or not to write in Marc's name. For the last two years most of my Christmas cards, postcards, presents had all been addressed to Kate and Marc – *so when do they take your name off?*

'To Kate – fuck I don't know what to say.' He waited, pen in air, 'when I look at you, all my problems seem so bloody ridiculous...'

'I didn't know you had any problems, Nick,' I said.

He held up the book again and wrote, "To Kate: Never any more, While I live, Need I hope to see his face, As before, Once his love grown chill, Mine may strive: Bitterly we re-embrace, Single still. All love, Nick XXX."

'I hope he's not making you pay for it!' laughed Anna as she peered over our shoulders.

I read the lines.

'What's this mean?' I asked. Nick shuffled about.

'Browning. I thought –'

And before finishing his sentence, Nick was led away by his agent.

I was left with my sister. I felt angry at her. First because I felt guilty I'd overheard something I shouldn't have, I had to keep a secret from her, and second, something bad was happening in her life and she wasn't paying attention - she was the one who deserved these cryptic lines, not me.

'What a great evening!' she said falling into me. Her breath smelt of apples and her hair was in the process of forming itself into animal shapes.

I felt sad and scared for my sister, but part of me was exhilarated. I'd never thought Nick was fair or honest with Anna, he'd never been good enough for her. And now I'd proved myself right. But who was I to judge other people's husbands?

I was seventeen when Anna first brought Nick Davenport to our house for Sunday lunch. We met this lanky, laconic boy, supercilious, self-assured yet at the same time nervous, which I perceived as an affection to make people even more indulgent to him than they were already. Every time he spoke, which wasn't often, my sister looked at us, beseeching her family to fully appreciate every syllable that came from his beaky mouth. No one had ever managed to impress Anna before, she had always been other people's prize.

'Nick's godmother lives in a palace in Sri Lanka which has hundreds of white peacocks on the lawn! His parents have a Turner and a first edition Oliver Twist. Do you know, he was kidnapped when he was at prep-school?'

My parents made the appropriate 'Oohs' and 'Aaahs' but dad's always been intrinsically wary of people who don't have jobs, as clearly Nick's parents didn't.

'I don't think mum and dad liked Nick,' said Anna on the phone that night when she'd got back to her digs. 'Katie, did you?'

'He's very thin...'

'He's got the most delicious cock: full of poetry and intelligence and –'

'Is that what he's going to write with in his finals?'

'I'm going to marry him.'

And that's what she did. She dropped ideas of a Masters and put all her energy into organising a large, social and very stylish wedding. It even appeared in Tatler – the first and only edition my parents ever bought. Anna and Nick travelled all over the world for nearly two years, only stopping when she got pregnant. But even when the babies came, Nick never changed his lifestyle, he continued travelling, drug-taking and found, to his surprise, that marriage had increased his sex appeal, especially if his lovers knew of Anna's reputation and wanted to score double points.

'I never want us to be like them, Katherine,' you said, after we'd stayed with Anna and Nick one turbulent weekend. 'We will always be monogamous, trusting and in love with each other.'

Someone was walking up behind me. I turned to see that friend of Anna's, Gideon.

'I think we got off to a rather bad start,' he announced.

'A bad end.'

'Oh don't be like that. Look, it's only just gone ten, nobody goes home at this time. Fancy a drink?'

'Not with you.'

'So I acted like a complete prat. I am a prat. I didn't disguise it very well. I'm just not used to being around beautiful women who actually do things for a living, like life-saving surgery. I was overly impressed by you. I was thinking of going to a club that's just opened. The Nadir, I've got a spare guest invitation –'

'Have fun.'

'Won't you come too?'

'I'm a married woman.'

'But Anna said he'd walked out on you?'

'Listen you little freak,' I hissed in Gideon's ear while pinning both his shoulders against a parked van. 'He didn't "walk out." Something's happened to him...something happened...something...' I whispered, loosening my grip as the power went from my arm muscles.

'Okay...Okay...I wasn't suggesting anything...Are you okay?'

I fell to my knees, my ribs were closing in on me, my skin was freezing cold, but sweaty. Nothing, nothing made any sense around me. My heart was banging inside my head and I couldn't focus my eyes. I heard the screeching of car brakes and Gideon's arms hooking themselves under mine. He dragged me off the road. Eventually the black and white strobe-light effect in front of my eyes faded and I regained a consecutive line of even breaths.

'Let's get you a drink,' he said.

For the first twelve weeks after you left I'd wanted to stay at home in case you returned or got in touch. Even if I dashed to the corner shop I'd experience rising levels of anxiety that you may call at that moment and I wasn't there. But when summer was over, I decided I needed a change of strategy: I was going out to look for you.

I'd heard you talk about this club – you often went out dancing after your work – and I remember you mentioning the owner, Johan. It was a start. Staying home certainly hadn't done me any good.

'Want a toot?' asked Gideon.

He took me into the unisex toilets which were made of glass and mirrors for the ease of snorting drugs. I copied what I'd seen you doing occasionally with your friends and waited to feel what you must have felt sometimes. Nothing too different from a trip to the dentist, but still! I tugged at Gideon's arm and we followed the music into the basement, pushing our way through to a space where we could move.

You loved dancing, for you it was like other people go to the pub or jog around the block. Very often we'd be sitting in front of the TV and you'd say, 'Let's go dance.' And we did. When I first met you I wasn't at all used to this idea – I'd always needed a few days' warning and several drinks before hitting the dance floor. I remember confessing to you that I was embarrassed by the way people exhibited their sexuality to music - wriggling and writhing, thrusting their genitals at strangers - you looked at me quizzically – you said, 'But that's the point, mon coeur, a person's sexuality, it's for everybody - sex, that's just for one person.' I'd read a lot of philosophy before I met you, but everything you said was a radical departure from my way of thinking.

Back on the dance floor, Gideon shook his body like he was being electrocuted but he still couldn't keep up with me. I was sharing my sexuality with anyone who wanted a piece; see Marc, what I'd learnt from you?

'Gideon, do you think Nick's having an affair?' I shouted over the music.

'Probably, they have an open marriage, what d'you expect? Anna's madly in love with some married man...oh, she's always got someone hanging about.'

'Really? She never told me that...'

I was worried about Anna, but I was desperate about you – it didn't cross my mind to put the two together.

'Gideon, I want to meet the man who runs the club. Introduce me.'

'I don't know where he is.'
'Well you're a journalist, aren't you? Find out.'

Forty five minutes later Gideon returned to where I was sitting on a banquette upstairs talking to someone.

'Kate, all I've found out is that the club's owned by Johan – he's some Arab-German poof who doesn't talk to anyone. Can't help with that one. I thought you wanted another dance?'

'Gideon, meet Johan.'

The men looked away from each other. Gideon mumbled something, slinking off.

'You see darling, why I don't do interviews? Those people!'

'Tell me something, Johan. Anything.'

'If I knew anything, darling, anything, I would say. I loved Marc too – really. Sometimes he came here, late, after work, we'd have such a great time – having a good time, it's an art form with some people, and he was a maestro, eh?'

Johan dabbed a tear from each eye.

'Did he need money? Did he take drugs? Were there women? Johan...please?'

'Marc was a professional – he worked hard, he played hard: one night he DJ-ed for us! Yah. One of the best nights here. He was a crazy guy, but to just disappear...no one could believe it. And that he would leave you! Especially you. He was uxorious! Always talking about his doctor wife. Hand on heart, I never saw him show attention to a particular woman...or man. Never. He had every opportunity. He flirted, he teased, yah. Maybe because he could play at love-making, he didn't need to go outside for it. He was one of the very few men I would say was honourable like that.'

'So, where is he?'

Gideon brought me a drink and positioned himself by my feet like a whippet.

'I don't know.'

'Johan, can you really not think of anything...?'

'Okay, darling, there was something, but...'

'It doesn't matter how silly.'

'The last night I saw him, it must have been April, there was a woman here, red hair, French, I saw them talking – they were arguing. I could tell she was upset. It's not...particularly revealing, *yah? But he didn't say goodbye to me that night. And that was the last time. He didn't say goodbye.'*

Johan and I held each other before I turned to Gideon.

'You can take me home now.'

Gideon was heating the milk for my Horlicks. He turned around. I was in his kitchen with no clothes on.

'Hit me,' I said.

'Kate, your drink's nearly ready –'

'Hit me. Hard. Around the head. Hit me and don't stop.'

*

After the night I met Gideon, I went in pursuit of men who resembled you. It wasn't running away from but towards you. I was reinforcing my fidelity, my rage and a loneliness which caused me to pound my head against the bedroom walls for hours. I'd go out after work with the nurses and junior doctors, we'd go clubbing, drop some ecstasy tabs, then I'd pick the man who looked most like you. And something would happen. It made me feel better and worse at the same time – but it made me feel something. And I needed to be desired, to show you that other people wanted what you didn't. You would have seen me in a club, and you wouldn't have liked what you saw, and that was a way of getting your attention, even if it was only imagined. Very seldom did I see the same man more than three times, and it was always just for sex, and some of them were nice, Marc, some of them thought they were in love and I hurt them, just to pass on the infection you gave me.

sunday morning

After a stroke, it's not uncommon to lose your memory. Forget how to tie your shoes, what a toothbrush is for and how to get into an orange. And then you meet your family: someone you apparently married, children that claim you, friends who assume your trust. They ask questions, and another person answers back. Over the days, the weeks, you get to know each other again, tentatively, politely, biting one's tongue and leaving the room before outbursts. Strangers become part of one's intimate life: and sometimes a love develops, and sometimes it doesn't. But whatever passes between you, it isn't what was before.

I have my memory – it's all I've have left. We are not what we were.

It's Sunday and neither of us opens our eyes to see what we have dragged into our bed. Even in your sleep, your hand circles my buttocks as though shining up a piece of furniture - or is it to check if I have scales?

And last night you wanted a new love to develop, but I am not what I was before. Did you think I would be packed up in ice, stored away, paralysed, while you dallied and dithered about coming home to me? No, I took what was left and sprouted a different thing, a new Kate who you are only just beginning to meet.

'Are you on your own?'

I avoid crushing one-liners and for simplicity's sake, answer you with, 'Yes.'

'Can I buy you a drink?'

'Vodka and tonic, please.'

You lean in front of me with a fifty pound note. I wonder where you got it from – but I let the game go on.

'Do you like Techtronic music?' you ask. I laugh.

'Yes, but I need one of these to really appreciate it.'

We share an ecstasy tab and think of what to say next when I feel a warm hand on my back.

'Is this man bothering you?' Johan kisses me on the lips.

'Johan, do you remember Marc?'

You clasp onto one another, pat backs and softly punch each other's arms.

'So where've you been?' asks Johan catching my eye.

'All over – but what's important, I'm back. You know my wife, Katherine?'

'I know your wife. I've been looking after her for the last three years. There are ten people on the permanent guest list – and one of them is Kate. She comes here...a lot eh? She's coming to my opening in New York – in two weeks – the new club – it's going to be crazy. January Jones, Brad Pitt, Madonna... Everybody –' and with that, Johan is needed downstairs.

You frown. You are genuinely surprised by this.

'You come here?'

'Weekends, if I'm not working.'

'Why do you come here?' you ask.

'Follow me.'

I walk into the toilets where there's a crowd who know me. I snort a few lines of cocaine with them, laugh a little with a Brazilian lady boy I sometimes dance with. You stand behind me, watching. You don't join in. When I've finished I push you into a toilet cubicle. With your back to me, I lift your shirt, move my breasts against your back, unbuckle your belt, your jeans. I turn you to me, kiss down from your navel, licking the salt off your skin. Dropping to my knees, I curl my tongue around your balls, slide your cock in and out of my mouth. From my pocket I take out a black, rubber line, I – you catch my wrist with your hand.

'Katherine. What are you doing?'

'This is what I do with people I first meet.'

I snarl at you. Someone bangs on the door. You pull up your trousers, shaking your head at me.

'You think you can shock me, Katherine? You think I'll be impressed with...this?'

You flick the rubber cord in my fingers.

'I just wanted you to see –'

'I've seen enough.'

'But we haven't even started.'

'Katherine, all I see is that you've confused pleasure with happiness. Let's go.'

We walk through the West End, hand in hand, fast enough to counter the night's frost, but not too fast that we are tired. We set a good pace, you and I.

Passing the Ritz Hotel, we walk alongside Green Park. Peering through the bars into the darkness between trees, you say if my shoes hurt we can get a cab. But outside is better, there isn't that pressure to talk, and there isn't just you and me.

Safety in numbers. Couples pass us, and we could be any of them. And I'm relieved we are in the world. Grief makes you feel like such a freak, I really had begun to wonder.

Our arms stretch over each other's waists, and I'm acting like I trust you but I don't because I'm only just getting to know this Marc. And I wonder if I would have gone on a hunt to find you if I'd known then all that I know about you now. Because I was looking for you and I found someone else, and then this man came to my bed and said he had come back for seven days.

That's why walking across London fits our situation, because we too are crossing from what was, to what is.

'You always talked to me like you were such a brave, worldly man, someone who thought about things and made considered, balanced judgements. And yet, you weren't like that at all. The hypocrisy! You were too scared to tell me you wanted to leave. Those first few days, you must have known I would have thought you might be dead or hurt – I can't describe the anguish...unbearable, violent pain – and all you had to do was text me! That's what I can't forgive – not that you left, but the way you did it.'

My shoes are hurting now. The early birds are swooping from tree to tree, scouring the streets for breakfast. No more couples pass us, just the homeless and the brain impaired. And questions shape themselves in the misty air, do I want to be here, now, doing this, with you?

'Because when I first met you, at the hospital, I thought if I could love this girl, and she could love me, all would be right...and yet...I was living a lie because you didn't know me, so I wanted you to know me, to really have experience of what I am capable of.'

'Once I knew that, Marc, it was very unlikely I'd take you back...so what was the point?'

'Suicide was too easy, too kind, so I found a worse punishment for myself – killing the part of my life that I wanted the most, you.'

'But why, why all this suffering?'

'You didn't find out why?'

Because you couldn't break a promise to Yasmeen.

*

There was the day after, two days after, the first week, month, first birthday and Christmas, New Year and then a year, that day, June 6th, that you'd been gone.

That date had been waiting ahead of me like an expectant crowd at the gallows. I'd worked the night before at the hospital and it started with the journey of slow-rolling tears at each side of my temple. Hot, airless, in the little doctor's stay-over room with grey nylon curtains and khaki lino floor. My hairline was wet and itchy, my eyes stung and my nose was blocked. Is that all I had to show after a year without you?

That day last year I'd had a husband next to me. And for some reason, I'd hoped that you'd have been there beside me again. If clocks could go backwards and forwards an hour at the season's change, why not one year?

I showered. With the warm water running over me, it was the best place to cry. I dressed in black, had two strong coffees in the doctors' staffroom, a short spell on the PC to check any emails and I hit the wards.

I moved through each second of that day as if flicking through snapshots of that time last year. Each breath, each corridor, each conversation was like a reconstruction scene of the day one year ago. Every time I had to write down the date I felt the earth turning its full 360 degrees, 365 days and 8760 hours since you'd been missing. I didn't want it to turn any more – I wanted to stay affiliated to the day which commemorated my ignorance of what was to come a few hours later. I wanted to remember that 52 weeks before, I'd looked forward to coming home and never once questioned whether I'd see my husband again. A year ago that day, you were my life because you were in it – not out of it. Only one year ago – it was almost near enough to grab hold of and pull through – close enough to touch.

I followed in the shoes of my former self, the married self, the one who started so many sentences with, 'Marc and I...' That time last year I'd had lunch at the sandwich bar, prawn cocktail sandwich, and that's what I had a year later, each mouthful like a toll bringing me closer to the inevitable. I'd had a strong coffee in

99

2007 and, having been awake all night, I needed to do the same. It tasted disgusting.

The afternoon passed like most and at 5:30 I finished for the day but continued for another hour writing up notes and checking up on the patients I didn't see earlier. I'd just collected my things from the stay-over room when Callum came in and dropped his bag on the bed.

'Ah, home sweet home. Not!'

'Wasn't too bad last night...' I said.

'That doesn't bode well for me...having said that, with a three-month-old baby at home I get a better kip here.'

Carpe diem. Hold on to the one-year-after-day. It hadn't been so terrible. Not too bad at all. And was nearly over, but for the night ahead, which I planned to spend alone. Sally and my sister had said I should do something to mark that date, but it was my grief, and what they didn't seem to understand is that you were not dead – it wasn't a matter of putting flowers on a grave or lighting candles. It wasn't about letting go, but holding on.

I had thought that if it had been a pleasant enough evening, I could have gone to Primrose Hill or fed the ducks at the Serpentine like we used to, but it wasn't – London was dusty, grey and smelt like a dank cellar.

Perhaps I'd re-read the emails, post-it notes, cards that you'd written me over the years, maybe I'd go through your clothes, squirt some of your aftershave on my wrist - the one you saved for special occasions - and the one I used as a very, very last resort when I had to breathe in the smell of you.

The Central Line was down and I had to take three different tubes home. The people on the train looked just as sick and tired, unhappy and depressed as I did.

Walking from Bayswater, there was little distinction between the colour of the paving stones and the colour of the sky about to burst open with rain. I walked as fast as I could but my feet hurt and my muscles were stiff from carrying my overnight bag. Anniversary of a disappearance or not, all I wanted to do was whack up the heating, put on an episode of 'Prison Break' that I'd recorded and drink a few glasses of white wine before passing out. It was, after all, just another day.

Turning into my street I reached in my bag for my keys. But I couldn't feel them. I moved my fingers over my wallet, diary, pens, scrunched up pieces of paper. I opened and checked my wash-bag. They weren't there. When I heard the first crash of thunder I was emptying my bag out onto the pavement. I checked my pockets, my briefcase, my bag again. Then I remembered the last time I saw my keys, they were on the bed when Callum put his things down.

I sat back onto my heels as the first drops of rain drummed onto my things.

I couldn't see any lights on in the building. No one was in. No one was on the road. Maggie had keys to my flat so I pressed her bell, once, twice, again and again. No answer. Again and again. Nothing. I'd just have to wait for her or, if the rain let up a little, I could have trudged back to work and slept. I collapsed against the door, clinging onto my bag as if it were driftwood.

The clouds shook out the rain like pins from a box. It scratched my face, my hands. I bundled up and cowered from it but the dam burst in me too. I could no longer hold back the torrent of sadness that moved through me whether I wanted to feel it or not. So this was where I'd ended up one year later.

If only you could have seen me then.

'Are you...'

I looked up but couldn't catch what someone was saying against the sound of cars sawing through the puddles.

'...someone?'

I was aware of a dark shape moving into me – I thought, this is how I am going to die, battered to death on my doorstep on the anniversary of your disappearance. And I didn't care. I pressed myself into the wall and hoped my attacker would be quick about it.

'Are you waiting for someone?' he asked.

His face levelled with mine, hidden inside a hood. It occurred to me that maybe I was at the wrong house. Maybe I'd been going to the wrong house every day for the last year and you were at home all the time looking for me.

'Are you waiting for someone?'

'My husband,' I said, looking around for people.

'Okay,' he said, scratching his nose where the rain tickled.

He took out a bunch of newly-cut keys and put one into the door.

'Do you want to be let in?'

'Yes,' I managed to say through my chattering teeth.

It hurt to unlock my joints and stand up again. He waited with the door ajar, holding my bag. The door banged behind us and the boy turned on the lights.

'Right, that's better.'

I could feel cold, minty droplets snaking into my neck. My shoes squelched as I tried to see if I could move my toes but there was no sensation in my feet.

When he opened the door to his flat we were both blasted by the heat and heady smell of perfumed candles. He swung off his leather jacket and helped me unload my coat.

'You live here?'

'Yup.'

I'd forgotten all about the first floor to the building. As long as I'd known it no one had ever lived here, there'd been developers working on it and then nothing, even before you left.

'Just chuck your stuff down anywhere.'

I was afraid of getting the parquet floor wet so I shivered by the door looking out at all that space.

'It's a little bare, I know, I only just moved in y'see. I'm Tom, by the way.'

'Kate.'

'So you live upstairs then?'

Tom pressed a switch and a galaxy of halogen lights glowed above our heads.

'Yes.'

'I thought there was a doctor living there.'

'That's me.'

'That's you! Cool. Well. We should've met before...not like this...but, sorry, I'm crap about all that...stuff.'

There was nothing in his flat, just a telephone and an enormous plasma T.V. screen with a 1930s club leather armchair placed directly in front of it.

I looked at my new neighbour with his soft skin, his hair smartly cut and his Labrador brown eyes. He couldn't have been more than twenty-two.

'When are your parents coming back?'

'Huh?'

'Your parents, are they away or...?'

Tom laughed.

'My parents live in Wales. Abergavenny. No, they wouldn't come to London for anything...especially me.'

'I thought this flat was empty.'

'It was. I bought this place over two years ago now but I've not had the time to move in. The record company found someone to do it up, one of those minimalist people, so it's a bit...you know, minimal. I just came back from ordering some furniture and stuff to fill it with really, when I saw you. How long have you been in the building, Kate...Doctor?'

'Since 2005. Record company, are you a musician?'

'Guilty.'

'What instrument do you play?'

His turn to laugh.

'I don't, it's all...' he wiggled his fingers. 'Machines. I do clubs, private parties. Mixing, mash-music.'

'Silly me. Like you imagining that Dr Brenton was an old man with whiskers and a white coat.'

'Busted!' he laughed. 'You know, it's funny cause when I saw this place there was another flat I liked in Holland Park. My manager insisted I buy this one because there was a doctor living in the building. He thought I'd be safer!'

'Ah, and here you are, looking after me,' I said. He put his hand on a radiator and beckoned me to stand by it.

'Well now I know the heating works...shouldn't need it in June but there you go.'

'Am I keeping you from anything?'

'Not at all. I should offer you something to drink but I haven't had time to do a food shop – stay, I'll just run out and get us something. What's your poison?'

'Oh no, please – it's pouring.'

'Not at all - I need my Starbucks' fix anyway. What about a hot chocolate? Skinny latte with caramel? I'll be back in a minute – make yourself at home.'

He grabbed his keys as if they were a baton in a relay race and charged off down the stairs.

I started peeling my steaming clothes off and lay them over the radiator. Would it be taking advantage to go to the bathroom in search of a towel for my hair? I took my shoes off and tried to guess which room was the bathroom. I padded around trying not to drip on the glassy floor.

I found his bedroom. It was only a little smaller than the living room and done up in shades of white and beige around a bed the size of my living room. There was hardly any sign that anyone lived there apart from three suitcases at the other end of the room. Leading off was a bathroom which looked like it hadn't been used either – nor had the piles of white, springy towels resting on warm radiators. I took one and started soaking up the rain from my hair. I tiptoed to my bag, took out my brush and my collection of creams and moisturisers, samples I'd collected from shops and the insides of magazines, a system I'd found to lighten my bag as well as economise.

I tiptoed back to the bathroom still feeling guilty that Tom was out in the rain. I went to check if it was still pouring down – the sky looked like it had a giant bar-code stamped across it. Turning back into the flat, something caught my eye. What I saw on the ground was such a familiar sight it took me right back to those days of you: a scrunched up packet of Marlboro reds, your lighter and a bottle of Sancerre.

'Only me!' said Tom, lowering his hood and shaking off the rain, 'This is my first night in for...I don't know how long...to tell you the truth, I was getting a little creeped out being here on my own. I'm used to having lots of –'

'Tom. Where did these things come from?'

'- people around me all the time. What's occurring?'

'These?'

'Not me! I don't smoke...never have. They could be anybody's!'

'Who has keys to this flat?'

'Oh, quite a few people, actually...see, I've not been here for –'

'Who has keys to this flat, exactly?'

'My manager, Bill, the decorator, the builders, my PA - Skye - that's her name – probably her PA – and she probably has an assistant! - a mate of mine from back home, er...and me...Oh, and the French chap who lives upstairs...there might be others, too, I don't know really.'

The room spun around me, 'Who...upstairs?'

'Listen, I don't like smoking much either, dirty habit. But as long as people do it outside, it's their lungs, though I imagine as a doctor...'

'What Frenchman upstairs?'

'I know it's irresponsible but it's not like there's anything to nick! One advantage of minimalism, eh? Hey, relax! Here's your drink...'

'The French guy...'

'Yeah. What? Oh him. Well, after I bought the flat I came round one day to meet with the decorator, see. I ran into the man who lives upstairs – we chatted and he suggested taking my keys in case I needed anything delivered or if there was an emergency...What? It's what neighbours do, don't they?'

'Where is he?'

'I don't know – never saw him since. I said, I only arrived today.'

'When did you give him your keys?'

'I don't know, last year some time? What's the matter?'

'He was here...he was here...he was here all the time.'

*

Since Christmas I've spent Sundays with either my family or with Anthony's and sometimes, if his brother's family couldn't host lunch, his mother would come to my parents. Everyone got on very well.

We'd probably be going there now, if I wasn't all tangled up in bed with you.

You and I used to spend Sundays together, at home. We chose to be together because we wanted that more than spending time with anyone else. I know I did. Doing nothing, like this, being warm, wrapped up, touching, kissing, saying any rubbish that came into our heads, was my favourite way to spend the weekend. Making plans, changing plans, finding different things that we found pleasurable, just being ourselves with each other. On Mondays at work when colleagues asked what I did at the weekend, I couldn't think what to say! I'd be so relieved if we had seen a film or an exhibition – something I could talk about. But usually we hadn't left the flat or even our bed and somehow it didn't seem appropriate to say that.

You move, get up and return bringing me a glass of water. After a few sips I start talking, it comes out in a croak and I've a splitting headache but I need to talk.

'When I first introduced you as my boyfriend everyone was thrilled. They thought you were great. But when I said we were getting married they were shocked. They said I was making a terrible mistake. No one approved of you, you know. My family didn't think you were "husband material"!'

'Do you remember our wedding?' you ask.

Of course I do. We married in July at Anna's old college. It was a simple, beautiful day, and whatever reservations anyone had about you disappeared in that clear blue sky above the flowers in full multi-coloured bloom. It might sound corny or clichéd, but that day, I felt reborn. Every time I looked at you, I fell in love with you, over and over.

'Since you left, I've looked through our wedding photos trying to find a sign that you weren't happy or that you were looking for a get-away car...but both of us looked so...sure. So in love! Had I missed something? Did you know then?'

'No, I loved our wedding too. It was great, eh?'

My eyes moisten. Thinking back to that day is a guaranteed way of making me cry. The expectations, the hope, maybe it's too much for any couple to live up to.

You lift the glass as though toasting the two newlyweds we once were.

'The night before we married, remember I cooked that meal for all your family and guests? Well, your brothers came in to the kitchen – they were looking for Nick who'd slipped off somewhere but I knew they'd been talking about me. I asked if everything was okay, and Richard said there was a slight issue about seating. Usually in the church, the bride's family and friends sit to the left and the groom's people on the right – he said they couldn't do this because I had "no people". You know your family – they hate to do things differently!'

I laugh at this, it's true, particularly with Richard my older brother. You continue speaking as you stare at the wall. 'I said people could sit where they wanted, it wouldn't be a problem for you. Eddie looked embarrassed, then he said, "Yes, well it may not be a problem for Kate now, but it might be in a few years." '

'Really? You never told me that!'

'That night I said to you, "Katherine, I am not like the kind of husband your friends and family want for you," and you said you were prepared for anything.'

'No. Marc, I said, I was prepared for anything as long as we faced it together... And then you left me.'

'I believed you were better without me.'

'What more could I have done to prove to you how much I loved you!'

'Maybe this. Being here now, taking me back, making a life starting from the truth.'

'What happened to for better or worse? Couldn't you have taken my word for it?'

'Eddie was right. All the people who warned you about me were right. We were so different. I just didn't know how to deal with it all.'

'Tell me, tell me now, what happened, that morning you left? Had you planned it or was it some sort of dissociative fugue?'

'A what?'

'You know, where people just...wander off, forgetting who or where they are...it happens to some people, did that happen to you?'

'I didn't plan it if that's what you want to know. That morning, I was getting ready for work, after you left and...I was shaving and I stopped. I looked at myself in the mirror and I didn't know this man. Those last few weeks my past was coming back, people, memories...the lie I'd built about who I was, it was all falling apart. I wanted to tell you about me but I didn't want you to see me like that, how I really was. I didn't want to disappoint you. I dressed and I was about to go to work and I just...didn't go. I walked out. I believed that you would be better without me. I believed I had made a mistake in marrying you.'

'Because you didn't love me?'

'No! No! Katherine, that was always true. I loved you. I love you now. It's why I left!'

'Of all the reasons I came up with for why you left, it never occurred to me that it was because you "loved" me so much. What do you take me for?'

'Think about it. It would hurt for a while, yes, I'm really, really sorry about that - but you had family, friends, your work...eventually you'd get on with your own life, you'd get over me, find someone interesting, intelligent, balanced – I knew you would - or else what? No, listen Katherine –' I struggle free of you.

You bring your eyes to mine, your voice is firm and resounds from a part of you I've never heard before. 'Or what else? I could tell you everything I was ashamed of, bad things – horrible! - show you what a shit I was, what a liar, I could bring you into all my mess and the disasters I'd made around others – and you are loyal and good Katherine and you would have felt obliged to stay – and maybe too proud or too sorry for me to leave – it didn't seem fair. That morning, I believed the best way was to go.'

'Didn't you care what would happen to me?'

'Of course I did. I watched you.'

'That's creepy...I know you stayed at Tom's.'

'Yes, I did. I watched until I knew you would be okay. And then I left to work it all out on my own, give you space to make a life away from me.'

'Fine. So you were right. I must be completely transparent to you! I did move on. I did find someone else who's interesting, intelligent, balanced and he loves me and I was going into a new life without you...well done. You knew.' I look at you questioning if you ever could have imagined the insanity, the anguish and the desperate sadness. And I think that you could have.

Which leads to my question: 'So why the fuck did you come back?'

'Because now you can choose. You're free to decide.'

'Do you think I'm free when you've humiliated me and used me and I let you back so you can do it all again?'

'You are free, and you are stronger than you think.'

'I feel so weak when it comes to you, it's like I just say "yes" to you all the time...'

'Ah, good...do you say "yes" to this?'

You dip your finger in the water, trace around my heart. You lean against me and I feel your body against mine. I answer the question in the only way I can. And we fall asleep again in each other's arms.

It's just like Sundays used to be, although this time, I know who I'm lying with.

*

After France, I spent the rest of that summer working in my father's research lab in Oxford. As my friends returned from their holidays, my sorry romantic tale was circulated. Anna, who'd not gone on holiday because Nick was still in Libya camping out with Berber herdsmen, vented her boredom in a "hate Dave" campaign. She lay on the dogs' tartan blanket in the middle of the garden surrounded by her children, phones, books and friends forming a nucleus of gossip and loathing towards Dave, who was reportedly back in London and hadn't got in touch with me, 'even to apologise!' shouted Anna down the phone at someone I'd never even met.

'Anna, I'm just not the kind of girl men feel that way about...' I argued, trying to assuage my sister's outrage.

'Bollocks!' Anna said.

But when I said that about myself, it wasn't entirely to do with Dave. It was the way the Frenchman at the bus station had put his hand on my neck and run his thumb across my mouth and refused the goodbye kiss I'd waited for. 'I will kiss you, Katherine, but not now. You are not ready.' This I kept to myself.

'Shall I tell you about men?' Anna said. 'Men are only happy when they are unhappy,' she stressed, smacking Plato's Symposium against her thighs. 'Read this – it'll teach you all about love.'

'I was thinking of taking up French actually.'

That August, Oxford was particularly hot and crowded with weltering tourists swaying in front of entrances, holding up maps and toppling into courtyards. I was ready to leave for London and what my father laughingly called 'the killing season' – those months when Foundation House Officers begin practising and patient mortality apparently goes up.

But it hadn't been what I'd imagined. Sally, whom I was supposed to be living with, had started seeing Paul, a student she'd met while island-trotting in Greece. He was doing an MBA at LSE and had his own flat where Sally spent most of her time. I was left with Ng, a Chinese student who rarely left his room and Julie from Ireland who was rarely in hers. Apart from a book group which Anna had introduced me to, I was terribly alone. I worked hard and by the end of that first term, came top in our exams – anything to distract me from the flat's yellowing walls, the carpet which had worn through to the rubber lining, a half-collapsed seventies sofa which took over the front room like an obstinate drunkard. The kitchen served no dietary purpose – no oven and only a warm fridge which came alive at night with rounds of explosions. So whenever I had the chance, I went home where mum fed me, left me to study and returned me to London with a full bag of clean, ironed clothes.

My parents knew what to expect from their child's next decade specialising in medicine, they'd been through it themselves and then with Richard, their eldest. But with me, they worried: they worried that I was too thin, unhealthy and clearly lonely.

There were moments, such as on the coach heading home or wandering around the flat when it was empty, listening to music while washing up or braving the bath, when the little scenarios I scripted during the day turned into full-length two-hander performances between you and I. Marc, since that day we met, you'd taken my mind hostage. My thoughts followed the memories of your voice, the fixed blue stare of your eyes on me and the longing for your touch. You had possessed me, and yet a part of me was relieved we were separated by a sea – that you were confined to my fantasy world – the real you, you had made me afraid. Sartre had said vertigo was not the fear of falling from a great height, but the fear of jumping. I wasn't afraid of you – I'd been scared of myself when I was with you.

The weeks built into months, your image became even stronger in my mind. I hadn't said goodbye at all. I was waiting, and not that patiently.

Saturday, Oxford Street. The January Sales. Sally's Granny had sent her money for Christmas and she was shopping for a coat. As we browsed, she surprised me.

'Kate, do you want my opinion?'

'Erm...No,' I answered, standing in front of a mirror in a shop changing room.

'Tough. I find your entire appearance depressing.'

'Depressing?'

'And frustrating. Depressing and frustrating. Sorry,' confessed Sally.

Out of pride and habit, I prepared to defend myself, but in fact, I'd come to the same conclusion a while before, I just hadn't known what to do about it. Looking good wasn't exactly a quality that would've got me anything I wanted – until that moment when you'd seen through me.

'Why? I don't look that awful, do I?'

'No, of course you don't look awful - you couldn't ever look awful. But you don't make anything of yourself,' Sally sighed and went on, 'when we go shopping you spend ages with me deciding which clothes I should buy and when it comes to you, you just pick out the same navy blue cardi from John Lewis every time. You dress like your mother.'

'But my mother buys my clothes!'

'Exactly.'

'Exactly what?'

'You dress like you're in some kind of menopausal camouflage gear – hiding yourself from anyone who might want to fumble with your bra strap.'

And again I was back in France looking to the empty space where you'd been standing.

'Kate, are you all right?'

'Course! Just need to sit down with a strong coffee.'

After bustling through the shoppers and queuing for ages in a café, we collapsed as soon as two seats were free.

'I hope I didn't upset you or anything. It's a compliment really.'

'What? Oh, yeah. That. It's just...How can it be a compliment again?'

'I'm saying, listen, I'm saying you're gorgeous, Kate – tall, slim, fantastic legs, cheek bones to die for – most people would kill to look like you but you just cover it all up in baggy jumpers, lesbian haircuts and this kind of fashion asceticism which, in my opinion, is a waste of a very beautiful, feminine being.'

'Urgh!'

I tried to laugh it off, but the truth of it hit me. It wasn't just about clothes.

'It's true, it's true. I don't look like a "woman",' I said, infusing the word with as much irony as I could.

'Course you look like a woman...but a...a traffic warden woman!'

Despite not having thought much about the way I presented myself to the world, a self-realisation came to me instantly.

'I think it's to do with Anna. It'd always been so important to my sister to be "the beautiful one" – to be adored - I never wanted to compete, I just let her have that glory unchallenged. Everyone in my family has their own particular characteristics: Richard's brilliant, if a little boring, Anna's beautiful, Eddie's quirky and I'm...reliable.'

'Well if you're happy with that.'

'I'm not. Sally, would you...would you give me one of those...make-overs?'

'Top Shop. Quick. Before you change your mind.'

That weekend Sally worked on my "look" and I was ready for you.
Waiting for that kiss.

Several weeks later, on a Monday morning, Mona took the crash bleeper from me as long, gluey strands of sunlight rolled down the corridor walls, along the skirting boards and through the queue of patient trolleys. It was Spring, and I hadn't noticed.

It was into my seventy-ninth hour of work that week - stupid to count the hours but competing over "who'd done the most?" was the game we played in the canteen. I was winning having seen over sixty patients admitted since Friday morning and had only managed to lie down in the vacuum packed on-call room for two hours on Sunday morning before I had to tend to the aftermath of Saturday night's casualties. I wasn't really prepared for my first social conversation of the week.

'The weekends are just the bloody worst, aren't they?' sympathised Mona, 'having said that, we spent the day in IKEA which wasn't that different from A&E! You look so pale, Katie, why don't you pop out and get us carrot cake for later. There's a lecture lunchtime, we can scoff it down then. No time for proteins – let's cut straight to the puddings!'

'Wait there.'

I walked through the building in an etiolated daze, the adrenalin and caffeine was wearing off and my legs weren't moving the way I wanted them to. I wondered if it was possible to catch peritonitis. I nodded to a receptionist who was coming in after the weekend away. I deliberately avoided eye-contact with the patients who were queuing up to see someone. I stifled a yawn – something I was getting very adept at - while nodding goodnight to one of the night porters leaving for home. I had to rush, get that cake for Mona and I to eat after our compulsory Pre-Registration Doctors' lecture on "Applying Stomach Drains". After that it would be home until the following Thursday.

Once outside the building, I listened to the messages on my phone. Sally: the landlord's coming around to fix the broken window. What broken window? Friends from Cambridge: planning a reunion in a Soho wine bar on Tuesday night. My mother: on and on. These voices came across like ever-dimming light waves from remote stars. My mother's message was an excitable ramble which I shut off before she'd even gathered momentum. The star receded a little further.

Then I heard someone calling out to me.

'Katherine?'

I twisted around and you were standing in front of me.

'Hello,' you said.

You were smiling. In the time it took to look at you, all the accumulated tiredness and hunger and need for natural light completely disappeared. I was wide awake, more awake than I had been in months, well, since...

'You.'

'Yes. Me. Remember, from France?'

'Marc.'

'Marc, yes.'

'How did you...?'

'Your mother.'

'My mother?'

'Yes, I looked up your name in the telephone book.'

'Oh,' I said.

You looked so handsome in a soft black suit and black t-shirt with something scrawled in white on it that I couldn't read. I hadn't seen a well person for so long, and certainly not someone who emanated the energy you did.

'I called your mother. We talked for a long time, now we are both worried about the long hours you do, your diet and not exercising enough. Interesting jacket Katherine,' you said, looking at my doctor's coat.

My eyes were stinging and I was wondering how filthy my hair must look. So much for the makeover, the one time I wanted to stun you with my metamorphosis...there I was, exhausted and *stinking in my M&S Cosy-Toes shoes which I'd assured Sally I'd thrown away.*

'You were looking for me?'

'Of course. I told you we would see each other again. Remember?'

'Yes. How long have you been in London?'

'About three weeks.'

Your eyes were sparkling with amusement; your arms were crossed over your chest, like you were waiting for something.

'Are you happy to see me?'

'Yes, yes I am...' *I answered. I noticed my group of junior house doctors congregating at the lift.*

'I'm really pleased. How long are you staying for?'

'Forever. This is my home now. I was offered a job and I wanted a change, I thought well, I know of a good doctor in London, that's all I need.'

We just stood there looking at each other.

'Are you free tonight?'

'Yes.'

'Come meet me at my work – here's the address, and my number.'

You gave me a card for the restaurant and your mobile number written on the back. I took it in my unsteady fingers. All sense of there being anything else in the world but you was zapped into insignificance. My breathing was fast and shallow.

'It's good to see you again, Doctor. A ce soir.'

'Yes, thanks for...Bye,' *I said.*

I watched you as you walked through the main exit doors. Was it my imagination or was everyone else looking at you as well?

'Why don't I ever have patients like that,' *opined Angela as I stepped into the lift. I couldn't help laughing.*

'He's a friend actually.'

We moved inside the lift, squeezing up for a family.

'Why don't I ever have friends like that?' *she added.* 'And I thought you were all work and no play Dr Brenton. I see you got his phone number.'

'And a dinner date, for tonight,' *I said unable to keep the rampant excitement out of my voice.*

'Dinner, eh? Lucky you, I'm taking part in a study on Pancreatic Enzymes for the third year's research project. Enjoy your meal.'

sunday, midday

The intercom buzzes. My heart jolts into systolic overload while the rest of my muscles are still locked in sleep. I run through the usual questions following a Saturday night at *The Nadir*: Who am I? Where am I? And who's he?

Another buzz.

Most weekends when I wasn't on duty I'd go out, find someone who looked as much like you as possible and take them to my bed. On a good morning, the frogs leapt back into their ponds, but sometimes they flapped around croaking on and on until I returned them to the wild. This morning, you lie next to me, my prince is too hung-over to stir.

I roll on track-suit bottoms and socks, keep on the T-shirt I slept in and move as quickly and quietly as I can down the stairs. I can hear the rain outside like soft gun fire in the distance. The front door requires two hands to open against the wind.

Anthony is already walking to his car. If I leave him a few seconds longer, he will go. But when he hears the creak of the door, he turns, grinning despite the rain. He sprints back towards me.

'I've been trying to ring you for days! I thought you'd gone home for the weekend – and then I saw your car.'

He aims a kiss on my lips but I turn and he catches my ear. He trips a little on the threshold because I won't let him pass. He stops in front of me.

'I was just on my way to Rachel and David's – we're all meeting up for brunch. Fancy coming?'

We both know it's out of Anthony's way to come down my road to get to Rachel and David's. He must have taken a long route just to pass my building, even though I was supposed to be away. What might have been a cute act of sentimentality at any other time, has proved a dangerous error of judgement. He must have been thrilled to see my car there. That's why he is smiling.

I stand inside the corridor, keeping my face in the shadows. Anthony waits while drops of rain barge past him to get to the ground. I force myself to leave him in the cold: if I can't even bear to see him shivering, how am I going to tell him what I have to tell him?

'I can't come to lunch.'

'Oh shame. Work?'

He puts his hand on my arm as if I'm frail and he is about to lead me across the road - or is to lead me to what I have to say?

'Marc.'

The name means little to Anthony: he isn't from the past, but the future. A future being brutally aborted.

I find a few more words might help.

'Marc, my husband. He's come back.'

Anthony takes a few seconds to understand what I'm saying. And then he does.

'He's there? Now?' he asks, looking up in the direction of my flat and back to my bare shoulders. I nod, refuse to look sorry. Apologising would be to insult him.

'He's come back,' I repeat as though reinforcing a lie.

'So that's...it then?'

'He's my husband.'

Anthony steps away from me. He is a decisive man, a man whom I have watched after hours of surgery who never tires or angers or loses his equilibrium. Please don't now, I beg him with my eyes.

'Kate...'

He doesn't know what to ask first. A relief for me, because I've no idea how to answer anything he might confront me with.

I don't dare speak in case 'sorry' comes out.

I give a Gallic shrug of the shoulders, learned from you.

His eyes search my face but there's nothing to be found.

Anthony turns, paces slowly to his car. He presses the bleeper to open the door, it takes three goes. He holds the door open, looks to me again, just to take a parting snap-shot of the girl he recently proposed to. I watch him as though I am a sniper, spying on him from a long way off, unseen. But the bullet's already been fired. It's raining harder. He looks at me again, to check I'm the same person. And I'm not.

'Oh, congratulations about the job.'

'Sorry?'

He has to repeat it again.

'The job, The Heart Hospital. They want you. You should get the letter tomorrow.'

He bangs the top of the car twice as if to spur on a coach load of weary horses.

And he is gone.

When I turn back into the corridor, the door closes and the light behind me withdraws. There's only your silhouette on the stairs. You are sitting, watching me. I walk past you and into the flat.

'Katherine?'

'I don't want to talk about it.'

'Okay.'

'God knows there are enough things that you don't want to talk about!'

'I said okay, Katherine. It's okay.'

'It's not fucking "okay!" Don't you get it?'

'No. Maybe I don't –'

'That was the most hurtful, cruel, unkind thing I have ever done. That man - he's a good person, Marc. He trusted me. He took on this basket case, he wanted to spend his life with me, share everything with me - never leave me - and I just shut the door in his face because you wandered in for the weekend. Oh I forgot, for *seven* days.'

'You didn't have to Katherine.'

'No. I didn't. But I did.'

You put the coffee on and lean against the sink, both hands on either side of it.

'You've changed,' you say.

'What did you expect? Of course I've changed!' We face each other. It's a standoff to see who can put a name to the difference between then and now. 'I was thinking the same of you.'

You turn, look out the window, and I wonder if this time you'll stay and face it.

'No, it's just that you have new eyes. And he is a good man, I'm not.'

'And nor am I a good woman....' I say, thinking back to last night.

'No Katherine, you will always be good...'

'Oh Marc, you just don't know.'

'I can go anytime.'

'I know that, Marc. I know that!'

'You are angry. I understand. What are you doing?'

'I'm making a cake.'

*

'What's this?' Anthony asked, walking into the Conference Room of the Kensington & Chelsea Hospital and stopping in front of a side table laid out with food.

Mr Cole from The Heart Hospital answered, 'The rabbit food. Yes, Dr Brenton is responsible for that.'

'Oh, I thought I'd wandered into a petting zoo by accident!' laughed Anthony and the consultant.

I looked up from the papers I was arranging.

'I just thought it was ridiculous that we have so many meetings about the health of the heart while we're munching on chocolate biscuits and drinking coffee. Surely if we are to advise people about diet we should take our own advice?'

Mr Cole and Anthony gazed at the selection of crudités and wholemeal breads. Cole smiled, 'Care for a carrot, Anthony?'

The man by his side laughed, 'Could I have it administered intravenously?'

During the meeting I was aware of Anthony catching my eye and making a point of biting into the apple slices.

At the break, Dr Henderson introduced us.

'Kate, someone I wanted you to meet. This is Anthony Blanchett, he worked with your father at Johns Hopkins. Anthony, you were asking about Dr Brenton - this is she, why don't you hand her some oats?'

Anthony turned the carrot in front of his eyes as if he'd never seen one before and nibbled at it.

'Healthy foods for doctors, eh? I think the medical profession is probably a population cross-section you'd never succeed in converting, but good for you for trying,' he said. 'I'm Anthony, worked with your father. We really, really thought a lot of him over there.'

'Good.'

'We have met before, though, haven't we? At Gina Brightman's dinner party, long time ago.'

'Here's a napkin,' I snapped, switching off the PowerPoint projector.

Of course I remembered meeting Anthony at that dinner party. The night before you left. He was the reason my old school friend had rung me out of the blue and invited me to her house. Anthony, a friend of hers, had returned from doctoral training in the States, he'd talked about his mentor, my dad, and it'd come out that I'd been at school with Gina, so Anthony asked to meet me. That's why she threw that little dinner, for us to get together.

Well you're not stupid, Marc, you saw the set up for what it was. That night, that last night, you were in a sulk anyway because you hadn't wanted to go out, we were at the stage in a marriage where we no longer had to feign interest in each other's friends. I'd coerced you into coming out, you thought it was a concession enough that you'd agreed, but you weren't going to be civil as well. You were difficult even before she introduced us to the tall, handsome, starring-light of the medical profession. Anthony hadn't disguised his excitement at meeting me. It was innocent enough – my dad had rather taken him under his wing, his father had only recently died, and then he'd returned to London and was lonely, he was interested in my work, in me – but I could sense your chilly petulance turn into a long-term freeze over.

You found the people dull, Gina was 'boring' because she'd given up trying to ask you questions and wasn't listening to the answers anyway. And the dinner – a perfectly ordinary meal Gina had spent the day repeating from a trendy recipe book – was, for you, inedible. In the taxi home you ranted about everything that was wrong with the middle classes, with dinner parties, with globalisation, the English, but I picked you up on your subterfuge and, buoyed by Anthony's attentions, accused you of being jealous. Then you'd said it, said what was in our minds that night: that Anthony was the sort of person I should have married. That he was the kind of man I needed. And I didn't deny it. I said something I never meant to say and left the incision open.

That last night.

Whatever Anthony had subsequently heard about my marriage, he never let on, he gave me room to be me, to be the person I was supposed to be.

After the initial meeting – the carrots and my presentation –
we worked together with Mr Cole on a paper. One night after
work, Anthony and I ended up in a small Italian restaurant in
Hampstead. At that time, my criteria for men was simply whether
or not they looked like you. But he couldn't have been more
different, his complexion was fair, his accent very English; his
words precise, unadorned with adjectives, let alone imagery. He
talked as if he were reading from a text book and when he asked
about things, his questions were set like exam questions, "Examine
the restaurant menu and briefly assess your choice of starters in
order to evaluate its strengths and weaknesses..." When I
answered his questions, he nodded as though we were attending a
viva. He made mental notes – remembered everything – and once
I think he even laughed.

Half way through the meal, Anthony asked, 'Have you noticed
the other people here?'

'What?' I said, looking around.

'They're all couples...'

It was true, we sat in a line of couples and I saw a red rose
between each one.

'Anthony,' I laughed. 'It's Valentines' night!'

He blushed.

Of course, all day there'd been commotion at the nurses' station
with flowers arriving and anonymous cards being sent, giggles
and jokes with the patients.

'Well this is the first time I've ever had a date for Valentine's,'
he'd said.

I didn't say it, but it was mine too. Remember? Valentine's
night was such a busy time for you at the restaurant so we never
made plans for us – not that we'd ever have bowed down to
institutionalised romance like that, you disapproved of the whole
idea although you were thrilled that it brought you a full house
and guaranteed vast sales of champagne.

A pleasant enough evening. Anthony and I cut and swallowed,
made room for the silences which squeezed past us like overweight
strangers until relevant conversation resumed. Anthony surprised
me by ordering a pudding, he didn't seem a Tiramisu sort but he
scraped his bowl while telling me that since his father had died
he'd spent his free weekends looking after his mother who was
alone and desolate after nearly forty years of marriage to a man

she adored. His brother was married with children so the onus was more on Anthony to care for her. It was a change to talk about our mutual families; with you, the subject had been so taboo.

When our meal ended, Anthony kissed me goodbye. Just the one peck on the cheek.

'Thank you for being my Valentine's date,' he said, adding that he had a Saturday free in two weeks and he wondered if I wanted to visit Kew gardens. His sister-in-law had bought him a year's pass as a Christmas present and he'd never used it. I must have said 'yes' before going on clubbing that night with Tom. I took too much Ecstasy and was sick into the sleeve of my jacket in the taxi home.

Kew Gardens with Anthony. It was nice, Marc, it was a relief to spend a day in fresh air not being whirled around by my anger. We talked about pollination and the host family he'd stayed with in the US.

I was there by accident – he'd turned up on my doorstep and I was too embarrassed to say I'd forgotten we'd made a plan. But for that day I wasn't someone who needed to visit a counsellor twice a week, who took sleeping pills at night and whose only respite was having a 22-year-old boy lick between my legs until I passed out.

For those few hours, Anthony lent me a little time in a world without you.

Tom was watching TV when I returned from my outing. He looked me up and down and said, 'You're going to marry him, aren't you?'

'What?' I laughed, prizing a joint out his fingers.

'The date. Dr Anthony. You're going to marry him.'

'You and Maggie saw it in her crystal ball, did you?'

I drew the smoke into my lungs and closed my eyes as part of my face numbed.

'You get over your husband, and I lose you. I'm just a symptom, that's how it goes.'

I looked at Tom's sad face. When I kissed him, my bottom lip tasted of salt, but I didn't know which one of us was crying.

sunday afternoon

I'm whisking. The oven's preheating. It's still raining.

'Do you love him?'

'You're not French by any chance, are you?'

'I am,' you smile. 'How did you guess?'

'Questions like that. The obsession with love! Sally says it's just an overwhelming desire to recreate one's family of origin...a yearning to re-find that face we once looked up to and got stuck on. Wanting to go home. And we dress it up in all this medieval, superstitious, opium for the masses clap-trap.'

'Apparently it makes the world go around.'

'Apparently it's free. You should have seen his face, Marc. That's the price! What have I done? Love's...just not a good enough reason. A husband like Anthony is what a girl wants –'

'- needs.'

'- needs! Yes, I need a good, solid, tax-paying, meat 'n' two veg man...'

Your mouth is over my mouth. Your fingers enter me and I lay down over the breakfast bar, wrapping my legs around your back, knocking over a glass of water and loose change. You hold my waist, push into me, going right through me as I move closer into you. When our eyes lock I am all heart, all feeling, all an extension of you as much as you are so much a part of me. And as you are about to come, you cry out, *'Oh ma cherie! Ma Katherine!'* You give yourself to me, are helpless to me, and all I know is that if this is love, I love you, and I never loved Anthony.

'So, still need a meat'n' two veg man?' you asked as I wriggle out from under you.

'I need to get out of here.'

'Katherine – where are you going?'

'Out. Just...away...from all this - you!'

sunday evening

'Kate! You're soaked. Come in. Come in.'

Sally shouts up the stairs, 'It's Kate! Sorry about the mess... We're trying to get the kids off to bed: we thought if we started earlier it would be less of a rush...in fact it just prolongs the agony!'

'Hi gorgeous,' says Paul, bounding down the stairs shaking a baby's bottle.

'Sorry, I didn't ring or anything before.'

'No, you're just what we need - some sane company! There's a bottle of white already open in the fridge. Welcome to what we call the suicide hours: the children's supper, bath and bed...not necessarily in that order.'

'What's all that banging up there?' Paul shouts to the top of the house. He looks back at me, 'We planned to take the kids to the zoo and it's been bloody raining all day so they're pretty stir crazy. And as for us!'

'Paul would you do the bath, let us have a little girly time? Then I'll do the stories, or Kate, would you?'

'Sure, I'll read to them...as long as it's not Greek myths again!'

Sally shuffles into the kitchen, grabs the wine, kicks away the children's toys and sits us both down. I can still smell their Sunday lunch.

'Ah, that's better. This weather. You okay?'

'Yeah, I just got a bit restless, thought I'd walk over.'

'You walked!'

'Well it looked like it was stopping when I left –'

'Coming to book group Tuesday?'

'I...I don't know...'

'What?' Sally calls up stairs, leaning right out of the chair to try and hear him better. 'What? I can't hear?...It's in the laundry bag...doesn't matter, just take it out. Well, then it's – Oh for God's sake - Kate, just a sec.'

When Sally returns from finding a towel for the baby, I'm gone.

I'm running. Running in the rain, running in the dark. Running away from now, from today, my best friend, you and me. I'm running to catch up with the time when you came back for me.

When I was the person you wanted me to be.

✻

The night of our first date. The bath filled with a milky oil which Sally claimed Cleopatra used to bathe in. I dried my hair afterwards like people do on TV, swinging from right to left, curling the brush out in the air. Since the day you left me, unkissed at the coach station, I'd been growing my hair, trying to become the woman you wanted.

'Now that's what I call a real scrub in, Dr Brenton,' said Sally.

'I am so nervous. What do you know about French men?'

'Errrm...They have long lunches, are obsessed with oral sex and dressing up in women's clothes. Oh, and baguettes, they eat a lot of baguettes.'

'Where d'you learn all that?'

'I had a French exchange once. She was a nightmare so I got to watch a lot of TV, and ate baguettes. Hang on a sec...'

Sally rummaged in her room and returned with a necklace.

'Here you go, treasure it. It's New Look's finest. I'm going to crash now - wake me up when you get back tonight...if you come back!'

'Are you still cross I didn't tell you about him?'

'Well, yes. There I was in my tepid bath on Sunday night and I answered the phone to this deep sexy voice asking to speak to "Katerrr-rine," and then he says, "Can you tell her Marc rang, Marc from France, last summer." You're a dark horse, you are.'

'Sorry, but...I sort of...wanted to keep him to myself.'

'The cat's out now. Everyone at the hospital knows and after his call to your mother all of North England will be gunning for you tonight.'

'Wish me luck.'

'You've had enough already, Mademoiselle.'

Walking home from the hospital since I'd moved to London I'd been weighed down by a feeling of - I didn't know how to identify it - but maybe I was just afraid of the word "lonely". Everyone I passed seemed to have somewhere to go, friends and lovers to meet, events in their lives that they rushed to and from, while I left the hospital to sleep a few hours, change clothes, eat what I could and return to work. I couldn't see how my life would ever change. And then came that night. There was nothing in the world I would have preferred to do than to see you again. I was fizzing down those streets to get to you, gravity had nothing on me. And loneliness?

You were in London. You were waiting for me.

The restaurant was off Knightsbridge. I watched from across the road, trying to calm myself while updating all this new information about you. I braced myself, and walked into where you worked.

'Madame?'

'I'm here to see Marc?'

The man spoke fast and in French to one of the waitresses.

'Crystalle will show you.'

I followed her through the restaurant and the swing doors to the kitchen.

You didn't see me at first, and although I knew it was you, it took a while to take in this Marc I was re-meeting, the man pacing that big white and metal room. You moved from one person to the next, pointing, suggesting, taking over, shaking your head. You, in your white chef's jacket, your bass-line voice filling the kitchen, your employees frowning in concentration, twitching in anticipation of your disapproval. You said something, they laughed. You orchestrated: set the pace, syncopated tasks, inspired. Even I, standing at the door, was under your command. It would never have occurred to me to compare a chef of a restaurant to a surgeon – but your kitchen was also a theatre and you, my date for the night, were its star.

'Katherine! Là voila!'

Everyone looked up to see who'd come to see you. You introduced me to your team as they relaxed momentarily from their jobs and smiled, amused that their boss had another life which he was sharing with them. Your good manners Marc, they have got you everywhere. You waved them goodnight, dumped your white coat in the laundry basket, just like I did at the end of my working day. You brought me to the front of house. I didn't understand what you said to the man, but he shook my hand and said, 'So, this is the reason Marc has come back to London!'

Once on the street, you held me by my shoulders. You kissed both my cheeks, slowly, deliberately. You stroked my arms and pressed me against you. No one had ever held me so long without talking.

'It's my night off but I have to...babysit them a little. Anyway, I wanted you to see where I work. You like it?'

'Yes, everyone seemed terribly nice.'

You laughed and repeated what I'd said, 'Terribly nice'.

I could feel the heat of your muscles under your cotton shirt. You were so alive. The antithesis of all the old, disfigured, decaying bodies I patched up all day long. With your palm against my back, you walked with me through Knightsbridge and onto Brompton Road.

'I want to cook for you Katherine but where I'm living at the moment...it's not right for you.'

'You should see where I live! Ng, my flat mate, has identified eighteen different types of fungus in our bathroom.'

As we walked, women looked at you. I could see them in their cars, at the traffic lights, feeding on you with their eyes.

'Shall we go for a drink first, then dinner?'

You circled your thumb around the curvature of my shoulders.

'Have you made any friends here in London?'

I sounded like my parents.

'Friends? There's a group of us Frenchies who go out at night but as for the English, most people who come to the restaurant can be a little...they think they are better people because they arrive in a limousine, you know?'

'Most people I meet arrive in an ambulance.'

That night, our first date – and traditionally speaking – my first ever 'date' - walking around London in the Spring with you, eating dinner and you taking me back to my flat before midnight because you wanted me to get a good night's sleep – as if I would sleep! - was probably the happiest night of my life. I was in love – you dropped me in it from a great height– you worked me, flattered me, seduced me. You made me feel the most special person alive. You gave me just enough of yourself to leave me wanting you forever. And when you stood at the door of my flat, you put your arms around me.

'Katherine. Are you ready now, ready for me?'

'My hair's grown a bit,' I said, tugging at it.

You turned me to face you. The back of your hand glided across my jaw bone, from my ear to my chin, your thumb stroked my bottom lip. I opened my mouth a little, closed my eyes and when I opened them again, I wasn't sure if you weren't laughing at me, just a little.

'Katherine, I was a little cruel, what I said, remember? I wanted to kiss you so much that afternoon. But then, it wasn't the

right time. You were so vulnerable, you were on holiday and going home and it was not real. But now, I have come here for me, yes, but also for you. This is real.'

You touched my cheek, stroked my neck with your fingertips. It wasn't the first kiss I'd been given, but it was the first one I gave. This time, kissing you, I didn't feel asphyxiated, concerned about the exchange of microbes, I wasn't counting for it to end so I could catch my breath, wipe my cheeks and have my face back. I had to give to you, so I could get more. And you gave me more. I was locked into you, your heat, the softness of your mouth, the motion of you against me. You knew what you were doing, and I had no idea. Not one thought of anything but you. Your touch formed me, creating something just for you. Your lips, your tongue claimed me, your hands on my back, clasping my waist - if I could be useful for anything, it had to be for you. I would never have stopped, but you drew back, sealed what had passed between us with your lips on mine, just as we had begun.

You spoke, 'I want to cook for you. Next week come to my restaurant, bring a friend, anyone, but not a boyfriend, I would get jealous. Bonsoir, Katherine.'

Today, Marc, I know where you were going that night. But I couldn't have worked it all out then, I wouldn't have known where to start. And me? I must have been such a cinch to you.

*

'I'm really sorry to disturb you on a Sunday.'

'Oh, don't worry, love, you're only keeping me from cleaning out the cat litter. You look like a drowned rat.'

'Thanks, I feel like one.'

'Fancy a rum and *Coke*?'

While Frances finds a seat near the fire, I order the drinks and look at the same faces I've seen in every pub. They've had a good look at us and are now contemplating the beers in front of them. They wait, as though filling out the duties of some job description, 'Man sitting at the bar', 'Man by the juke box', 'Bartender rinsing a glass and keeping an eye on the football scores.' I want to ask Frances how everything seems so normal when I'm in such a mess.

She switches off her mobile phone when I put the drinks down on the table. The fire's flames light up the amber swirls in our glasses.

'Cheers,' she says.

'Thanks for coming out tonight. I had to talk to someone. I went round to my best friend's but I just couldn't speak to her...I ran out. I feel like such an idiot.'

'I remember that when I was getting divorced, I'd find some total stranger on the bus, tell them my whole life story - every intimate detail - and my mum would ask "How are you?" and I'd bite her head off. It's like that sometimes.'

'I didn't know you were married.'

'Briefly. It wasn't for me. All that, "I'm making a cup of tea, do you want one? I was thinking of having a friend over, is that okay? I'm gonna do a wee now if you were wondering where I was..." Drove me mad. And other things – I worked, he spent – sort of thing. But when it came down to it, I just couldn't – wouldn't - share my life with someone – and I was a relationships' counsellor at the time!'

Frances laughs her solid, woody laugh.

Our pile of coats, hats and scarves lay next to us under the windows. Outside the wind flaps the rain around like tinsel under the streetlights. And you are out there somewhere, wondering where I am. And I like that.

'How did you know Marc was back?'

'I was watching the Hounslow house, saw him go in.'

'Why were you there?'

'I don't know...I had a morning off and...intuition.'

'No, Frances, you wouldn't drive to the other side of London and watch that house unless something...'

'You want my job?' Frances laughs and sips her drink. 'Okay, you're right, Katie. But this needs to be checked out...I was searching the records for missing people in California – for another case, an adoption thing – but a man's just run out on a young woman from San Francisco – he was the chef at her restaurant. It looks like your friend's M.O. So I thought, if your Marc was on the move, that's where he'd go...and I was right. I'll get more info on the US story early week. So, how's it going with lover boy back?'

'He wants us to have a week together. A week to decide.'

'That's very...specific.'

'I think he wants it to be the way it was in the beginning. God knows so do I, and sometimes it's just like he never left – in bed – and then, it's like...he's interrupting my life, my grief even.'

'Yeah, honey, sounds right.'

'He won't really say anything or answer any questions. Just keeps making me cups of coffee and asking if I've eaten.'

'Hum, nice.'

'It's irritating actually. I'm used to helping myself.'

'Oh God, don't get like me!'

'I broke off my engagement with Anthony. Frances, what happens when people came back?'

'Roughly the figures work out that 20 percent of people return after they've been located –40 percent make some sort of contact but don't want to return, and the last 40 percent don't want to be found. It's grim sweetie, but you're someone used to dealing in facts.'

'I'm just wondering where Marc comes into all that.'

'He doesn't. He never did. But this is also about you.'

'I want him to know what he's done – I want him to really understand what he did when he left, right from the beginning –'

'You could write him a letter?'

'It would be a book.'

'Why not? It'd help you and maybe...your husband. I get the feeling he's someone who either believes or justifies his actions by thinking that it won't make all that much of a difference. He doesn't stay around long enough to see what he does to people. Kate, you deserve to let him know what you've been through.'

It was after that chat with Frances that I started writing this to you.

You've tidied the flat, you're reading the newspapers. A soup is bubbling on the low burner. The flowers you put in water on Friday are browning at the edges. There's music playing on low and the heating is up high.

You look up when I come in. You don't smile, you turn the page and you begin reading again. You bide your time before saying, 'Sally rang.'

'Did you talk to her?'

'Of course.'

'I bet she was surprised to hear your voice.'

'Yes, she was. But it's okay, we had a good talk.'

It's better not to articulate the sarcastic quips that come to mind. How easy it must be for Sally, always half-fancying you, missing you but then able to have a flirtatious natter after a curious two and three quarter years.

I take off my damp clothes and change into a grey, velour tracksuit that I usually reserve for nights in front of the TV on my own. I wring out my socks and add them to the bulge of dirty clothes in the washing machine. I turn the settings' dial thinking back to Frances' last words as she ran me back in her car.

We'd stopped outside my flat, I'd thanked her for the lift home.

'Why aren't you telling him what you know? Why are you keeping his secrets? On some level, I think you're acting as an accessory to his actions – it's not like you, Kate, to be passive like this.'

'This is between Marc and I.'

'Okay, I'll butt out –'

'I don't mean it like that, Frances, it's just...while he's been gone, I've been living in the past, and for just a little bit longer, now he's back, it's like, I want to pretend. And I've had a change of heart.'

Frances looked up at my kitchen window where the man she'd been hired to follow was adding spices to a broth.

'This time last year we had a ten-year-old girl waiting for a heart transplant. We were running out of time and couldn't find a donor. Then a call came through that there was a heart for her, the heart of a 65-year-old man – we had no other option – so we went ahead with the operation. The heart of a grown man is much bigger than the size of a child's, of course it wouldn't fit in her body so we attached it successfully and it lay outside her chest. Several days later it'd shrunk to about half the size, after a week it was just small enough to be closed in. Now she's running around... The heart re-shapes itself to fit the person, to match the experience. Do you see? That's what's happened to me.'

This was probably going to be the last time I ever saw Frances, and there was something I'd always wanted to ask her. If I didn't then, I never would.

'You never told me who it was that you lost.'

'Oh my days! You want to rummage around my past now!' she laughed.

'I just wondered.'

'Well, I was a war-time baby, apparently my dad was an American GI, "Bob" my mum thought he was called, but then she said it might have been "Bill". He promised he'd come back for her after the war, marry her and all...but I guess something came up. She was always waiting for him... I made it a vow I'd track him down, put his name on my birth certificate, but I never found him.'

We sat, thinking about 'Bob-Bill' and Frances looked different to me now she was half American. I wondered how old that made her.

'Thanks for everything Frances.'

'Just doing my job.'

'No, you did so much more.'

Before closing the car door, she tapped the window. It lowered itself down. She asked, 'Shall I pursue the San Francisco connection?'

But she already knew the answer.

Forty degrees. *Eco Wash*. Start.

You put an arm around me.

'You would rather be out in the rain than with me.'

'I just needed to talk to someone.'

'Him?'

'No, not him. A friend...'

'Sally said you ran out on her.'

'I just...couldn't cope with Sally, and Paul, explaining everything. I knew what they'd ask and I didn't know how I would answer. Anyway, I'm sure you made her feel better.'

'She was upset. And then four hours you were gone. I was worried – you turned your phone off.'

'Can you hear yourself?'

sunday night

You make supper while I soak in a hot bath that you've run for me. I'd spent the last half an hour slamming things around and not speaking to you, then I tired myself out, got in the bath.

I'm thinking about the girl Frances mentioned, the one looking for you in San Francisco. I hear you moving around the kitchen, and she doesn't.

You poke your head around the door.

'Katherine, a woman rang. Mrs Wheeler? I said you'd call her back.'

'Thanks.'

You spend a few minutes looking at me, the soap bubbles sit around my shoulders like a cloak, crackling in my ears. You close the door, respectfully.

Sunday nights if I'm not at the hospital, I call my mum, and I call Mrs Wheeler. I don't know why, it's a homage to grief, I suppose, and guilt. I know what it's like when you've lost someone and everyone else goes back to their lives and you have no life to return to.

I don't know if you'd be interested but I thought I should tell you what happened to Dave. Your predecessor. I can't say my hands have no blood on them either.

*

I left Dave in France with Tatyana, and I met you later that morning. I never looked back, didn't think about him again until about eighteen months after you left. His mother had tracked me down to say that he'd been living at home and was having some 'difficulties'. She thought it would be good for him to see old friends again. I had three weeks off to revise for exams and Tom was recording, so, in search of distraction, I went there, to Northampton, to fulfil some obligation to a mother who sounded anxious and afraid for her boy. And I wanted to open links with my past, get in touch with old friends who didn't know you, or us. It was easier to be with people who weren't looking at me and wondering where you were.

I remembered Dave's mother from the times his parents came to take him out at college. She'd been a small, lively woman with dark hair swept back behind her head and a face whose little features seemed to have been painted on rice paper. When I met her again, the rice-paper complexion had been scrunched into a ball. She was hunched over and there was a warble in her voice as she led me into their house where I'd expected to see Dave.

'Bill, this is Kate. She's one of David's friends from Cambridge. You were in Jesus College, wasn't it? Did you want tea?'

Mr Wheeler was in a large armchair by the fire reading The Telegraph. *He put it down to look at me, then returned to it while his wife talked from the kitchen.*

'Was it ghastly getting out of London? The traffic these days well we rarely have reason to go there anymore although once a year for the theatre with friends - friends who live in Edgware, do you know it? On the A41? It's very nice, nice - or a very special exhibition like the last one at the British Museum which I do really enjoy and then you make a day of it but with all the pushing and shoving, the rushing about, people spitting on the roads, the congestion charges, parking, pollution and the rudeness! It's not what it was for a start there are no English people there anymore, I can't understand a word anyone says, David says you're not supposed to say that but it is true really so really it's just not worth the... sugar?'

'No, thank you. Would you like a hand?' *I asked, going up to the Aga, pressing for warmth.*

'So how's your life at the hospital? He's been upstairs in his room you know he probably won't come down till lunch time writing, writing, well I told you on the phone. Hard work is it dear?'

'Yes, it's pretty tough but nothing compared to the House Officer years.'

She's not listening; she's busying herself with putting the sugar from one bowl into another.

'Poor thing, you must take care of yourself or you'll get ill and then what will the ill people do?'

The house was making my nose itch.

'And then on your day off you come all this way to see David. So kind of you. He always had such good friends, some even from primary school, we never moved, see? I say, David, why don't you ring up some of your friends? Have a get-together – like a dinner or something, I'd do the food - but he never does, never does. Come in dear sit down I won't call him because he usually doesn't come if we do and that's a bit...I'll send you up if he doesn't make an appearance by the end of your tea –'

'Who?' *asked Mr Wheeler.*

'David, dear. This is Kate. A friend of his from Cambridge – come all the way from London - but I said I'll not call him in case he doesn't come down and then that's...awkward, so we'll just...wait.'

The tea was served in bone china cups with non-matching saucers.

'Have you still lots of friends from Cambridge?'

'A few. My best friend, Sally, some others.'

'He hasn't any friends now of course. Used to have lots of friends.'

Mr Wheeler put his paper down and stared at me.

'We've met you before, haven't we?'

'Yes, at college, a few times when you came to take Dave out for the day I came too. We went punting once...'

'You came top in your first year's − were made a Scholar, I recall. Doctor now?'

I nodded.

'How are you bearing up with the endless policy changes, hospital league tables, these 'Foundation' hospitals −'

'Whatever happened to Robinson's Lemon Barley Water and changing a catheter with a smile?' laughed Mrs Wheeler.

'She was a nurse,' said Mr Wheeler, as if informing me of something quite unbelievable. The floorboards above us creaked.

'David was explaining to us about how magnetic resonance imaging works last night. I didn't know how much medical treatment depended on computers these days, what would happen if there were a power cut, eh?'

'Hospitals have independent generators.'

'Finished your tea love? You'll have so much to talk about, not having seen each other since...since...'

Mrs Wheeler knocked on Dave's door and let me in.

Dave was standing in the middle of the room like an oil rig amidst a choppy sea of books, papers and clothes. He'd put on weight, it didn't look right on him, more like he'd been padded up for a school play. He'd also grown a beard from which his eyes looked out, dim and distrustful.

'David, someone's here to see you.'

It was then I realised he hadn't been aware of this visit, he'd been oblivious to his mother's calling all the people he'd once known and inviting them over.

When I took a few paces into his room, he stepped back, slipping a book over something he'd been writing. There were so many papers out, so many pencils over his desk, the floor. I'd forgotten that Dave always wrote in pencil, it had been a joke in college that he copied down all his notes from lectures, learnt them, and then rubbed them all out to re-use the paper for the next day. His reasoning was more economical than ecological.

Mrs Wheeler mumbled something about getting the lunch on and disappeared down the stairs closing the door behind her.

I wasn't sure how to approach him, so I just stood there, facing him, wondering what that unpleasant smell was.

It was a strange shaped mock-Tudor room in the rather odd looking mock-Tudor house. Dark, airless. There was the single bed against the wall where I'd lost my virginity.

'Has she sent you?'

'Who?'

'You know who.'

'No. I don't.'

Dave laughed, his chin bulged under the bristles. I'd been long enough in health care to know which types of medication cause that pallor and pudgy weight gain.

'Lady Davenport, that's who.'

'No, Dave. I haven't seen Tatty for a long time.'

'Good try. I knew she'd send her spies in eventually.'

He looked around his room as if he needed to find something, then he turned to me as if surprised I was still there.

'So. Not exactly one of Tatyana's residences but there you go, not as draughty though, eh? Small but well insulated. My Dad's in the aluminium double-glazing business, he probably told you.'

'You didn't finish your degree.'

'I did go back. Sat in the medical library trying to memorise anatomical diagrams and chemical formulae and Kate...I started writing poetry!'

The 'P' of poetry came out with such a splutter that Dave was temporarily lifted off the ground.

'Poetry! Lyrics! Dialogues! Lyrical ballads, pastoral ballads! They just came out...out! Out! I couldn't stop... I started reading them to patients, then aloud in surgery waiting rooms, on the wards in Addenbroke's Hospital and...people...were... getting better! So! What do you think happened when they found out - they *didn't like that, did they? The medical profession – oh no, have to put a stop to that...tut-tut-tut...can't have people getting better without pharmaceutical companies getting richer, and doctors buying yachts and younger wives with their fat pensions. You wouldn't believe the lengths they went to shut me up – they wanted me dead...yes, dead. So what better than claiming me mad and in need of....surprise, surprise...medication! They are still out there – watching, listening, I know they're there – they're not just drug pushers and thieves – they are murderers. But I'm a poet, Kate...they can't take that away from me. A poet: someone who heals the soul, not the body.'*

He fell into the chair, exhausted by his speech.

'I'm sure you're very good.'

'There's no good or bad about it – you either are or you aren't.'

'I'm sure you are, then.'

'I've already been published... Look...'

Dave thrust a local magazine into my hands, 'Read it.' He pointed his finger to a poem which was between an advert for a family run hotel and someone selling a 1989 Passat.

I read over the poem. It was an enthusiastic, clever piece. Anna had written similar poems for similar publications in her early teens. I found myself looking over the car ad.

'They're listening. You've probably not been in fresh air for months. Let's go.'

Dave's parents were sitting in silence in their armchairs when Dave announced, 'We're going out.'

Mrs Wheeler leapt to her feet and started on about scarves and hats and catching our deaths, but Dave pushed me ahead and slammed the door behind us.

The day was cold but very bright. At the end of Dave's road, the houses, the streetlights and the parked cars came to an end, after that, it was uninterrupted countryside. Dave crossed the road away from the line of houses and started running fast while rotating his arms around. I jogged behind him, trying to keep up as he shouted things out which I couldn't hear until he turned to me.

'Look at this! Solaris! Avarus animus nullo satiatur lucro!' Dave said, bending over to catch his breath.

For a while we traipsed fast over thickets and under branches until we relaxed into a regular pace.

'I heard you married.'

'Yes. But...'

'Oh no, "buts," don't disappoint me - if you can't make that ridiculous institution work there's no hope for any of us!'

'It's not a matter of it working or not, he disappeared.'

'Disappeared you say?'

'A year and a half ago, he vanished. I'm looking for him but...'

'Can you still love someone when they are no longer there?'

The cold air scoured my throat. Dave didn't wait for an answer before turning to me, putting his heavy hands on my shoulders and shouting into my face.

'They teach children that we all need water, oxygen and food to survive but throw physics to the dogs! We need Love. When you love someone and they love you, you can really live, and you grow! Without that, we die. Fuck cancer and heart disease: loneliness is the greatest killer of them all. And what can you prescribe for that, eh?' He jabbed his index into my ribs, 'Nothing. Kate, I thought I was going to die. After six years of medical training, I thought a girl would be my cause of death! But, look, I've made it! I'm getting better!'

Dave leapt up again and flung himself towards a clearing and up an earth mound. He sprang to the top of it and shouted down.

'They're a rotten lot, all of them. I'm better than the whole damn bunch of them put together! See, I can say that now. You can tell her I'm fine now. She doesn't have to worry about my calls or my letters. Fly, little spy, fly! Go tell her!'

Dave's eyes were darting in all directions. He started laughing loudly, a laugh with no echo.

'The Great Gatsby,' he said, jumping down and putting a hot hand on my shoulder. 'She bought it for me in Cannes at the English Bookshop...What, darling girl?'

I turned my face into his and kissed his lips in a number of ways before he opened his mouth. It was me who pulled him down on the little bit of grass, who heard a cuckoo as I put my hand into his jogging trousers. Dave's mouth tasted of copper. His jaw didn't seem to be doing what he wanted it to do – he'd smack his lips together, lick and re-lick them – before coming back to the exercise of kissing me again. I sat up to undo my boots, Dave rolled on his

137

back, wriggling on the grass like a large dog picking up the smells of spring. I took out one leg of my jeans, one side of my pants and rolled Dave onto me. Eventually, we managed to fit our bodies together although he never managed a full erection nor to ejaculate, but we went through the motions regardless.

Afterwards, I lay there, half of me freezing, small insects gnawing at my flesh. Dave chatted to himself, gathering ideas for something he wanted to write later that day.

What had I just done? Maybe I'd got back at Dave for hurting me that summer in France, but mostly, I'd completed a circle – as always, it was all about you.

I left after the walk, didn't stay for lunch. Said I had an emergency at the hospital to attend to. Dave's eyes filled with tears when he said my visit had changed everything.

'It's a shame you have to go off so soon, you've done him the world of good,' said his mother. 'He's already upstairs writing an ode to you. Oh, can you hear? That's him on the guitar...'

As I started to drive away from the house, Mr Wheeler leant through the driver's window.

'Stay in the middle lane, stick to 56 miles per hour. That way you save on petrol and reduce the risk of accidents... Thanks for coming to see our son, we really appreciate it.'

Dave called many times over the next two weeks, sent me letters, poems, cards, but I didn't take his calls and after reading the first two or three letters, I didn't even bother opening them. The next time I saw his parents was at his funeral. Dave had hung himself. His parents thanked me so much for my visit, and I promised to stay in touch. I kept my word. Sunday nights, I ring Mrs Wheeler or she rings me. It's always the same silly conversation, but it pays a dividend to my conscience.

*

While you make supper, I call Sally. She's miffed I didn't confide my big news to her, but very cheery after speaking with you.

'Isn't it wonderful he's back? You must be over the moon!'

That's exactly why I didn't want to talk to her. I'm ashamed of not feeling the way other people think I should feel – whether they expect rage or delight – my sensor must be defective, I don't function like I should.

'Whatever happened, he's been miserable without you, and you've been so unhappy without him – even with you trying to make the best of it with Anthony. Oh, I so hope this all works itself out – he even mentioned maybe renewing your vows – well I said it, but Marc seemed to think it was a really good idea!'

Didn't you say once, it's not that we are attracted to others as much as how attractive they make us feel about ourselves?

Sally, like everyone I knew, adored you.

You found all our points of vanity, made us fall in love with ourselves over and over again every time we saw you.

I watched how you operated, how you were different with everyone: from the moment you met someone new, you seemed to pick up from a conversation started years ago. With some people you argued politics, with others it was intense discussions about jazz, food, others you cuddled like a big bear. With Anna it was all double- entendre and innuendo; with Sally you were everything her husband wasn't – sensuous, attentive, romantic – good around the house.   And it wasn't just the women. Even the kids at the restaurant you berated every night, they couldn't speak for sadness when, as the days went by, they realised you weren't coming back. My dad's lost for which wine to serve without you advising him. My mother has no one to tell her that her eyes go so well with her dress; my nieces and nephews have no one to climb over after Sunday lunch. You didn't just leave me.

'Kate – you're pleased, aren't you?'

'Yes, he's alive. He's here.'

'Where was he?'

'He worked on boats for a while, travelled and settled in America.'

'And do you know why?'

'He was very confused. He needed to sort his head out...'

'Aarh! Kate, I know it's going to be all right, in fact, it's going to be better than before.'

There's a silence.

'Would you both like to come for dinner next week? We're free Thursday or Saturday...'

And now you're back, we're no longer fractions, but complete. Happy ever after. It's as simple as that for Sally.

It never bothered me that my best friend was half in love with you. There were so many people who loved you and I felt big and generous lending you out to the world.

You let me flatter myself into imagining that I was above all those impromptu scenarios – that I had the real Marc your fan-club didn't see. You had moods, the 'black attacks' as we called them. No one else was privy to those. Sometimes you hardly spoke for days and at other times, you were a little too euphoric, bouncing into the flat having spent your week's wages on an olive oil or handbag for me. I recognised the look in your eyes when your past was pulling you down, and I treated it by keeping you calm, secure, loved, or we'd go out, change the mood. I thought that our relationship was the authentic one, all those other people, they were just the tasters, the *amuse-gueule*. But after you left, who was the biggest sucker of them all?

Sally's invited us for dinner, like nothing ever happened.

But it did. Doesn't Sally remember those first few months? Like the night she came to pick me up for Reading Group. It was just another night, Marc, one of almost three years of nights.

*

Sally had called in the day to remind me it was book-group night. I could tell she was hoping I'd forgotten or would bow out. I hadn't, although I'd planned not to go, but when I could tell how quick she was to write me off, I said how much I was looking forward to it - just out of spite.

All day at her surgery the phone rang with members of the book group asking if I was really coming and what was the latest news on Marc - should they mention it? – how was I...really? I'm sure she wanted to scream at them, ask her yourself! But people didn't ask me, it was easier to get all the information from Sally and have silly, meaningless conversations with me.

Sally didn't know what to say anyway, because I didn't tell her much. We were best friends but having a giggle at a film once in a while or having Sunday lunches together is nothing until it's tested by something like this. And Sally had failed. Every time someone asked her how I was, she came out with a big zero. I'm a giving person, Marc, and I wanted to share some of the shit you left me with.

That day had been a particularly bad one. I'd been on-call the night before, a night we actually had theatre tickets booked for – if you hadn't have left, we would have been sitting next to my parents watching a play about a Californian therapist having an affair with her mass-murdering patient. We'd probably have all gone on to dinner somewhere in the West End or to your restaurant. It was something we did every few months. I'd thought we'd enjoyed that. Even weeks after you left, I was still cancelling plans we'd made.

At one point that morning I went to the nurses' station to ask for something and I heard a song on the radio that you used to hum, so I spent lunchtime in the toilets crying. I'd had a stupid disagreement with one of the orderlies and when I got home there were no messages, no post, just the flat, the way I'd left it two days before. I hadn't slept properly for weeks. I'd not been able to gauge, Marc, how far off-centre I was moving; those days, the days when I thought the blackness would chew me up, and I was disappointed when it didn't.

I was on the floor in the 'recovery position' when I heard the buzzer. I shouldn't have answered it but I thought it might be you. I heard Sally push in the light switch where there was the Missing photo of you. The cheap black and white home-printed copy, Sally knew it well because she had one up in her surgery. 'Yer friend found her ol' blue eyes, then?' her receptionist apparently asked every morning. Sally hoped that one day they'd take the picture down, retell the whole story with a happy ending.

I'm sure that when Sally climbed up the three flights of stairs to our flat she fought against a shameful urge to run in the opposite direction. It was like that with me then. I made people feel hopelessly inadequate and trivial, often depressed. Sally didn't want to talk to me about her life, her nanny problems, something her mother-in-law said which niggled and what to cook for Christmas lunch. All her life's preoccupations seemed vastly gratuitous and smug in light of my anguish. Or maybe I just liked to think so.

Your leaving affected the whole building. The air of something not-quite-right started from the street outside us. Gloom in the trees, the empty basement flat, the first floor had been recently bought but no one had moved in, the For Sale sign rotting by the bins. Inside there was a sinister quietness. The doors of the other flats were shut, locked and bolted; our neighbours barricaded themselves against the frightening, unpredictable world. The corridor smelt of damp and that's when the light outside my door stopped working. I was waiting for you to come home and fix it.

The last time Sally came to collect me for reading group was a May evening, you were playing a new CD of Italian jazz, the flat was filled with white flowers you'd bought me on your way home. You were tanned, wearing a white tunic shirt and matching trousers. You had a silver fish around your neck hanging from a silver chain, you were barefoot. Most men would look absolute arses dressed like that, Sally said later, but you were always so comfortable in the way you filled your skin. You offered my friend a glass of wine while she was waiting for me to change out of my work clothes. She said she shouldn't, but after a taste, couldn't resist. You lit a cigarette; she took a drag from it. With you, people couldn't say no, you made everything seem too tempting, such fun. I heard you both from the shower, talking about the kids – our godchildren - about your plans to see Paul's new offices in the city. You never made that meeting, Marc, and Paul thought you were his friend. He thought you might not come home to me, but that you'd certainly keep your date with him. You didn't.

This time Sally was in no hurry to get up the stairs, she lumbered, rallying the strength to say the right thing, still thinking there was a right thing to say. She couldn't even think what it would be like to lose her husband. She once insinuated that it wasn't so bad for me because we'd didn't have children, but when I asked her to imagine what it was like to know I would never have kids by the man I loved, she realised that you couldn't weigh up one person's loss against another's. She felt guilty. That's one of the reasons there was a rift between me and everybody else, I knew people left me and clung on to their loved ones, relieved that disaster wasn't knocking on their door. That's what I'd have done. Isn't that how pity works?

But, to be fair, Sally had lost you too.

She must have been hoping I wouldn't look so tired, so blatantly miserable when I opened the door.

'I haven't read the book.'

'It doesn't matter. We'd all love to see you.'

'Who'd love to see me?'

I'd recently developed a talent for picking people up on words they used and becoming particularly argumentative about them. I could even find a crushing response to an innocent, 'How are you?' But Sally didn't answer. All she wanted was for that night to go well.

'I can't face it...Sorry. Again.'

'Come on Kate, it's no big deal.'

'Okay...Okay...Where are my keys?'

'In your hand.'

I had seen Sally a bit since you left, but I noticed she always tried to make it when Paul was around. He had a way of calming me, bringing out the rational, dispassionate side of my character. He questioned different methods of finding you as if he were referring to a lost file on a computer or an earring. 'Have you tried his gym club? What about down the sofa? Why don't you make a documentary about yourself? Are you sure you've checked all your pockets? Shallow graves?'

When Sally said, 'Just come as you are', she didn't exactly mean it, or at least she'd anticipated I'd change out of my slippers, but no, I came to the book club exactly as I was.

'Come in, come in – isn't it cold? Lovely to see you Kate.'

I walked into Jessica's home for the first time since you'd left me. The conversation lulled. I'd got use to that. Eyes shifted, people didn't want to stare. Jessica brought me some mulled wine and an ash-tray when I pulled out cigarettes from my bag. It is the last habit one would have ever expected of me but you smoked so, when you left, I took up the habit, to be close to you – I liked to think that somewhere in the world, you and I were lighting cigarettes at the same time. While someone was talking to me about their holiday, Deborah stood behind, leaving her hand on my shoulder for a short time. She didn't need to say anything, but I felt how much she cared.

Many people - from close friends to people I'd never met before – had reached out to me those first six months – shown me great kindness. I don't think I ever thanked them for it. Loss of gratitude was just another symptom of my pain.

We didn't begin discussing the book because we were waiting for Becky to arrive with a new member. Sally noticed my eyes darting around when they mentioned a name I hadn't heard before; Sally knew that this would make me nervous.

Bells was a tax lawyer and Becky's friend from law school. She seemed unnecessarily tall and loud, Becky stood behind her, introducing her to the group, and I wondered what she'd said about me when she briefed her friend about us beforehand. We had our polite faces on, talked as if there was an echo and nodded pointedly at astute comments - a new member always provoked a bit of showing off.

Half way in I had to come clean about not having read the book. Bells piped up with 'Naughty, naughty' which was ignored by the group.

Over Thai food we went from talking about the book to the lives of the readers.

'I've got some news...' flushed Elspeth, 'I'm having a baby!'

'Becky was saying in the car here,' announced Bells, 'that we should dub this the "breeding group" instead of the "reading group"!'

Then Bells went through the members, 'So you've got two, I've got three, Jessica one...Sally two...' She stopped at me. 'And what have you got?'

'No children for me.' I answered.

'Too bad, too bad...better hurry up and get hitched now or you'll end up with other people's left-over pickings!'

Becky trod quietly over her friend's toes. Elspeth came to my rescue.

'Kate's got a husband...'

'Arh, I remember Becky saying something about that...sorry, well, I put my foot in it!' said Bells contemplating my ordeal and dipping a chicken wing into the satay sauce. And into the embarrassed silence she threw in, 'I'm sure he'll be back when he gets tired of her.'

Driving me back I looked out of Sally's car window and said, 'I shouldn't have gone.'

'Wasn't it good to see everyone?'

'No. But I guess I had to see.'

'See what?'

'See that...I am so...disconnected. Unplugged from real life. I'm a freak, a parody. It's only the hospital which keeps me functioning and even that is only on the barest level. If I think about why I'm doing it, even saving people's lives is pointless: they're all going to die anyway.'

Sally increased the pressure on the accelerator and resisted the temptation to pipe up with reasons that I should keep going – she'd already learnt that that really aggravated me.

'Bells is ghastly. She won't be invited again.'

'Isn't she my replacement?'

'What are you talking about?'

'It's quite obvious, we were eleven tonight, I wasn't supposed to be there. Since Marc's gone it's like I've gone too...people look at me like, "are you still around?" '

Sally turned into my street.

'What are you doing for Christmas?'

'Work, I'll give someone else the time off. I can't face my family at the moment...Anna's a mess over Nick, she thinks he's having an affair and mummy's a nervous wreck about me...'

'Come to us if you want.'

'Thanks, but...'

Sally stopped outside my flat, waiting for me to hop out and leave her to her life, but I didn't move.

'So what Bells said: does everyone think Marc's just left me for someone else?'

Sally was tired of fencing off my discomfort. She drew up the hand brake, 'It seems the most obvious explanation.'

'Is that what you think?'

Sally's fingers circled the steering wheel. She couldn't answer.

'Okay, maybe he met someone, but why didn't he tell me? People break-up all the time, it's no big deal, that way there aren't Missing posters of him all over London – there aren't police wasting tax payers' money looking for him: he would have got half the flat, had work references, friends, that way I wouldn't be going mad...' I breathe in to give me the strength to shout, 'Why didn't he tell me?'

'I don't know.'

'Paul used to meet up with Marc, did he suspect anything?'

'He would have said if...'

'Did he? Did he think Marc was unfaithful? Tell me Sally, I won't hold it against either of you if you know something.'

'Never. Paul never said anything. We both knew Marc loved you so much, Kate, really loved you –'

'You say that but he's gone! He's gone Sally! Everyone says how happy we were, how much he loved me, but look at me now! He must have fucking hated me! He must have loathed the very sight of me! He must have wished this hell on me! That's the only explanation!'

I slap the tears around my face. 'It's the only way he could have done this to me. And you know what? If he's not dead, I'm going to fucking kill him myself!'

I didn't see Sally for a long time after that evening. I'd lost you, I'd lost her, I'd lost me.

All I'd gained was a search. That night, I didn't go to bed. I sat at my computer screen running through the names of every missing person until the winter light went from dark grey to light grey. I thought I was being thorough, but I must have passed over your name several times, I just didn't know it.

late sunday night

You sleep, I don't.

You turn in the bed, flinch into the pillow. Your arm makes a barrier between our heads. Your fingers are curled like a baby's and when you exhale, the hair on your forearm trembles. Where have you been sleeping, my darling?

It was sometime after the second Christmas that you'd been gone, I'd got a call from Tatyana at three o'clock in the morning. I thought it was a wrong number at first. It was difficult to understand her, her voice was slurred, she was half giggling and blowing smoke into the earpiece. I think she said she was ringing from Miami.

'It's Tatty! Kate, I've got something to tell you...'

I could hear laughter in the background and the sound of people singing Karoake.

Tatyana said that she'd spent the last year and half travelling around South America and every time she woke up in a new place,

146

she'd stick up a poster of your face with an announcement that you were missing and her email address. Then she met some American students on a bus who said that there was a man living rough in Mexico who fitted the poster's description. Although the man's appearance wasn't exactly the same - this one was darker with blonde streaks in his hair – they'd remembered the tattoo. This man, the *loco,* had made himself a cabin and spent his time drinking Tequilla and playing with the village kids. Sometimes, when he got it together and needed money enough, he'd cook amazing meals for travellers who could afford it.

'It's this gorgeous place by the sea – off the beaten track – like *Puerto Escondido* used to be in the sixties, y'know? - backpackers go there to sleep in hammocks, campfires... Anyway, apparently that's where he was! So, I thought I'd visit for Christmas, why not, eh?'

The day Tatyana arrived, the man had just left for California with two sisters. These girls were wealthy Americans and one of them had fallen in love with the drifter.

'I'm going to California now, I'll do what I can...but it's something, isn't it?'

Something.

Why did you leave me so you could be homeless, penniless and spend your time with strangers?

monday morning

'Look at you! You're positively beatific! He's a doctor here, isn't he? Which one is he? Don't! Let me guess.'

To get Anna to leave the hospital I had to tell her something to satisfy her curiosity, but everything I said only enflamed it. Anna was in London for the day, ostensibly researching something at the British Library, but in reality, to find out about this Frenchman who'd called my mum asking for my number.

'I've got to meet him! Does he know all about us? About me?' asked Anna.

'Yes, we talk about you a lot. He doesn't have any family of his own, so he's interested, sure.'

'Everybody has a family, Kate, is he married?'

'No! And he grew up in a foster home.'

'Oh Kate, people like that...'

'You don't know anything about people like that.'

'Invite him to tea.'

'Why, so you can interrogate him?'

'No, well, yes. I know! May Day!...Bring him to the May Day Ball and I'll do a big dinner party – you know Eddie's going to be over – let's all get terribly drunk and stay out all night, dance on the bridge! Yes! Oh please Kate!'

'He's not a "ball" sort of person.'

'Don't be silly, all men love looking like James Bond for a night.'

'I'll ask him. I have to see what my schedule is and you know, he works nights too...'

'So he is a doctor...or a porter...or a –'

'He's nothing to do with medicine, actually,' I said. 'He's a chef.'

'Oh how delicious. I love him already. Tell me, what's it like to French kiss a French man?'

'You can add that question to your agenda.'

'Adieu! Au revoir! Voulez-vous couchez avec moi, ce soir!'

✿

'Don't go,' Katherine, you say, clamping me in your thighs, your arms, your mouth.

'Work, the pressure, the patients, the routine. It's what kept me sane, Marc, when you were away, I need it now...'

'For what?'

'To get some perspective.'

'I can pick you up some at the supermarket.'

You squeeze me. Those corny jokes I used to giggle at in our first year don't make me laugh any more.

'When will you be back?'

It's been almost three years since anyone's asked me that.

'Six-ish.'

'I'll be here. Or would you rather I wasn't?'

'I don't know, I don't know,' I say, sweeping the duvet back and heading for the bathroom. I hold onto the towel for support, bite into it, press it to my chest. I don't know. I don't know, I keep thinking. I don't know what I want for dinner, and I don't know anything about you and I'm wondering if I know even less about me.

You come in, find me like that, put your hand on my shoulder, rock me back and forth as I hang off the towel.

'You've really fucked me up, Marc, really.' It comes out in one long moan, 'First by going, and now by coming back.'

'I understand Katherine. I want to make it better, now, for you. It's for you to decide if you will let me have that chance, that's all, *ma chérie*.'

'What did I ever do to you for you to treat me like this?'

'Okay, if that's what you think, Dr Freud –'

'Don't laugh at me! Tell me! Tell me that you love me, that what you did was wrong.'

'I love you. What I did was wrong.'

'You're only saying that because I asked you to.'

'So don't ask.'

A tremor begins at my feet and builds through me, whatever stood between my anger and you, breaks out of me, and like some flimsy, comical, damsel in distress I slap, kick, hit you. You take the blows, absorb the pain without even blinking or losing your balance. Then you catch my wrists. You hold them up to my face. I get the message. Exhausted, I fall into a heap. Fighting has to be learnt, practised, perfected. Just like leaving somebody.

'I'll dress myself today, thank you.'

But I don't know if you heard me. You were tidying the bathroom, putting everything back to where it was. All but me.

Dressed, I gulp the coffee that you've made. I open my bag and throw in my phone, my wallet and my keys. I look at you, open the door, walk out.

When I pass Tom's flat, he is standing in front of it.

'Kate?'

'Not now.'

'Kate.'

'What?'

'Are you alright?'

'No.'

'Please...can we just...?'

'Oh. Your money.'

I turn and step into his flat. He closes the door behind me. I open my bag and take out my cheque book. Tom stands by my side.

'Don't worry about the money, I just wanted to ask if you were okay.'

'Well, I'm not. I'm not. Marc has come back, Anthony and I are done, I'm going to be offered a job I don't know if I want, I've got to perform surgery today and I can't stop shaking and crying and...Tom, this isn't a good time for us to have a chat.'

I continue writing out the cheque for money I owe Tom.

It's rent. Tom has been my landlord since last year.

I was getting into debt trying to pay the mortgage on my own. I was scared I would lose my job when my private life was cracking me up. I wasn't able to pay for my car when it needed a service and I couldn't accept any more money from my parents. When I was refused a third loan, Tom offered to buy my flat. He had the money sitting in an account. He insisted it was a good financial deal for him, maybe he'd buy the next flat up, take over the whole building eventually. He even mentioned we might live together one day.

It was a simple transaction with a cash buyer, an offer I couldn't refuse. After I sold the property, I was solvent again. At least money was something I no longer had to worry about.

'So he's back.'

'So it appears.'

'And you're going to just let him come back, like nothing happened, like he's −'

I whack my hand across his face.

150

Unlike you, Tom is knocked off his feet. When he steadies himself, he is stunned. His eyes moisten. He looks at me in horror. When he takes his hand away from his face, there's a red mark on his cheek.

Why couldn't I hurt you? Why doesn't your skin redden and bruise? Why can't you cry?

'Oh God!' I rush to him, 'Oh Tom, I'm so sorry.'

We stand there, crying together, in his large, bright room with the TV screen showing the morning news.

'It's so easy to be angry with everybody but him...and you've done nothing but be good to me!'

I take an ice cube out of his ice-maker and dab it on his cheek. 'Let me look at you.'

'Why can't you love me like you do him?' he asks.

'Who says I love him?'

I wipe my hands, tear the cheque out of my book and put it on the table between us.

'Tom. I've got to go. I hope you find someone to give your love to – someone who deserves you.'

'I'll see if Anthony's still available.'

'And don't be cheeky to your elders.'

'I got it wrong, didn't I? I thought I was more to you than just a kid to boss around or a quick shag on your way to picking up your post. We spent so much time together. You meant a lot to me.'

'I'm really sorry.'

'I'm not accepting sorry. You used me big time. You let me think I was more than just a shield against being lonely. That's what I'm thinking.'

'Tom, don't start thinking.'

'You think that's funny? You are *so* patronising. You think 'cause you're posh and a doctor and some dickhead shat on you that all the world owes you something. You don't know what anyone deserves. You don't know shit. Thanks for the rent. We're quits.'

Dr McKendrick is in theatre inserting a mitral valve into my patient. This is the second procedure that I've missed this morning.

'I owe you one,' I say, while he rinses his hands. The anaesthetist behind him lifts her eyebrows under her surgical cap and leaves the room.

'You certainly do.'

151

He wipes his hands, looks at me and turns. I follow him into his office.

He closes the door behind me, but we don't sit.

'Do you remember a baby, Jamie? ICU – one of yours. They came in last night. We couldn't get in touch with you Kate. Your pager was off, so was your phone. You didn't answer our messages. Then this morning. You've never done this before – don't let it start now.'

'How is he?'

'He isn't.'

He looks at his watch.

'I don't need to tell you what'll happen if you ever do that again.'

His phone rings.

'Get to work.'

monday, midday

I've been longing to be out of the hospital and just walk, fast and mindlessly, as far away as possible. The last few hours I worked like an automaton, keeping to the routine, the dosages, the same script with everyone I met, and then, just as my lunch break and my chance to get out arrives, I put on my coat, look up and see Anthony. I'm shocked that his misery is so physical, as if he's been struck down by a tropical virus overnight. He holds onto the door, one arm above and one across, as if the impact of seeing me might hurl him down the corridor.

'Kate?'

The smile isn't there, the cheery 'hello', the sneaky kiss in case anyone's looking. When Anthony gave me his heart, he gave me his heart.

Often on Mondays we'd go swimming together, either at lunch or after work, there's a pool only five minutes away which we used. We went this time last week, now the idea of it is out of the question.

'Can we talk?'

'Sure,' I say.

Neither of us are big talkers so I wonder how this is going to work.

We walk out of the hospital side by side but not together. I can't look him in the face. I think I should touch his arm, tell him it will all be alright. But I can't.

I don't know who leads who, but we turn into the street.

'Do you want to eat?'

'No. You?'

'No.'

Anthony hasn't thought this through.

'Let's get a coffee then.'

He doesn't even answer, just follows me into a take-away place where I order two coffees. I pick up a flapjack in an optimistic effort to jolly up the exchange to follow.

I remember challenging my mother about why she never really asked me how I was getting on without you. Out of everyone I knew, she was the least surprised that you'd gone. She even acted as though you were always going to leave and I was just being melodramatic about it.

She said, 'I became myself when I had children - from Richard to you - each child filled me with love, purpose, real joy – of course, it was difficult at times - but I suppose I was one of those women whom feminists must loathe, because I sincerely believed that everything I'd done in my life was a prelude to motherhood. It was my vocation. And then you all grew up and I was out of a job. In a flash, it was all just...over. Do you know Katie, every minute of every day I miss you children. You've all left home and sometimes you come for lunch or not, or Christmas, or Anna comes by to leave me with her children - it doesn't really matter to you, but for me...I miss you all the time, all the time. Getting older is just a process of missing people, missing them more and more as the days go by, like watching a boat go out to sea with all those you love on it, receding into the distance. I even miss daddy, how we used to be, all those friends from school, my parents, my grandparents. I'm sorry Marc has left you, I really am, but you were always going to lose him at some point or another.'

Anthony and I sip at our coffees. Already I miss him.

We sit on a bench. It is freezing.

'You must be relieved your husband's back.'

'The last time I went to identify a body that might have been his I was disappointed when it wasn't. I wanted all this finished.'

'So it is finished, isn't it? You got the best-fit result, now you can go back to how you were.'

'Can I?'

'How should I know?'

'Marc's return, it wasn't planned you know, I haven't been keeping anything from you.'

'When were you going to tell me?'

'He came back just before the weekend. He's given me till Thursday to make up my mind.'

'Surely he's not in a position to start laying down the law – well, it's none of my business.'

'It was just an idea, I was confused, he came up with the week. Seven days to work something out together.'

'How generous. The fact that you were engaged to someone else didn't come into the equation? Shouldn't take a week to say "yes" or "no".'

I look at Anthony from the side. His chin jutting out a little, his nostrils flared in disgust, lips cracked, and his eyes so full of rage and worse, disappointment.

It was a mistake to think we could talk.

We watch the pigeons, a school trip troops past. Tourists meander and workers clip-clop in search of sandwiches. I wanted to stop anyone of them and ask them to take my place next to Anthony on the bench, take my life while they were at it.

'It wasn't you, yesterday, the way you answered the door. You were different.'

'You just saw something you hadn't seen before.'

'Is your husband different?'

'I can't say I ever knew him.'

'But you still want him? Kate, I have to ask.'

'I loved him when we married, and he was there, and then he wasn't there, but I still loved him and now he's back, does the continuum stop?'

'Whether you love him or not, I have to ask you, as a friend, do you really want a man who walked out on you three years ago?'

I don't say anything and in my silence, Anthony has his answer. I love you, yes. I want to say that love is meant to be unconditional, but what kind of moron would believe that? A romantic partner, the person who we are supposed to love the most, is the one most constricted by the highest level of conditions and restrictions. I'd never demand fidelity from anyone else, that they spend most of their free time with me, render up all their secrets, ration their pleasures outside my jurisdiction. We say I love you, you're mine, I'm yours, and we believe it. It's slavery.

This idea only comes to me now, but it's probably not the time to air it.

'The Johns Hopkins' Hospital offered me a position a few weeks ago. I talked to your father about it, but didn't mention it to you. I turned it down because of our...er...our situation, but, now, I might ask if it's still open. I liked America, despite their foreign policy and lack of irony. It'll be hard on my mother, of course, but I don't want to stay here now.'

I imagine Anthony in Maryland in brightly-coloured Converse trainers eating waffles. I suppose he's asking for the last time if this really is the end.

'Sounds like a great opportunity.'

'Hum? Yes.'

Then I remember my engagement ring. I start twisting it off.

'Here.'

'No. Keep it. Sell it. Send the proceeds to some medical research centre.'

He looks at me like a puppy whose owner is tying a brick around his neck and dropping him down a well.

The talk is over.

We are over.

We stand up, face each other. I'm waiting for him to shake my hand and ask me to consult his secretary for a follow-up appointment later in the year. He says he's walking to South Kensington tube station, points to it as if I'd just asked for directions. I'm about to say something – to say something that might put all this right, but I can't. Instead, I mutter about heading back. We say goodbye: hands in pockets, faces giving nothing away. He says 'Thank you, Kate', but I don't know what for. I get the feeling, however, that he is the one being released. I watch him turn from me and start walking. The puppy's neck is out of its noose and he wags his tail all the way down the street.

*

'Jesus! What are you doing in here?'

'I don't want to sleep on my own, it's boring...'

'How did you get past the nurses?' I laughed.

'I have my way. Come here...'

'If anyone catches you.'

'I'll say I'm very sick and you're making me feel better.'

You kissed my ear while untying my hair.

'Viens ici ma belle...'

We undressed each other as if we were being timed, all the while I shook my head at your audacity. But I couldn't stop you. I pecked your arms with kisses as your hands unclasped my bra.

'My bleeper's going to go off any minute –'

'So's mine baby!'

It'd been six weeks since you'd found me. We'd spent all the time we could together, usually in my room because...because...why Marc? How did you always manage to keep me out of your life? I think you said you didn't want me to see where you lived. I went with anything in those days when our skins were like Velcro and every moment was spent plotting and planning how we could keep it that way.

'Katherine, I want to show you something.'

 You took off your shirt.

'Look.'

You turned your arm to my face.

'It's not real!' I said.

'Yes, it's real. I did it last night.'

'But...but...it could get infected...'

'You don't like it?'

'Well, it's not a matter of whether I like it...it's a tattoo...of my name...'

'K-A-T-H-E-R-'

'Yes, I can read!'

'I was bored, missing you, maybe I had too much to drink but I wanted you to know how much I love you. Whatever happens to us Katherine, your name is here, under my skin. No one can change that. Now let me make love to you and then go back to sleep...'

'But...but...Marc...'

'Hey Katherine, it's not such a big deal. I love you so I put your name on my arm, come here, come here...'

The tattoo was permanent: we would be permanent. You wanted everyone to know that you loved me. The details didn't matter. Your huge, giving and undeniable love blew away all my feeble defences. You were in a strange country, without friends, family or any security and you were offering your love. That's what it said on your arm.

'But what if you split up?' asked Sally while we ladled a curry onto our plates. It was a night we'd put aside to revise together but an episode of "Sex and the City" and some beers had taken priority.

'Well he says he'll just put dates under the names, you know, like birth and death.'

'Or he could just carry on going out with Katherines.' I looked at my friend, 'It's the most romantic thing anyone's ever done for me....the only romantic thing!'

'That's for sure. I think he'll propose soon...God knows what he'll do for that! Write your name in the sky or chop off an arm!'

The commercial break ended, we went back to our programme.

'I can't concentrate on watching this. I feel as if I've been pumped full of helium...I just think of Marc and I float away...I can't stop smiling...'

'That's the serotonin. Watch out, it's the hormones drugging you into thinking it'd be good to throw away your life on a bloke and kids. You'll come down with a bump in a few months – by that time, it'll be too late.'

'That's very cynical.'

'I'm a doctor,' answered Sally tilting the beer down her throat.

'I'm just a love thing!' I said beaming, while ignoring Sally's quizzical frown. 'Everything looks so different these days – from black and white to technicolour! I had no idea how big the world is! With Marc...anything is possible and life is to be enjoyed! Why didn't anybody tell me that? Life is to be enjoyed! Marc says –'

'Are you going to finish those Poppadoms?'

*

Three people died today in front of my eyes, under my hands. And no, they didn't go peacefully. They contorted, clawed at their chests, were thrown from side to side, they fought with all their strength for their next breath, their eyes bulged in agony and their tongues turned blue. And then they lost. It's not called a heart attack for nothing. People find that out too late. On two occasions the families couldn't get there in time to say goodbye. This afternoon Jamie's father and grandmother came by to hear the results of the autopsy report and deal with the administration to release his body. They came from the funeral parlour and were still undecided about the colour of the coffin.

I catalogue the losses to the on-duty doctor, watch the night-nurses come in and transform themselves from students, mothers, lovers into guardians of the sick.

'Going back to your family, doc?' asks the last patient I check up on.

This is too difficult a question to answer.

Before leaving the hospital I check my emails. There's one from Frances. The message is short and there's a phone number.

I don't let myself stop and think before I start dialing.

The woman answers after the first ring. Of course I hadn't thought what time it would be in San Francisco.

'You're looking for a Xavier Rocher?'

'I was, yes. Who is this?'

'His wife.'

I know she is attractive by her voice, and that she must have been sleeping, fitfully, on the alert for any news to come through.

'He's not coming back to you, he's come home. To me.'

And now it hits her that the man she was looking for might not be the man she was looking for.

'That's not...possible. Who is this?'

'My name is Katherine, you know, like it says on his arm.'

'You're saying Xavier's married?'

'He is married.'

'Why are you calling?'

'To save you the pain and the waste of time. The woman he left me for enjoyed knowing I was suffering, going mad looking for him. I'm not like that. You can either believe me or not. It's up to you. But he's here, with me, his wife.'

'You're British.'

'Yes. We live in London.'

'Can I speak to him, please?'

'No. It is very unlikely you will ever hear from him again. Leave it. Even if he comes back to you, it's finished.'

When I say that, the phone, the office, the world wobbles around me, tears roll down my hands and into my sleeve.

'Lady? Is this some kind of joke?'

'I'm doing you a favour –'

Through the glass door I see Dr McKendrick standing outside talking to someone. I have to finish this conversation and get back to work.

'Right, well, thanks for your concern but you got it wrong. My Xavier called me this morning. He just went out of town. He's coming home at the end of the week. Home to me. You've either got the wrong person or you're a very sick lady.'

monday afternoon

You are outside the hospital entrance, standing under the bike shelter reading the notices about ante-natal programmes and the new – now old – legislation prohibiting smoking in public buildings. It doesn't stop you blowing smoke into the light rain. The fleece top I bought you at the weekend looks all wrong. I stop and watch you and I want to tell you that I know it's all wrong.

Your eyes follow a sparrow as he bounces around the puddles. I realise that I put you in a world where you didn't belong. And I see that you tried and almost succeeded in covering up from me that you were suffering until that morning when you closed the door and you walked away from me.

'You must have been waiting ages.'

'It's okay.'

We don't talk much as we make our way home, I didn't have the kind of day I want to think about again. And you, well, you just don't want to tell me anything.

'Did you have a nice time with your friend at lunch today?'

'You followed me?'

'I wanted to see you.'

'You spied on me?'

'You spied on me.'

All those shelves of folders, boxes and letters about you. I suppose sometimes I was intrusive, but you left me to choice.

'I was looking for you Marc. That's not the same.'

'I was gone. That's all you needed to know at the time.'

Time. Do you know, I want to ask you, that I have never had a watch? Before I could tell the time, I knew I'd be working in a profession where they were considered unhygienic. I meter out the days by how many beats the heart makes per minute, how fast blood can travel down a vein, how long a person has left to live. And then I loved you, so I never counted the days or the blood cells left between us. I love you now, as you sit in my car trying to find a radio station you like. I love you now and I have about three days until the 'ping' of our timer goes off and I have to decide about us.

Stepping out of my shoes I open the letter saying that I was successful in my interview. I have been given the job I wanted at The Heart Hospital. There's another letter. The lawyers have confirmed that following a meeting and the signing of relevant documentation, our marriage will be annulled.

'Good news?'

'Yes, I suppose so. I got offered a job I wanted,' I answer, slipping the lawyer's letter beneath a pile of papers.

'Well done, *félicitations!*'

'Thank you for doing the kitchen, it hasn't looked like that in –'

'I'm going to cook you something really nice, *ma belle*, and then massage and early night for you. Forget about today, I'm here now.'

You wink at me. It should be a devastating, heart-warming wink. But it isn't.

I'd just read Frances' text message on my phone:

No mistake. Phone call made to SF this morning from your home phone. Best, F.

tuesday morning

'I used to relish the feeling of getting over an illness, like a bud unravelling out of the winter frosts: everything was a little brighter, tastier, scented. I even thought I looked a little handsomer...dare I say it? I don't know if there's a medical reason, probably that one appreciates life more after being out of it, you want to get back in the game. But these days... The mornings come and I don't really wake up, not really, my timetable's full of pills I need to take and doctor's appointments, what hurts and how much. I've been forced into a career of being ill.'

My patient's purple lips barely move as he catalogues his post-operative existence. I don't normally see adults but this man is part of a research study I'm involved in. I've been used to answering the questions that children ask concerning their experience, and it strikes me how much more terrified, bewildered and attached to life an adult is by comparison.

'Some people feel completely different after a heart transplant, full of life and new beginnings, but others don't. They feel like you described. The body has had a lot to deal with – your heart attack, the operation, adapting to new parts. The heart transplant has maybe given you another ten years, possibly more, Mr Miller. Time with your family: time to do what you've always wanted.'

'I know, I know, I'm not ungrateful, I just...I'm not myself. I just I don't feel the same man. I keep wondering whose heart I've got.'

'You know I can't tell you that.'

'Was it a bad man? Was it someone with a wicked heart and I'm going around with it in my chest –'

'Mr Miller, the heart is just a pump. Like a pump on a washing machine or a swimming pool. It expands and contracts to propel the flow of blood around the body. That's all. In most cases, the only difference between a good and bad heart is how much fat is on it.'

'The other consultant said that my old ticker problems were as a result of a flu I might have got thirty years ago.' He clasps his chest to him as if to keep it safe.

'Possibly. Every illness, meal, cigarette, stint in the gym or creamy cake contributes to our heart's well being – our lifestyle from the time we are children catches up with us at some point.'

Mr Miller touches the stitched wound left by my blade ten weeks ago.

'So I'm housing the balance sheet of someone else's life. Don't you think that's the stuff of nightmares?'

'I really wouldn't think about that aspect of it too much. The earliest experiments with heart transplants were done with pigs' hearts and no one took on porcine attributes...anyway, looking at these test results, it was a good heart –'

'But did it come from a good man?'

When I left you this morning you were sleeping and now you are sitting in front of me, shaking your head at a menu. This is the restaurant around the corner from my work where the consultants come after management meetings, but this evening, we're the only people here. It's the first time we've been in a place like this, one that, in the past, you would have deemed an insult to food. We used to go to places that had just opened, were renowned or exclusive, often owned or run by friends of yours. We'd make a night of it, dress up, drinks beforehand, often with friends but sometimes just us. It was more than just an evening out, for you it was a passion and an education – otherwise you liked cheap, authentic, regional food – bagels baked overnight from the East End, or curries from Brick Lane, British fish and chips. But this sort of place you despised: expensive, mediocre, derivative. So I don't know why we are here except that you wanted to spend time with me before I returned to work for the night. But I've a suspicion that this is an exercise in compromise: you are demonstrating to me that you can spend money on food you resent just to be with me.

I'm out of the hospital but my mind is still pacing around the wards. You look shattered, defeated, in that brown suede jacket you came back to me in. You touch my arms with your fingers, it's meant to reassure me, bring me back, but right now, that's asking too much.

'What did you do today?'

I ignore your hands sliding over my forearm.

'I went to the restaurant. They said I can start my job whenever I want.'

'Really? They'll take you back just like that?'

'Why not?'

I don't want to start on the reasons why not.

'They must have had a shock. Seeing you.'

'Yes, I guess they did.'

We're quiet for a while, rolling our thoughts around, tasting them, seeing if they are worth carrying on with. Most aren't.

I keep asking myself why you'd want your job back when there's a woman in San Francisco who's expecting you to return this weekend. How many lives have you been keeping on the go, how many promises do you plan to break?

'So were they thrilled to see you? Or maybe just a little pissed off, I mean...'

'It's work Katherine, the hospitality trade, eh? We're trained to be nice to people's faces if it's good for business.'

'Still, must be a problem trying to find work at your age without any references. Most chefs of your calibre and experience have their own restaurants by now, maybe working towards a star – but you, you just keep coming in at the same level, must be...frustrating, huh?'

'Not really.'

I'm going for the low jabs, punching on behalf of those who you let down and abused, those who've just rolled over and let you scratch their tummies. They've done nothing. Like I've done nothing.

'But you were ambitious, like anyone, you wanted to have recognition and –'

'I make a living cooking food, that's all, it's for other people. I don't need to get myself on TV and write books, cook like a celebrity. That's not what I do.'

'Was the food good in California?'

'Yes, fish, seafood, very interesting. Are you ready to order?'

When the waiter leaves, you ask me if I kept any of your things. I haven't the energy to keep my guard up, and I've forgotten what we are fighting for, so I tell you, honestly, that I couldn't have thrown away your things. I couldn't really have let you go, but an act of providence did. A broken washing machine did.

*

I was returning home after three days and nights at the hospital, a lecture, a viva and a 45 minute tube wait in a tunnel outside Tottenham Court Road. Opening the door into my building, I could hear voices, loud and blaring, at first I thought Tom's TV had been left on. Coming up the stairs, the sounds became real. Then I saw my door on the other side of the landing. All my towels and sheets were on the stairs leading into my flat.

Then they saw me. A fire-fighter asked if I was Kate Brenton. Good question. I answered, kept my focus on his black thumb nail which moved up and down the wall like a swollen black slug extending from his sleeve. He explained that he was sorry, but they had to force entry. Chantal, the American banker who lives upstairs, came out of my bedroom with your dressing gown in her arms. She stopped, opened her mouth and then a rush of words came out. All I could think is that she looked so much younger in her pastel jogging outfit with the stain of tears at the sides of her face. She kept repeating, 'so much water' and then 'pouring, pouring down...' and she wept. An arm touched my back, lead me to our bedroom. 'Trying to save all we can before it goes!' she called after me.

It was raining outside and inside the flat. The ceiling was a voluminous belly unable to bear the load of water. There was a constant flow running into our drawers, into my clothes, my books. Your suits were piled on my bed, my shoes in a mountain on the carpet. It was already starting to smell. Someone said 'cup of coffee' – and 'a Cognac in the cupboard.' Chantal's Blackberry rang. Gerry, her boyfriend, was on my sofa, yawning. He said something about only just having arrived from Hong Kong. His downturned mouth and standing-up hair, the fire-fighters trying not to gawp at Chantal's little breasts, my computer equipment in the bathtub. I was hoping a commercial break would come soon and end this soap opera that had become my life.

'Don't touch those!' I said as a woman carried your CDs across the room.

'Sorry, I was trying to –'

'This is my sister, Louise,' said Chantal. 'She's the one who called the fire brigade.'

'I'm really sorry...'

'Just...I'll take those. They're my husband's.'

Louise and Chantal exchanged a look, 'Sure,' said Louise, 'I'll put them down right here. It's all dry. Right here.'

I walked from one dark grey wall to the next as Chantal kept saying 'sorry' and 'insurance' and 'top priority'. Then more people. Maggie came down with the telephone directory and some filthy herbal remedy she tried to make me drink. She said everything would be alright. But I thought, unless you came back right then and there, nothing would ever be alright.

We all stopped when we heard the sound of the bedroom ceiling tear - the crack – the deep, ripping crunch of weight through the wood, plaster, the rumble – there was the inevitable crash as it split, no longer able to hold back the mass of water. We just stared as the contents of Chantal and Gerry's sitting room began to fall onto my bed.

While the others did things to prevent further damage, I stood, distracted at how our bodies made shadow puppets against the remaining walls with the blue light of the fire engines coming in from the windows.

'Kate Brenton...B-R-E-N-T-O-N. Well, get him over here now to do the report!' shouted Chantal down her phone as she lined up my bras over the bathroom rail. Two men in overalls nodded to me.

'It's a right mess...'

'We've done all we can...'

The speaker had an uncharacteristically high-pitched voice. I kept my eyes on his colleague's thumb which was beginning to get infected.

'We've cut the water, the electrics...it's safe but...'

Gerry stroked Chantal on the shoulder and padded out of the room waving his hand up in the air, half for goodbye, half for surrender.

The blue swirl of the fire engine lights moved down the street onto the next call, doors closed in our building and I too, shut whatever little there was to close so I couldn't hear Chantal and Gerry arguing – we were almost in one flat now. I sat on a plank of wood across the sofa, looking at the wreck until the candles and the torches sunk into an umber glow. There was the stench of old water in your books, soggy plaster on your clothes. There was a washing machine turned upside down on my television, there were plants tossed over my files. The Montblanc pen you gave me our

first Christmas was floating on my desk next to my sodden diary.
Under my feet our home looked like the bottom of a drained ocean
and you were nowhere to be found.

✿

'I wish I'd been there for you.'
     'Me too. All your things.'
     'Just things, Katherine.'
     'Things aren't just things when they're all you've got left of someone.'
     You hold my hand, squeeze and let it go, sit back as the waiter comes to take our plates.
     'You wouldn't have believed the destruction, it was the like the flat expressing its grief, expelling you from its walls...'
     Your mouth turns down into a pout: you're unimpressed by the image.
     'Anyway, I guess it forced me to have a big clear out – find things I'd probably never have known were there...'
     'Do you want dessert?'
     'No. Coffee.'
     You order two coffees. I wonder why it is that events only seem to have really happened when I shape them into a story to tell you.
     'It's a shame it didn't drown that little shit downstairs.'
     'Tom?'
     'Yeah, him.'
     'What's he ever done to you?'
     'I don't like his attitude.'
     'What attitude?'
     'Every time I walk past his flat, he stands there, staring at me. You know, with this look,' you scowl like Tom does. 'Oh, Katherine, if it makes you laugh! I don't find him funny.'
     I don't want to talk about Tom with you, I've given you so much - I want to keep my shame to myself.
     'Tomorrow's Wednesday.'
     'Katherine, if you need more time –'
     'No, Marc, you said "a week." I need to pull the plug one way or another. You stay or you go, either way, I can start living.'
     You turn the palm of my hand up, gaze at it as if it's a compact mirror.

I only have 25 minutes left of my break before I need to return to the hospital for the night. In that time, I try to explain to you the bond between Maggie, Tom and I in our building, the solidarity of the 'singles' against the 'couples', but you are not really listening. Hearing about the people who have gone some way to filling the chasm that you left isn't particularly interesting to you. Every so often, I draw in my breath, hold it until the weight of its force presses so hard against me I have to release it. I let out one long, metered exhalation. When I get to the end of it, there's a second's relief in the emptiness. Then I fill up and feel it all over again.

I can't identify if it is the sadness of what's gone before, or the sadness of what's to come.

'Can I sleep with you tonight? Remember how we used to, when I'd come into the hospital at night?'

'No Marc. I need space.'

'And tomorrow?'

'I made plans for tomorrow, Marc, it's not like I knew you were coming back.'

'Plans?'

'Yes. Plans. Family commitments. Nick, in fact.'

'Anna's Nick?'

'You kept his secret from me.'

You push my hand away, look around the restaurant as if you'd only just noticed where you were. And then I added, 'And hers.'

'Why would I tell you something that would've hurt you? I'll get the cheque.'

*

People never appreciate the destruction that water can cause,' said the insurance company surveyor. He snapped off the window frame. 'Well,' he concluded, catching another clump of wall in his hand, 'The ceiling's come down, so the anticipation's over. Let's get the electricity back again, then you'll need to take up all the carpeting before things start sprouting in there. Could you just give me a hand lifting this cupboard away from the wall?...Sorry to have to ask you...Thanks.'

He picked up his folder.

'You won't be able to repaint until all the plaster's dried through, course March isn't the best month for that...what's the date today?'

It was 777 days since you left.

After the inspection, I started the process of filling black bags with stuff – a bag for me, a bag for you. Mine was to stay, yours to go.

I wondered if I was sad that you were gone, or that you ever were.

I wiped a cloth along the back of the cupboard I'd just moved, and I saw the letter. The envelope was black with dust and damp. It was waiting for me, curled up like a tarantula.

You never kept anything. That was your creed, use it or lose it: what did you used to say? 'Yesterday's history, tomorrow's a mystery,' something naff like that.'

But the letter was in my hands. You'd slipped up. Time had pulled a fast one on you.

My heart ran faster than my eyes could read. The clearer the message, the more confused I got. The sentences recounted meetings and retraced conversations, pages and pages, all about you. All in my sister's handwriting.

Tom stood in what used to be called 'the doorway'. He'd only just got back from New York and was still holding his suitcase. He was laughing when he joked: 'Ever had the feeling that the sky's just fallen in on top of you?'

'My sister was in love with my husband.'

'Huh?'

Tom came to kiss me. I was still staring at the letter.

'I found this... All the time Marc and I were together, she...she says...look... "Kate has no idea how she is stifling you, she just wants a husband...she doesn't understand you...she hasn't got the capacity to love you like I do..." ' I tossed the page down, picked up another, "Listen, 'Please Marc, just give me once chance to show you how happy I could make you..." What kind of teenage, clichéd rambling is this? "You and I are free spirits, passionate, wild..." ' I slammed the pages down.

I looked at Tom, 'All that time...Anna was in love with Marc.'

'And do you think they did it?'

It took me a moment to understand what Tom was asking. But in short, he'd got to the heart of what was tormenting me. Did you two do it? That was the question.

Did you 'make-love' with my sister?

'No. I don't think so... she writes of her pain, that he ignored her, he didn't reply to her letters...apparently he told her he would tell me if she carried on. She says, here, "Go and tell my sister. I don't care...tell her and maybe she'll let you go...If she really loves you, she'll set you free..." I can't believe it! I just can't...'

'Yeah, well,' Tom sighed, looking around him, 'looks like Basra in here. Just forget about all that, here, come down for a drink...hey, hey, it's all over.'

But not for me. I thought, not knowing who you were was bad enough, but not knowing Anna, and being completely unaware that she relished her betrayal, that she despised me, that probably you both did.

'Where have I been all my life?'

Tom piled my clothes on top of his case before lifting me off my knees.

*

We stand outside the hospital, the two of us are laughing at Mona's embarrassment. She'd bumped into us. I'd introduced you and for the first time seen her blush.

'You have good friends, Katherine. They love you.'

'I've put them through it.'

'Thank you for having dinner with me.'

'What will you do now?'

'Go back to the flat. Watch some television. Think of you. Maybe go out for a drink with the little shit downstairs.'

'I'll be home early tomorrow morning.'

'Come into the bed, naked, it's the best way for me to wake up. It might be the last time,' you say, catching my hand.

*

After two years it might have seemed that I was getting on with my life. I was doing placements at different hospitals around London, and the change was a surprising tonic at the same time as exhausting. Spending my days where I didn't have memories of you was a distraction and a relief. When I wasn't working or studying, I relaxed with Tom. It was an easy, recreational and heart-free affair between two single people who lived in the same building and enjoyed each other's company. We'd made our own little world together that was, at least, another digression and at the most, a comfort. That's how I wanted to think of it, if ever I thought of it at all.

When I spoke of my husband who'd disappeared, it might have seemed like the trauma was receding. There were even days that went by when I didn't speak about 'him' at all. But I had times, times when I fell apart and I wondered if I'd make it back again, and then, somehow, I did. I was impressed to discover that time does actually heal: whether I was in fact being mended on the outside or just simply that I was exhausted and beaten by the search, I didn't know, but the episodes of grief were arriving at less frequent intervals and when they hit, it wasn't as hard.

But then, the days after the flood, after finding Anna's letter, those were the blackest days. Where I thought I was getting better, it was worse, worse even than the first weeks after you left. I couldn't work, I couldn't sleep or eat or speak to anyone and my home was unrecognisable. I couldn't talk to my family, least of all my sister – I lost you, and then her. I was told to take time off work and required to see the counsellor at the hospital. I stayed at Tom's, hardly got out of bed for days. The counsellor asked if I'd considered suicide, and it surprised me that she thought I'd have the energy or resources to contemplate ending my life. To have been suicidal would have been something.

'Yeah, stinks all right,' said the plasterer from his ladder as Chantal passed down a coffee through the ceiling. 'I'd get that husband of yours to take you away for a few days while it dries out.'

'He's away,' I answered, fitting a sheet over my new mattress.

'He'll have a shock when he gets back, eh?'

'I'd have a bigger shock, he left two years ago!'

'Oh,' he said, smearing the plaster across the last section of ceiling, 'What, just left left?'

'That's one way of putting it, yes.'

'That happened to me. I was engaged to a girl, we'd been together seven years and three months. Then, two days before the wedding, I came home and she'd gone. Lock, stock and barrel. I had a complete nervous breakdown. It bankrupted my parents – literally - keeping me, my mortgage, cancelling the wedding. We looked everywhere – it was the same time as that little Maddy McGann went missing but no one was looking out for Tracy, police said it wasn't a crime to get cold feet about a wedding. They found she'd been on internet chat rooms and started up some sort of romance with a bloke from New Zealand, that's where she went. She later got in touch with her nan. Said she couldn't explain why she left, she just didn't want to spend the rest of her life with me but couldn't face letting everybody down. And that was that. Some people have no manners, no guts.'

Usually I would have defended you but I couldn't, this man had lived through what I had and he knew what it felt like when someone wants to move on and can't be bothered to hang around long enough to say goodbye.

'I used to be so frightened of seeing her again, I just didn't know how I'd react: thought I'd kill her or maybe beg her to come back, depended on my mood...then, about three months ago there she was on the high street. She'd married the chap from down under and came home to show her mum the baby. We said "hello" and then went our separate ways. It's a strange old thing, but the heart keeps going. I thought the world of that tart, but now, nuh, I wouldn't want her back, she'd aged badly and apparently her new man is pretty quick with his fists... There, all done.'

Frances drew up a timeline and plotted where you'd been. It started when you'd lived under me in Tom's flat while it was empty – you must have left when the decorators came in. About a year later you were in Mexico and after that, probably San Francisco. Then it peters out. Frances was still working on the hypothesis that you had someone in England who was hiding you. I wanted to know where you were, of course, and I wanted to know why you went. I could admit that much. But what I really wanted to know was, what did I mean to you? Only one person could answer that, and I was starting to forget things about you, like your laugh, the spectrum of your moods, the exact shade of your eyes.

Finding Anna's letters had confirmed to me that you had secrets from me, that you could betray me and that while our marriage had been everything in my life, for you, perhaps it was just background noise.

It was during those 'bad' weeks Frances and I met in Hyde Park. She had something to tell me and she was being slow about it.

'Kate. This is where my line of work gets philosophical. I have to ask, what difference does information make? I can see you're pretty fragile right now and what I might tell you...well, I risk either sending you over the edge or helping you turn away from it.'

'Ah, but you've got me all excited now.'

It was the first time I'd noticed that summer had broken, there were people scattered all over the park, lying in the sun alone or in groups, some seemed to have carried out most of the contents of their living rooms for the day.

'You look anything but excited!' she laughed.

'The hospital has put me on to a counsellor. She says I need "closure".'

I mimic the way my therapist always uses her fingers to indicate a ring-fence around this word.

'Closure, yes. Usually comes just after you've absolutely bloody had enough.'

Philosophy over, Frances told me what she'd uncovered about your life before me.

The information came as if from a long distance and seemed to fly around me, but didn't hit me directly. Perhaps I just couldn't humiliate myself any more by showing interest in anything to do with you, or it was the body doing its thing to protect against shock.

I walked Frances to Bayswater Tube Station.

'I've got time off work next week, maybe I should go to France, maybe going back is the only way forward. It's better than just staring at the wall,' I said, thinking out loud.

✻

If you took the roof off the hospital and watched from above, the people in the white coats must look like pinball balls, shooting up and down, rolling across and back again over the same routes all day long, but at night, the choreography slows, the corridors lay empty and the pings aren't so frequent or loud, apart from the odd emergency when we gather round pushing and shoving to save a life. We do or we don't, either way, we write up the notes.

I tot up today's tallies.

A few hours into the night shift. The patients' faces are dimly lit by the corridor's fluorescent lighting. There's hardly a sound apart from muffled footsteps on lino floors and the regular bleeps of heart monitors. I already know the beds that will most likely be refilled tomorrow night.

'Ah, barely a ripple tonight,' says the night-nurse flicking past a perfume ad in her magazine.

'I might turn in,' I answer, tapping my bleeper. 'Don't hesitate...'

'Sweet dreams,' she sings.

I want to call you, see if you are back in the flat and that you are okay. I want to check that you are where you said you'd be, but I'm not up to facing the fact that you might not, so I don't phone.

Last night you slept with your arms around me, chaining me to you. You breathed regularly. You have spent your life on the run. You came in search of me, because I had a good heart, and you needed a good heart to tell you that you were forgiven. I could only forgive if I had personal experience of your crime, and so you wait for judgement Thursday when I'm to tell you if what you did was forgivable.

Walking from ward to ward, I see a coffee machine and I see two people. That's us, eight years ago. So long ago. The two people who didn't make it through.

tuesday afternoon

I never thought that I'd go to France without you. I asked you so many times if we could take a trip across the Channel, if you would give me a guided tour around your past. Of course, you thought that was silly, school-girl sentimental. Of course, I didn't question why.

After one gin & tonic, I wept on the plane.

When I saw the main fountain in Aix, the one we stood by that hot day, I was prepared to be torn apart - I'd allowed myself to crack at that point - but as the taxi approached, it was just a fountain. I'd over-prepared myself. I didn't disintegrate; I looked away, unmoved. So, there it was. My memories couldn't kill me.

The taxi pulled up in a side-street. I walked into my hotel carrying my laptop, a file of photos and a change of clothes.

I tried to speak French but the way the receptionist looked at me was so derisive, I switched to English to let her stumble around her dimly lit vocabulary. The hotel I found for myself was clean, quiet and expensive. Alone in the room, I paced from the bathroom to the window, waiting for someone to walk in and ask what I was doing there. I unpacked, claimed my space. I missed you. I talked to you. I missed you more because you didn't answer.

The hospital was as I remembered and I saw myself by the entrance, moments before you came to change everything.

This is where Frances' research brought me. A Frenchman, Xavier Marc Rocher was last seen at this hospital the day we met. He was last spotted where he'd left his girlfriend and their new-born baby.

I passed reception, the long corridor where we waited for Max and then the coffee machine where the two of us first spoke. I kept walking towards the maternity wing.

At the nurse's station I asked about that day when this man was there. The nurse looked at your picture. Another woman joined us. They knew what I was talking about but were suspicious of why I was asking questions, they didn't understand what it was I wanted. The two women found someone else, they stopped to gather around, repeat the story.

When I said I was a doctor, it confused them more. I added that I was looking for my husband who had disappeared. They relayed what I'd said back and forth, and from their frowns and shaking of heads, I wasn't sure if they'd understood too little or too much.

A mother padded over in her hospital gown, looking pale and holding her stomach. She asked something, one nurse went off to help her, another answered the phone and I was standing alone in the hospital corridor.

If I went to the coffee machine maybe I might find you there. I walked, light-headed, my feet unsteady, the ground seemed to be moving under me. I couldn't find my way back. A porter wheeling a trolley motioned to the lifts. More doors. More corridors.

And then a voice called out, and a nurse rushed up to me. I prepared myself for being told off again. Through the scrabble of words I understood that a nurse who was there that day would be coming in later, she was due for the night shift. I had her name: Magali.

Needing air, I re-traced our steps back to the centre and to the restaurant where we'd had lunch. A waiter moving around inside saw me and gestured that they were closed. I stood there, looking at where we sat the day we met. How could I have known that as you poured me wine, your son was being born?

The waiter came to the door, pointed at the Fermé sign.

'Could I speak to the man...the owner?'

'Madam, Closéd,' he stressed, holding the sign in my face.

'I've come to speak to the owner, the man...the boss –'

A man walked out of the darkness.

'Le patron. Is me.'

The waiter moved away and I was in front of the man who'd known you that afternoon. I took out your picture. He glanced and laughed. He looked at me, and laughed again. He put a hand on my shoulder and led me into the restaurant. He poured a liqueur for the two of us.

'Xavier,' he said, shaking his head. 'Is it Yasmeen looking?'

'No, me. He's my husband.'

He dropped his head in his palm and looked at me sideways. He was sleepy but amused enough to sit with me. He rubbed his eyes.

'Where? Where you married with Xavier?'

'London. But we met here – we came here to this restaurant – I remember you talking together; he knew you.'

'A little. He's a romantic...ça c'est vrai.'

'Two years ago he...vanished. Gone! Disappeared!'

I flicked my fingers apart like a conjurer over a black hat.

He was laughing again, like a private joke to himself.

'Et voila! C'est Xavier. Y' know?'

'No. Tell me.'

'Drink?'

He poured us another drink and lit a cigar.

'Xavier. I met him first time in very chi-chi resort in Théole-sur-Mer, near Cannes. Xavier arrived – no papers, no friends, no experience...but soon I make him responsable - he was very good, very good – speak English very good too – the persons like him. Yasmeen était serveuse – waiter? – there. Xavier had many, many girls – always – but she...like this...' He made a claw with his hand, 'like this, eh?'

I nodded and had to ask, 'What was she like?'

'Les yeux verts, Viper. She make beautiful clothes, sold them in market. Girl intelligente, very good English. When the season was over, he want to go in America, he has plans, rich people want him to make parties there. He has great opportunities for him. But Yasmeen many problem. She make baby...' He shook his head, sipped at the drink. 'Et lui? Pouf! Like you say, "disappeared".'

'Have you seen him?'

'No, no au revoir, no...I have friend who see him in Maroc.'

'When?'

'Months ago. He still run from Yasmeen! But you too! So he leave   you?'

'He didn't leave me...he just...went away. I'm looking for him, that's all.'

'You find him, you tell him he always has job with me. He's good man, but problem for too many women!'

I left him still clucking at the thought of such a problem.

After an afternoon sleep and a shower at my hotel, I waded back through the tourists to the hospital. Magali was on duty, she had been prepped for my return and, after finding someone to cover for her, led me outside to where she lit a cigarette and told me about that day.

Magali had been on duty the morning Yasmeen was in labour. It was she who had suggested her partner take a coffee break. She directed him to the drinks' machine. He was a little long and the pregnant girl was screaming for her husband. Magali reassured her that he'd be back soon. He needed to be strong too, so he could see her through the delivery. But the girl wasn't happy to let him out of her sight. When the baby's head could be seen, someone was sent to find her partner. But he wasn't in the corridor. The father had gone. The receptionist said she'd seen him talking to some tourists an hour before.

Magali shook her head and closed her eyes. 'Her screaming...like I never heard. I was saying, "he will come back...look at your baby..." But the girl knew. She said she knew he wasn't coming back.'

'Did she call the police?' I asked.

'To say what?'

Magali looked at me, her eyes dropped down and she glanced at her watch. I was keeping her from work.

'She was a young, poor, unmarried Arab girl. I don't think the police would have done anything. I was sad, really sad for her. She left the hospital early, before she was officially discharged. But she had to find this man. She was in no state to look after a baby...she was crazy, she made me afraid for her and for the child.'

Magali said all this in French but for some reason, I had no trouble understanding her, I wasn't even aware we were speaking another language; it was as if I knew all this already.

'I never did this before or since, but I found her address and I visited her. I was worried, about the baby, and her, and it was...' Magali shook her hand in the air and covered her mouth. 'It was terrible. The way she lived. She was crying, the baby was crying. To stop the noise she put sweets in its mouth. Oh! There was nothing in that room. They had nothing and the landlord was asking them to leave... I came back the following week, but they'd left.'

'What did she call the child?'

'No name, she didn't even give the baby a name.'

I showed her your photo.

'Yes. That was him. So, you found him?'

'No, I lost him too.'

That night I called Frances from my hotel. Within the hour she faxed me the details about Yasmeen El Jarri. It hadn't been difficult to find: she's now Yasmeen de Lancey. Even I'd heard of her. She's no longer the 19-year-old Moroccan whose family had abandoned her when she was pregnant. No longer the waitress you had a fling with and hoped to dump at some point, the girl you left bearing your child. She's now a very successful clothes designer married to a property tycoon.

I left the hotel and bought every fashion magazine in the newsagent's. Returning, I spent the evening cutting out pictures of her. There weren't many – just little photos of her fashion shows, clutching models and stepping out with her husband. The internet threw up a few interviews, but the woman talked about her work, not her private life. There was never any mention of a child. I stared at her face all night – it was an obsessive binge which I justified by telling myself I was looking for a link, a clue, a trap door.

In the morning I called her work numbers, tried to get hold of her at home. I left messages for her – she had shops in Paris, London and New York, but she didn't return my calls. Then, just before I left France, I received an email from her. It read: "Dr Brenton. Leave me alone."

The plane landed through London fog and as it taxied towards the terminal, a dark stain of dread spread through me.

It was a surprise to see Tom at the airport waiting for me. He was smiling, holding flowers, a gesture which was touching but at the same time wholly impractical.

'Good trip?' he asked

'What are you doing here?'

'Oh, thanks! Well, whenever I come through the arrivals hall I always look out for someone to be there waiting for me - and then I'm always disappointed that there isn't. Silly, isn't? But there you go. Anyway, I thought I'd come meet you, bring you home. Are you cross?'

'No, no. It's very sweet,' I said, trying to manage my bag, my lap top and the flowers without crushing them.

Yes, silly. But then, I hadn't seen Tom at first because I'd been looking out for you.

One decision I'd come to while away was that I had to end whatever it was I was doing with Tom. Somehow, despite never having started, it was already going too far. As the gardens of Victorian terraced houses zapped by the windows of the Gatwick Express, he chattered animatedly about his week. There was a high pitch note that rang out behind what he was saying. Through my own low self-esteem and self-absorption, I hadn't really listened to it before, just turned my ear and hoped it would stop. Behind his words he was telling me that he'd missed me. He thought he loved me. He imagined some kind of future together.

We shared the same home, our apartments had merged, our days and stories had fused, but the intimacy of our lives which he thought was fate was only consequential. I'd needed so much, he'd thought I needed him.

When we made love that evening, hanging onto each other as if we were falling through the bed, I didn't finish anything between us. If it wasn't him, it would have been someone else. And I wasn't up to ending anything.

A few days later I met with Frances over a beer in a garden pub after work. She put a file down in front of me. It was labelled 'Xavier Rocher'.

'It makes pretty hard reading,' she warned.

I put the folder away and passed her an envelope filled with cash I'd withdrawn regularly from ATM machines in payment for the info she'd collected.

She filled me in on a few details. Yasmeen had been in London to celebrate the opening of her South Molton Street shop. After the first night party she'd gone on to Johan's club, The Nadir. She was the girl Tom and Maggie had seen around our flat, and Johan identified her as the red-head you were quarrelling with at his club.

'Do you want to pursue this?' asked Frances. 'There's a chance they could still be in contact, maybe together.'

I thought about Yasmeen's email.

'I have to respect her feelings, after what she's gone through.'

'Yeah. If he could do that to her, to a little baby...but read the file, Kate. You'll understand him better. One other thing that's niggling...'

'What?'

'Yasmeen's never mentioned having a baby...there are no pictures, photos...nothing. There's the birth certificate, no records of a death. The child must be somewhere...'

tuesday night

I'm standing outside the hospital entrance watching the last of the visitors move quickly into the night air, relieved to be getting out and lighter for handing over flowers or toiletries. I called Anna a few minutes ago. I'd woken her up and she sounded groggy, breathless with the weight of the baby inside her. We agreed to meet at my flat tomorrow – it will be our first meeting for a very long time.

And while I have my phone out, and all is quiet, I ring my home number. You are watching TV, but there's nothing on. You too sound sleepy. You say you miss me. I say I'll be home early tomorrow morning, that I miss you.

I do too. I'm about to ask you to tell me about your child – but my pager goes off and I'm called to an emergency.

*

Late one night a few weeks ago, I was returning from a Missing Persons' charity event when, as the taxi pulled up outside my house, the driver said it looked like I had company.

There was a man curled up on my doorstep. In the darkness, it could have been you. All that day, I'd had this feeling, this was going to be the day you'd come back to me - but then, I'd had that feeling many times before and I'd been wrong.

'Marc? Marc?' I said, just like I did in my dreams.

'Kate?' croaked a voice from inside the coat.

I tumbled onto the body, pulled the hand away from his mouth.

But it wasn't you, it was my brother-in-law Nick.

It'd been over a year since I'd seen him. After reading Anna's letter to you, I broke all ties with my sister: whenever she rang, I slammed the phone down, refused to answer her emails, texts or open the envelopes with her handwriting on them. A few times she'd arrived at my parents' home demanding that we talk, but I'd leave immediately and gradually, I went home less and less. There was nothing to say. I'd read how she'd willed me to lose you and then you'd gone. Anna always got what she wanted.

'Has anything happened to the children?' I asked.

'No, no, they're fine...fine. Don't worry... This is about me.'

'Here, go in,' I said.

On the stairs to my flat, Tom opened his door and stood glaring at us.

'Alright?' he asked.

'Sorry, did we wake you?'

'No, I was up,' he said, staring at Nick. I saw the flickering of the TV against the ceiling inside his flat. He kept his eyes on Nick.

He imagined that this was Anthony, the man he viewed as his rival.

'Tom, this is Nick, my sister's husband.'

Nick wobbled forwards to shake Tom's hand.

'Pleased to meet you. Terribly sorry to disturb you at this hour.'

'No problem, mate.'

Tom looked at me. 'Night then.'

When I let Nick into the flat he took off his sodden coat and then his shoes.

'You thought I was Marc sitting on your doorstep. God I'm sorry.'

'It's not the first time. I think I see him everywhere these days. It was his birthday a few weeks ago.'

'I do that too...think I see him...I've even approached people –'

'Nick, if Anna's asked you to mediate between us - I won't.'

'No, no...Kate – there's something I want to tell you.'

'Sure everything's alright? The baby, everything?'

'Yes, yes, sure.'

I divided up the last of a bottle of wine between us.

'Do your neighbours often check up on you?'

'Tom? No...well, yes, he does. We single people have to look out for each other. So Tom's a little protective.'

'I noticed. I thought he was going to challenge me to a duel.'

Nick was so thin, in fact, scrawny. His yellow fingers grappled for a cigarette.

'Do you mind?'

'I'll have one too,' I answered.

'Really? I didn't know you smoked.'

'Occupational hazard. Nick, it's late. What's this about?'

Nick looked at me. At his wife's little sister. I don't know what the picture he saw was, possibly hints of the woman he'd married fifteen years ago, before the lust turned to domesticity, children, constant lack of money and whatever had brought him to my door. There was a time when Anna was slender and provocative, not always pregnant or breastfeeding or asleep. There was a time he wanted to spend his evenings with her, not cowering in doorways.

'I need help.'

'What help Nick?'

'Big help. I couldn't think who to turn to...'

Nick stubbed out his cigarette and looked around the room. He pushed his fingers through his damp hair. His eyes were bloodshot. I watched as his thoughts choked him. He gasped for breath. The words just didn't come. I took in a lungful of smoke, let it out, swallowed the wine.

Finally he spoke.

'I'm a heroin addict.'

I went over and held him as he cried into my neck.

'This'll be our fourth baby...and I still can't stop...help me, Kate...help me.'

'How long has this been going on?'

He sniffed in his tears. 'Since I was 17. Only on and off and then for the last five years it's been all the time...I need help, Kate. I don't know where to turn...'

'Does Anna know?'

'No...no one knows. Well, apart from Marc.'

'Marc?'

'He knew. The first time I met him he took me aside and said I disgusted him. He said I was a "low life-form". True.' Nick smiled a little, 'That's why we never really saw eye to eye. He said he'd been involved in drugs when he was a teenager, been in a gang, did terrible things. He never told you? I always wondered if he'd told you.'

'No,' I whispered. 'Never. There's a lot I didn't know. Do you know why I don't speak to Anna?'

'I suspect that she made a play for Marc?'

'I found a love letter.'

'Kate, I'm partly responsible for that. I had my secret - it was in my interest that Anna had hers.'

'You didn't write the letter.'

'No, but I saw how Marc could distract my wife from focusing on me. I exploited her being besotted with him. I didn't want to be the one who made Anna unhappy, I let Marc be the brute, and when he disappeared, well, he finished the job rather well.'

Having unburdened himself, Nick had become quite voluble. I couldn't let the chance go to investigate more about you.

'Did either of you have anything to do with him leaving?'

'No, no...but there was one thing - I couldn't have told you before without letting on about my problem. About a month before he left, we were at your parents for Sunday lunch. I was going up

182

to the bathroom to have a hit and he followed me. He touched me for a line, said he wanted to see if it was still so terrible.'

'He took drugs? With you? In my parents' house?'

'Yeah. He just snorted some heroin, looked at me and said something like, "I'm going to have to go back into my past and clean up the mess I made. One day, you will have to do the same...every day you fuck up now, is another day you have to fix up later".'

We sat in silence.

'Kate?'

'Hum?'

'When he left, I was pleased. I was grateful someone else was worse than me. I'm sorry, I knew you were in pain but I was relieved. That's what this demon drug has done to me. Messed up everything, more than you could ever imagine. I'm not me, only a sliver of what could have been...I'm not a man or a father, or a ...I don't know, I'm a...low life-form.'

'Stay here tonight. Tomorrow I'll make some calls, get you in somewhere –'

'No, I need to score tonight. I'm hanging out...y'know, withdrawing. It'll be my last night...can you lend me £50? Or do you have anything here?'

'Nick!'

'I just told you: I'm addicted - I can't go through the night without...'

Nick stood over me as I searched for money in my wallet, then I felt a tug and the bag was ripped from my hands. He was out of the flat before I had time to look up. When I shouted after him, he was already out on the street.

Anna was six weeks away from giving birth and her husband had disappeared. She called me and this time, I took her call. I couldn't leave anyone in a pain I knew too well. I said I'd come up to Oxford to tell her personally what I knew about Nick. I avoided her questions and ducked under her guesses. I was trying to protect her, needless to say, I'd made her worse. So that's how it felt to be on your side of the lies. To be the person who controls, edits and revises what another person knows. You chose to live that way, I didn't.

The afternoon I was due to go to Anna's, two policemen came to my work.

They sat me down in McKendrick's office and told me that they'd found Nick in a chemist in North London trying to use my prescription pad to get drugs. I collected him from the police station and from there, drove to the treatment centre which had agreed to give him a bed.

It was terrible being with him – that car journey, his crying amid strange self-conscious bursts of laughter. He asked which hospital he was going to, when I said the name, he tried to jump out of the car, 'That's where all the celebrities go! I haven't even got anything to wear?'

When I drove through the gate and pulled up the hand brake, we sat in silence, both of us with a sense that these were the last minutes before he signed off on what had been his life up to that moment. What I didn't know was that I was about to take a turn and step into yours.

Nick's counsellor, Ewan, met us at the door and welcomed us as if we were guests at his country house. He was our age but seemed a lot wiser. I attributed this to his many years as a recovering addict. After he'd told us about his own addiction, the disclosure, as well as promise of duck-down pillows for Nick, my brother-in-law felt reassured. We then went through a form detailing Nick's drug history. He listed every legal and illegal drug I'd ever heard of. He said he'd injected in his neck, his feet, that he'd overdosed several times, that he'd stolen from my parents and even pinched his grandmother's morphine as she lay dying.

Ewan wrote it all down without showing any reaction, I tried to stay impartial, professional, un-judgemental, even when he described burgling his own house.

'Did you not know about this Kate?'

I shook my head.

'None of us knew.'

'Right,' said Ewan, 'And how have you organised payment for the treatment, Nick?'

Nick looked down at his hands. 'Can't I smoke?'

'No, sorry,' replied Ewan.

'I'll pay for him to do this,' I said.

Nick looked at me, 'Kate?'

'I want to. We have to start repairing this family or there'll be nothing left.'

'But –'

'Don't worry Nick. Please. It's for Mimi, Bruno and Ella.'

I looked back to Ewan, 'His wife, my sister, is just about to have her fourth baby. Do you think he'll be ready by then?'

'Ready? That's up to him... Nick, we've got "group" starting in five minutes. But first...' Ewan lifted a camera out of a drawer, '...we have a tradition of taking pictures of our clients when they arrive and then we can compare it with how they look when they've completed the programme – a 'Before' and 'After' shot. May I?' asked Ewan.

Nick made a grim attempt at a smile into the camera, I was thankful that we didn't have the same practice in hospitals.

Nick left us to do the paperwork and when we were finished I stood with Ewan in the hall, at the foot of the stairs.

'I haven't spoken to my sister for over a year...what do I tell her?'

'The truth. Deceit, denial and lies, they're the worst symptoms not only of an addict but everyone around them. Breaking that down is the first step to attacking the disease. It doesn't help anyone to protect him. Here, I've got some literature you might like to –'

'Here he is, in this place, being fed and looked after, and she's got three children and pregnant with a fourth. He's the one who's been...It doesn't seem fair.'

'I know, it seems hard. It is hard. But she can call me, we can arrange sessions with a female counsellor. Come into my office and I'll find get a contact number.'

In Ewan's office, a juggernaut of fatigue crashed into me. My heart seemed to have stopped before pounding fast, my blood turned icy, white lights flashed across my eyes. Breathless, I couldn't speak to call for help.

'Sit down, sit down Kate, rest your head on your lap, there...just breathe.'

It wasn't easy. None of my senses could be relied on.

I moaned into my trembling knees.

'And what about me?'

'Sorry?'

'What about me? What about me?'

I was shaking, visibly pulsating, either suffocating or too full of air.

Ewan's voice was calm, experienced, gentle.

'What about you, Kate?'

I was held hostage by my convulsions. Ewan waited for it to end. I scratched at the tears on my face, slapped myself into some kind of coherence.

'How can they just go off and leave people?'

Ewan touched my arm and passed me a box of tissues.

'What's happened to my family, to Anna and me? We used to be...so close and happy and...normal. These people came into our lives, like viruses, they ate up everything good: look at us, we're just walking husks –'

'Sorry...Kate? Slow down...tell me...'

'My husband left me and I can't find him and this search for him, it's a compulsion...a torture...an addiction. I'm no different from Nick...'

I held my body in with my arms, keeping it together, heard myself yelling, 'What did I do wrong? What?'

Ewan returned to his chair, sat opposite me.

'Kate, do you want to talk about this?'

Yes, I did.

The grief was making a break for it – I'd reached a point when 'help' wasn't enough, I needed to be rescued.

When I finished telling Ewan the story of the last two years of my life, the crying didn't abate, I continued while Ewan listened. I heard the group finishing, voices around the building, supper being prepared enthusiastically downstairs.

'When one person in a family reaches out to find help, often the others follow – recovery is contagious like that. I get the feeling you've been carrying your own pain as well as everyone else's. You're a doctor. You're paid to look after others, be in control, have the answers. But you're also a woman whose husband has suddenly 'gone' – on top of a trying career and all the other everyday stresses and frustrations we carry around with us.'

'But how do I make all this stop?'

'You don't; you stop. Take it in. Feel it. The anger, the hurt, the confusion, the missing – all of it – you need to confront it in order to get through to the other side of grief – if not, these self-

destructive tendencies, these expressions of pain and rage, they'll overwhelm you like they did this afternoon.'

'I have a counsellor, someone at the hospital, but she's just someone else I vent my anger on. No one seems to really understand.'

He rubbed his forehead as an idea came. 'Kate, it's just a thought, but we have a patient here, someone who's been through a similar experience. I could ask her if she'd like to talk with you, sometimes it helps just to have someone to share things with. Would you like to meet her?'

I nodded. Ewan went outside, there was the mumble of considerate voices. I could hear Nick starting up a conversation with another guy. Yes, he was laughing. Ewan returned with a woman behind him.

I knew at once it was her.

'Kate, this is Yasmeen, she's in her last week here. I thought maybe you two could benefit from –'

Yasmeen studied me as her bony, brittle legs in their high leather boots crossed the carpet. Her eyes glanced down at the crumpled tissues in my lap. I saw a little smile, a smile for her, not for me. She had a gap between her two front teeth and grass green eyes set in layers of dark lashes. Settling her waist-length black hair behind her as if it were a pet, she seemed to be deciding whether to toy with me or just finish me off.

'We know each other. Yasmeen de Lancey,' she put out her hand. It was small, soft, like a child's hand, so different from the hardness in her eyes.

'Oh? Well, I'll leave you both to it.'

Ewan turned for the door, gave us another look and left.

Yasmeen sat down. I was taken aback by how attractive she was. Not like the photos I saw of just a pretty face. Her voice, the way she moved, her self-assuredness. I was jealous of her. Jealous because I could see what drew you to her, I could see you fucking her, your faces barely separated. You had a baby together. She was a part of your past, like me. Maybe I would be like her in the future and I didn't want that, there was nothing nice about her.

She began, 'If I believed in coincidence I would say, "Wow, my God, what a coincidence!" But more probably every woman involved with Xavier ends up in the nut-house, eh?'

I picked up a tissue from the floor.

'Still finding it hard, Mrs Doctor woman?'

'Didn't you?'

'Look where I am.'

'Because of Marc, you're here?'

'Partly. Whenever life is difficult, I drop in here, take time out, get straight again.'

She saw Nick's confiscated cigarettes sticking out from my jacket pocket. She took the packet, pulled one out and lit it.

'I thought you weren't allowed –'

She waved the thought away.

'Ça fait du bien.'

She blew the smoke out of the window.

'You had a private detective watching me,' she accused, looking straight at me.

'Yes, I... Sorry.'

'My husband hired one too...I had two following me everywhere, can you imagine? Certainly made my life a little more interesting at the time, but still.'

She blew the smoke out in one long line just above my face– you used to do that.

'Do you know where he is?'

'The last I heard he was in Marrakech. He had a friend called Momo – Mohammed - we worked together at one time, Momo was like Xavier's - Marc's - brother – Momo had AIDS. I heard that Marc was there when he died. Then Marc took over his bar and his identity. Well, a con artist like your husband wouldn't miss an opportunity like that.'

She looked at the half-smoked cigarette and extinguished it in her fingers. She slid the butt back into the pack and the pack into her boots. She seemed bored, got up and walked around the room like a show horse, all the time looking at me with the greenest eyes.

'I left you alone when you told me to, but I'd always wanted to see you, to talk to you.'

'What's the point? If it was right we met, we would, like this. Anyway, I was in a bad way. That's what brought me here, prescription drugs. From doctors. Ever since Marc left, I became hooked on Benzodiazapan. I needed them. He left me with nothing but pain and a baby. You know what some girls do for work, Dr Brenton, when she has a baby and no money? Men pay a lot to *suck on lactating nipples, when your vagina bleeds, they pay extra.'*

'I...I didn't know that.'

'Well, Marc did. He knew.'

'That's awful.'

'Yes. That's "awful".'

Her eyes were on me, pulling me to her face, but I couldn't look at her. I was ashamed for you, ashamed for me. When you left me, it felt like I had nothing, but in fact, compared to Yasmeen, I was spoilt: a home, family, friends, a career...I wanted to apologise to her for that.

'How is the little boy?'

'He's not so little. But he's resilient, well, he's had to be. I don't want to talk about him now.'

'But where is he?'

'Just leave him alone.'

The aggression in her answer was intimidating, she scared me.

'I was always curious about you. A young professional, English. You seemed so...excuse me, but...boring. Marc left me for you – left our baby for you – I've hated you. So, why give you anything?'

'You knew where he was? And about me? Why didn't you...?'

'I did.'

For some reason, she stopped being tough and clipped and sat down again. And then, without any prompting, she closed her eyes and told me the story of you and her. As she spoke, she relived it but it was like she was talking of another Yasmeen...and I suppose she was. A Yasmeen who had all the men in love with her except the one she wanted: you. You wouldn't let her seduce you, and then one night, after work as she was putting on her bike helmet a group of men surrounded her – she thought they'd rape her – and you intervened, saved her. That night she broke the code to you – you were tired of being adored, you wanted to look after someone, to protect someone more vulnerable than you, so she let you.

And she was more in love than she ever imagined possible. When she fell pregnant, the men in her family wanted to murder her and she came to you, her 'saviour'. The two of you moved to Aix-en-Provence where you planned to start a life together. She had no idea, Marc, no idea you were going to leave. It was you who wanted to get married, have the child and live together, she'd never have dreamt as much.

'Maybe you know a little of what it was like, but Katherine, I had his baby...'

She looked down into her hands.

'Why do you think he left you?'

'He was playing a part and then, he just walked off stage. Because he didn't – couldn't – stay in one place and be one person. He was afraid he would fail. Fail at being a better man. He always wanted to be the romantic hero. Like you are in the beginning of a love affair, unproven, untested, this is what he wanted. And, Katherine, your private detective, she must have found out about his mother? What do you expect?'

'What happened when you saw him again?'

I knew what she was going to say, Marc. She took out the cigarettes and lit one. She was taking her time: she was relishing the kill.

'It was after I left here for the first time – two and a half years ago – I thought my life was finally making some sense: I was clean, my husband and I were trying to make our marriage work, I'd just signed a big contract designing clothes...so we were all out one night to celebrate this good fortune. And the place that was chosen for our night out...was Marc's restaurant. Can you imagine? I always knew I'd see him again - I even wondered as I got out of the taxi if that would be the night. And when I walked into the restaurant, there he was, talking with the owner and clients, coming to greet us. He was shocked, really shocked to see me. I didn't want to talk then, and I wanted him to wait, huh? Sweat a little. So he came to see me, that next day, where I was staying, at Claridge's Hotel.'

She stopped speaking. She wanted me to beg and I had no choice.

'Yasmeen, what? Then what? What did he say?'

She laughed.

'Katherine, we didn't really get into all the talking bit,' she leant in and hissed in my ear, 'we spent the whole time in bed.'

And then she kissed me. Her mouth sucking at my lips, spreading them open and moving her tongue over my tears, the emptiness you left. In all those men I looked for you, the closest I came to finding you was in this woman.

Her jaw gradually closed, her lips pressed over mine, she left them there, hesitantly before a last tender touch, her lips getting tighter and drier. She leaned back, her eyes glassy. She was cold, brittle again.

'Katherine, you haven't been too bright about all this, have you? The secret is to enjoy the search – it's all you've got left. Okay, I'll give you a tip: 44 Hathaway Street, Hounslow.'

wednesday, sunrise

When I come out of three consecutive emergency operations, the violet sky is frayed with strands of gold. It's gone five thirty in the morning. The beeping of the monitors is regular, the nurses whisper in their stations, the delivery trucks and the catering staff will be arriving and soon there'll be bashing and clattering in the kitchens before the general high tide of people come in and out all day long. But for now, the new day lies dormant.

I'm writing up the night's notes. Looking up into space, hoping that enough words come to make a sentence, I see a smudge of black moving against the white corridor walls in front of me. A man's silhouette. Against the neon lights, you are just a dark shape, but I know your walk.

You slow down when you see me at the desk, pick the chair up and place it opposite me. You sit, drop your head in your hands. When I go to touch your face, it is wet. You take my fingers and press them to your mouth. I can smell alcohol on your breath. Your hands feel like metal in mine. You look at me and tell me without speaking, that it isn't that you won't talk, but you can't.

A nurse passes, she stops, widens her eyes at us. I lift my hand for her to leave us. She hesitates, raises her eyebrows and mouths, 'Sure?' All too frequently we have psychiatric cases, addicts and drunken men coming in off the streets wanting to fight, steal drugs or have sex with nurses, often just to talk. But this one's okay. He's my husband.

There was a time your eyes took me everywhere: Alpine skies, Mediterranean coasts, caves of lapis lazuli, but now, they lead only to sadness.

'Where does it hurt?'

You press my palm onto your solar plexus.

'I'm going to lose you,' you say, your voice breaking into octaves of sorrow.

'It's not just a matter clicking a switch off and on.'

'I know, Katherine, I know.'

The file Frances gathered on your childhood was terrible to read. Over the pages I learned that your mother had only been twelve when she had you. You'd never met your father. Your mother was what we'd probably diagnose now as bi-polar although her mental state is difficult to work out due to her drinking and drug taking.

She worked in restaurants, as a dancer, a cleaner, beggar and call girl – she did lots of things, but nothing for long. You both moved around regularly and every time you settled in a home or with a foster family, your mother would re-appear and insist on taking you back. She'd promise that she'd changed, reformed, learnt from her mistakes. She'd spoil you, indulge you, lure you back into her trust until a new man would appear in her life and you were dropped. Her relationships were always violent, obsessive and all-consuming, in no time she'd revert to drinking, drugs and paying for them by prostituting herself. The little boy she went to so much trouble to win over became a nuisance and someone only good for venting her anger on.

Either the social services got involved or she'd tire of having a child around, she'd drop you off somewhere, put you back into care, and you'd not hear a thing until she turned up again, unexpectedly, undoing your world with her plans for a new life. The day of your sixteenth birthday, the file was closed. You disappeared from the system.

We doze in each other's arms before day breaks through the wards. Voices shift up a gear from whispers to normal decibel range. Trolleys rumble along the corridors. The lift doors ping open and closed. Daylight. You stretch your legs, stand up unsteadily and walk away.

*

The day after I met Yasmeen, I went to watch the house in Hounslow.

From ten in the morning to two in the afternoon I sat in my car waiting for you to come out and explain how you could be connected with possibly the most ordinary house in West London. Two up-two down, 1930s' pebble dash front, crazy paving, one overflowing bin, sprouts of grass fighting for survival beside a half-built fence. No gnomes, no satellite dish, no stickers on the windows. Just house.

And the feeling that Yasmeen had taken me for a big ride.

When the man two doors down closed his door and started down the road, I got out and chased after him.

'Excuse me? I live just up the next street, I was sent a package for number 44 by mistake, but I wasn't sure of the person's name...'

'This one, love? 44? That's...er...Sam. Dunno her last name –'

'Is she married?'

The man tried to connect the logic in my questioning.

'I've seen her kids play in the street but...err...don't know 'bout that dear...'

He scurried off. I sat back in the car. Sam. I was ready to drive away but trembling so much I couldn't lift the handbrake. Children.

I wanted to start the car and leave. Who was I looking for anyway? I needed to pee. If you weren't really the man I'd married, what was I doing in your business? What was I doing badgering Sam's neighbours? But I was there, in front of the house: one council painted blue door away from my last chance to kill off the illusion of you. If I didn't do something now, I'd have to come back after the weekend, after work, however painful the truth, my imagination was torture.

I walked to the door, opened the gate and up the inconsequential path. I pressed the bell, heard it ring inside the house, muffled, irritating. Then the sound of fast, light footsteps in the corridor. A chain slid across the catch and I saw the face of a little boy.

'Yeah?'

'Is Sam in?'

The boy nodded.

'Could I speak to her?'

Without looking away from me he shouted up the stairs.

'Mum! It's her from the social.'

I could hear a door opening from inside the house.

'Mum!'

'Yeah, alright. I got it.'

Over his head I saw that the house was modern inside, it was well decorated, not like it seemed from the outside at all. There were children's toys scattered across the landing.

The boy fixed his eyes on me.

I saw Sam - legs first, cantering down the stairs in pale pink jogging trousers, her lithe, tanned waist punctuated by a diamond in her belly button. Above she wore a tight, Lycra pink top which enclosed overly large breasts. Then lots of blonde hair caught at the top of her head by a diamanté clip.

'Decided to have a look at us in person, have you?' she said.

194

She stood a foot away, hips slanted to one side, her hand, weighed down with bracelets and rings, resting on her mid-riff. She must have been in her early twenties but she had a worldliness about her that made her seem older. Having children young, I guess, must do that to people, and being able to pull it off.

We looked at each other as I searched for a place to start – I know, most of the day sitting in a car doing nothing, you'd have thought I'd rehearsed what to say, but I hadn't. Her directness, the little boy's eyes staring at me, not having eaten, the adrenaline high and lows, it had emptied me out.

'I saw you there, in the Megane 'cross the road. What's this about?'

'I just wanted to know if you knew this man.'

Papers and things spilled out from my bag, I grappled. She bobbed her head, her mouth a little open, her eyes on me, daring me to waste her time. I stood up, fought an overwhelming light-headedness and showed her a picture of you.

The boy immediately started chanting, 'It's Marc. It's Uncle Marc.'

'Nuh.'

'Your son seems to think so.'

'Yeah, well, he's got a lot of "uncles".'

Her voice was deep, it had a catch in it like something primal inside her was fighting to come out.

'That's –'

She put her hand on his shoulder, hard.

'Can I come in, just for a few minutes, just to –'

'No. No you can't. Who are you?'

'My name's Katherine. Katherine Brenton. This is my husband – I'm looking for him.'

'And what makes you think he's here?'

'Someone gave me this address.'

'The French bird…Yasmeen…the designer? Her, wasn't it?'

'Yes. She and Marc had a relationship, he abandoned her, he married me, he left –'

'Whatever.'

She started shutting the door on me.

'Please!'

'No, you "please". Marc comes and goes as he feels. What he does when he's not here, that's his business, get it?'

'I'm worried that he might be in trouble, or hurt...I just need to know...'

'Mum, she looks like she's going to cry.'

'There's nothing to say,' Sam said, increasing the pressure of the door against me.

'You don't have to let me in, but imagine if something happened to someone you loved.'

I looked at the boy, she let go of the door, walked down the corridor leaving me to walk in.

'But I've got to pick the others up from school at four.'

I followed her through to the kitchen. I sat down as a lemonade was put in front of me.

'Is Marc the father of your children?'

She spluttered out the drink she'd just taken a sip from, wiping her mouth, she was laughing.

'Marc's old enough to be my dad! He might be a lot of things, but he's not a kiddy fiddler.'

'So you're not...with Marc...like that?'

'Marc's like...like Harvey says, "uncle". To all of us. This is why I don't want to piss him off answering questions to you people who keep coming round. He's done nothing to us. I'm sorry about your romance, marriage – whatever - but, that's just him, innit?'

'I've been searching for him for over two and half years.'

'Well, that's your problem.'

'When's the last time you saw him?'

'Like I said, he pops in and out.'

'When did he last pop in?'

'I can't answer that.'

'If you're not sleeping together, what's your connection with him?'

She took the clip out of her hair, it rushed down her back and shoulders, then she went about twisting it all back up again. A gesture practised to draw men's eyes to her neckline and down to those expensive breasts.

'My nan was French. She was his social worker when he was growing up in France. They were really close, she loved him like a son, but the authorities didn't allow her to officially adopt him because his mum was around, but every time his mum did something bad to herself or to him, he was sent back to her. Then when my nan and her husband decided to move to England, to have a restaurant, he came over to London, lived here, worked in their place. As I said, he comes and he goes, that's just what he does.'

She leant forward, crossing her arms on the table. On the top of her right biceps were four letters tattooed in blue. She looked at what I was looking at, the name, "Marc".

'Oh that. We got legless one night, got them done, mine got bloody infected and all. Still, looks alright... Look, I've gotta run.'

'Can I speak to your grandmother or mother –'

'They passed away. Breast cancer, both of them.'

'I'm sorry.'

'S'not your fault. Listen. Marc's like a...fairy godfather to me, well, not the fairy part! – what I'm saying is, I haven't got any other family, nor has he. He looks after us. Please, Marc needs a safe place – people he can always trust – I really don't want to talk to you. Nothing personal as I said. Harvey!' she called up the stairs. 'I've got to go.'

'I was his wife. Why didn't he tell me about you?'

The little boy was playing upstairs, banging something on the floor.

'He didn't tell you nothing about him growing up?'

'He told me he had no family...no one. And yet he had you...why didn't he tell me?'

'It's complicated. Because of –'

'Because of what? Who?'

'Harvey! By the door now!' She took my glass and left it in the sink.

She looked into her garden, mentally listing the things she had to do later, it was a deflection tactic.

'Just one thing, please. Did he ever talk about me?'

She turned to me, roughly calculating how much this information would cost her.

'Sure. He said...'

Harvey was now waiting by the door.

'He said you was the best thing that ever happened to him, and that you made him want to be good and better every day he was with you.'

I never missed you so much as that moment when I heard her say those words. That's what you'd said to me the day we married.

'And yet he didn't trust me?'

'Someone has to know you completely before you can trust them, it's obvious really, he didn't want you to know him completely or...I've said too much. Please, you have to go.'

'Thank you.'

'Yeah, well. Sorry I can't help you no more, and...er...I don't mean it like it sounds but...don't came back here again, yeah?'

I helped her over the doorstep with a push-chair and Harvey in tow.

When we got into our cars, she gave me a quick business-like wave and a chirpy good bye. Harvey was in the back belted in his car-seat playing a handheld computer game but as she started the car, he looked up to me and smiled.

Sam drove off, relieved I was out of her life, and you were still safely in it.

wednesday morning

I drive from the hospital back home, over the edges of a creamy mist swilling out from the parks and gardens and into my nostrils, tasting of tin. I roll the car past my flat, look up at the windows. The blinds are down. I park the car, cut the ignition, drop back into the seat.

Programme will resume service in five minutes.

A bang on the bonnet and she's in front of me.

Anna. She's shouting at me through the windscreen. All in grey but for her red cheeks. Her blonde hair springs out from the top of her coat which she's unable to close over her pregnant stomach. Her arms flail on either side of her belly. She falls over the car when the loudness of her voice forces her off balance. She rolls around to me, opens the door and shouts again,

'You didn't say he was back!'

I hold my hands over my ears to protect myself from the screech of her voice. She continues ambushing me with her size, her loudness.

'You didn't say! You didn't say he was back!'

I start to get out of the car but she's on the either side, tugging at the passenger door. She throws it open and lands into the seat next to me.

198

'Just go! Go!'

I start the car again, just to shut her up. Disappointment closes in on me. I'm homesick. I'd so wanted to go upstairs, touch your skin, spend time with you and rest a little before leaving for the day. The last I saw you was at dawn in the hospital, your tearful eyes, the alcohol on your breath, I don't want that to be the last image of you in my mind today.

And I was hoping you'd have talked me out of collecting Nick from his treatment centre. I thought I'd have had time to blow my sister out; it was a gratuitous gesture of kindness to both Nick and Anna to offer picking him up and to drive them back to Oxford. Now I don't feel at all up to it. And this is the last day before I decide about us; I might not have the chance to come home to you again.

'Katie. Please. Drive.'

The car moves off. Her breathing is short and fast. She seals her hands over her eyes, either collecting herself or building up to another outburst.

It takes me a while to reverse out of the space. A bicycle passes by that I didn't see. He swerves, shouts something. I stop and let a car go in front of me.

'I can't believe you didn't say anything!'

'I told mum. I just assumed that she'd...'

'Mum! She doesn't tell me anything!'

'I thought we'd talk about it today, on the way to see Nick –'

'Kate! Can you imagine? I rang the bell, went up and there he was. Marc! I'm eight and a half months pregnant – can you imagine a shock like that!...Christ!'

'Yeah,' I said, 'Sorry, I didn't think. I was working last night and I...I thought I'd be back first but...'

'You didn't think! Fuck! Just drive!'

At the end of my road, I indicate. I'm about to move off but just before, I check the rear-view mirror to see the flat once more, and there you are, closing the door behind you, running up to the car. You open the back seat door and lean forward, kiss my cheek.

'Good morning, beautiful Katherine,' you say, your hand on my shoulder. You stroke my neck. Anna looks away.

I drive in silence, not daring to utter in case I spark off the charge of fury crackling around Anna. I catch the odd glimpse of you. Your face is somewhat crumpled and bleary eyed for lack of sleep, but it only adds to your appeal. I resist jumping over the seats and swallowing you whole. You catch me looking at you, wink at me. There's no medical explanation for how you make my heart spin, send everything inside me flying. I look again; you have a little smile on your face. I bite my lip and raise my eyebrows like a mischievous child who wants to giggle at being told off. Your eyes dart over to my sister, back to me and we both know what the other is thinking. What was it you used to call that? The connection between you and I, *complicité?* For you, it was the sign we were meant to be together, but when I looked it up on the dictionary, under British law, it's a criminal offence.

There's traffic gathering around the motorway junction which I sense that Anna blames me for. But she can't upset me anymore, not when I have you there, your fingers lightly pressing into the top of my shoulder. I'd forgotten how much easier life is when you have someone else who is on your side, someone else who loves you and doesn't really care about anything or anyone else. For a moment, we were there again.

Towards Surrey the roads clear, you suggest we stop off to have a coffee somewhere. I nod in agreement, but then you add that Anna has something she needs to tell me. She flinches, but doesn't contradict you.

There is a pub which serves breakfast. Anna and I sit down, take off our coats and scarves while you bring us some coffees. After the first sip, Anna goes through a series of long, even exhalations. The bartender keeps looking over to her, anticipating any medical emergencies that might arise on his premises.

'What do you want to say, Anna?'

She looks out of the window. Her renowned pearly skin is white, dry. It's the first time I notice the little fans of even pleats on either side of her eyes. She won't look at either of us. You stir your espresso. Anna writhes on her seat, then looks at me, willing me to understand what she has to say before she has to say it so she doesn't have to explain further. I realise that I have missed my sister very much since we've not been speaking. I can afford to be generous now that you are sitting next to me.

She sips her tea, winces before opening out her hands as an expression of honesty. She looks at you, you nod back to her. It's then I want to freeze you both, walk away from all this, go somewhere far, far away, unrecognisable from anything I've known before. I don't need to get a biopsy done on what's built up between us, if it's bad it'll kill us, if not, we'll go on.

'When you told me about Nick, you asked how could I not have known I was married to a smack addict - I must have seemed like the stupidest wife in the world...after you, of course.'

'Thanks.'

'You're welcome. The thing is, Nick and I have led very separate lives. Even when...well...I wasn't the person he went to when he needed help. It was you.'

You yawn. Neither of us really want to hear about Nick. Nick's been having three square meals, clean sheets, bedtime stories and cuddles every night – I'd like to hear something honest come out of Anna's mouth.

I know my sister, and I know when she cries, like now, that it is not because she is sad, but afraid. It's when she knows she has done something wrong and been caught out. I could save her from all this and just say I know, I read what she wrote, but all I can do is concentrate on the brown and orange geometric-patterned carpet in the pub and avoid the knowledge that this could be our last day.

And then she's off.

'They say love is blind, but it's not: lust is blind. You want someone so much it hurts, whatever gets in the way, you don't see it, you look past it. There's nothing else you can do. All you see are ways to get that person, how to wear yourself out of that longing, consume all that makes them them until you can get your breath back and see that they're just like everybody else. But love, love sees everything. That's why, after being with someone at the other end of desire, they no longer leave an impression, they bore you, they drain you. You just get too close. They aren't really what you wanted, and the same image of yourself looks back at you from their eyes, and you aren't the way you wanted. That's how I felt in my marriage – and then... Marc.'

I wait for her to take in a series of deep breaths and a sip of water.

'Marc is a tease, an ache in the groin, an orgasm that never reaches a climax –'

This gets your attention. For the first time in her discourse you react to Anna's summary of your character by blowing out your cheeks and nodding your head. Then you appear to see something out of the window much more interesting than us. Anna continues to talk to me, but really, she is talking to you.

'Marc keeps people in a permanent state of lust – that's why no one really looks at him, really sees him the way he is.'

You're listening to Anna's explanation of your power but she might be explaining string theory or how Blu-Ray DVDs work. Your elbow rests on the back of your chair and you lean your head close to mine, nod a little, all the time half-smiling, awaiting vindication. I look at you, to see you.

'I thought I was in love with him Kate, but I realise now, I just wanted to fuck him. Sorry, he's your husband, but I fancied him. I dressed it up as something else, something to justify and romanticise why I'd put so much at stake for such ignoble reasons – I convinced myself that ours could be the greatest passion of all time – because we make out that love is the ultimate, purest emotion and sex is just something for teenagers and randy old men – but lust is a fatal illness – you're paralysed, obsessed, oblivious to everything else around. It keeps you on the scent, leads you in one direction, makes you run everything else down – all I wanted was one fuck and I nearly lost everything because of it. I lost you.'

And now it's my turn to spin out of the loop. I thought I had my guard up, but Anna looks so small, defeated. Someone walks in the pub, turns to her, the blonde hair does that, or maybe it's because she is crying. The barman pours him a drink, both men make a point of looking away from us.

'I told him before you got married that I loved him. You were never right for each other. Marc should have been with me.'

You sit back. It's out. Anna puts her palms up to her eyes and cries just like Mimi, her daughter, does. I can't hate her for falling in love with you. I remember our squabbles over toys and books and friends that went from childhood into adolescence – and then extended to husbands.

'I found one of your letters.'

'That's what I guessed.'

Anna takes out a tissue, mops herself up.

'You need someone like daddy, or this Anthony mum's always going on about. Marc is a free spirit, he's a romantic, he needs to feel, to roam, explore – not be domesticated...not mortgages and roasts with the in-laws...of course he ran away in the end, what did you expect?'

'I read what you wrote – I couldn't believe you could be so bitter towards me.'

'I was in lust. Didn't you understand anything I said earlier?'

'Marc, why didn't you tell me any of this?'

You shrug, 'Why?'

'Because of what my sister was doing behind my back.'

'That's why,' you say. 'But I kept that one letter, just in case I did need to tell you one day.'

I look at you, then her again.

'But Marc didn't reciprocate, did he?'

Your face is calm, your eyes look around the café, then back at me. You raise your eyebrows.

'You really want to know?'

'Tell her,' you say.

'At daddy's 60th – he was drunk, so was I, I begged him to make love to me, I promised that if he gave me what I wanted, I'd leave him alone. We went into your old bedroom, he got me to take all my clothes off, he started me up like I've never known – I've never wanted anyone so much in my life...and then...he...he just got up and walked out. Left me there, like that.'

'So you didn't...'

'Oh no, humiliation was more his style.'

'She was being annoying,' you say, finishing your drink.

There's a crack in the cellulite clouds and a liquid blue runs beneath it. The light catches your eyes. You are untouched by all this, you make it happen, but you're not to blame, because we are not really talking about you. You're sitting right next to me, but I still don't know where you are.

You look back at me. If Anna wasn't watching us, I'd ask you to hold me, wrap me up, ward off the world. Instead, I ask, 'Is Anna one of the reasons you went away?'

'No Katherine, I loved you, your family and –.'

Anna cuts in. 'It was a fucking relief when he went away,' said Anna. 'For all of us. And you'd be a bloody idiot if you took him back.'

'Like you taking Nick back?'

'Yes, I suppose I'm a bloody idiot too.'

'Must be genetic.'

'Don't say that to a pregnant mother of three!'

She hugs her stomach and we laugh – like sisters.

Finding out about Anna had been a shock, and yet, on the other hand, I'd known it all along, somewhere. I wonder if your leaving was a search for integrity, perhaps my search for you was as well. And all we find is that we love people who can sometimes hurt and disappoint us very much.

'So. Are we finished?' you ask.

'I know I am,' says Anna winking at me.

*

Driving away that first afternoon after meeting Sam I knew I couldn't lie to myself about you. I couldn't continue loving a person who was only really as I'd imagined him to be. I didn't really know you Marc – and I colluded with your disguise - I loved a mirage, a romantic lead, the image of a husband I'd created for myself. Anna loved that same person too, and we'd both been left holding onto nothing.

Instead of going straight home, I drove to the hairdresser's around the corner from my flat.

'Got a special occasion?' asked the hairdresser picking up the ends and turning them disparagingly in her fingers.

'It's Valentine's Day tomorrow.'

'Yeah, and is your man taking you somewhere nice?'

'I'm not sure. But I've got a feeling he's planning something special. It's our first year anniversary.'

'Ow! That's so cute! Let's make sure you knock him off his feet, eh?'

Seeing Nick trying to break from his addiction, Yasmeen fighting for her career and marriage, I couldn't hang on to something that clearly hadn't really been there in the first place. I'd operated on enough hearts to know that you can seal up a valve, make another, channel the flow in a new direction.

As she cut, I thought about that moment at the coach station when you told me I wasn't ready for you. After that I'd grown out my hair. And I kept it long, for the day you came back. The pieces fell in clumps to the ground.

'There you go, that'll knock years off you,' said the hairdresser.

As I'd guessed, a year after our first dinner together, Anthony proposed. He went on one knee, presented me with a ring that looked like something out of a cracker – a small, simple diamond poking out of a gold band, a month's salary. I said 'yes'. We phoned my parents and his mother who were all delighted. Then you returned, just as I was having some good days back again.

wednesday afternoon

Nick stands at the door waiting for us. He hops from one leg to the other, bouncing his hold-all against his calf with an uneasy smile. Seeing the car he gives us a jolly wave, skips over to Anna and works up something close to a hug. He asks after the children, not listening to her answer. He rubs her bulging stomach. He doesn't seem to know what to do with this family he is meeting again. He tries to read Anna's tear-stained face, tugs his hand free of her grip. He does a double take when he sees you getting out of the car. You hug him – the connection is genuine, fond. He recomposes himself, stumped for ways to address you. He looks at me, I don't know how to present you either, what to say, so we laugh a little, awkward, yet excited. You pat his back, he pats yours. Neither of you ever thought you'd have so much in common as you do today.

'Do you mind staying for a little farewell bash they're putting on for me?' he asks.

The wind blows twigs and splatters rain into our faces as we follow Nick into the building. The meeting room is already filled with people. Ewan is there to make us feel welcome. When we sit I see that Anna's lips are trembling. Someone offers to bring her a tea. And the ceremony is underway.

Nick got a double First from Oxford and the *MacMillan Travel Writers' Prize* for his first book. His later books won great acclaim and on the back of the last he even presented a documentary on TV, but I don't think nearly as much a fuss was made of these achievements as his graduation from rehab.

We sit in a circle as his peers make speeches about him. They applaud, heckle, whoop and hug each other. They talk about a Nick I haven't seen. Much of the ritual, the vocabulary and the insiders' jokes pass me by but Anna, you and I, clap when prompted and try to look enthusiastic. All the time, what Anna said about you earlier has churned so much in my mind that it's now thick, sickening and stuck into my imagination. I can see it – the two of you – daddy's

60th birthday. Why my bedroom? How long did it take? Did you enjoy humiliating my sister? Is that what you missed from me? Is that what you went in search of?

Where Nick has found friends and support, a 'family' who love him, the three of us are fast orbiting away from each other. A nurse comes forward with anecdotes of Nick's late night hot chocolate drinking sessions and the group laugh. Ewan shows us Nick's before and after photos and says that Nick is someone who is full of love and warmth towards others. You drop your hand over mine. Ewan concludes by awarding Nick with a medallion, a book is offered which the 'inmates' have signed. After more applause, it looks like the session is coming to an end. But it isn't.

Standing behind Ewan is a visitor. He says that someone has come especially to say goodbye and *Bon courage* to Nick. It's Yasmeen.

She too has something to say about Nick. In her smoky French accent she says that she is sad they didn't have time to get to know each other better, that although she was leaving as he was arriving she was touched by his story and his courage. Apparently he helped her. She looks at him with those emerald eyes and wishes him luck in his future, returning to his family, his wife Anna – she searches the faces for Anna's – sees it, smiles to her. Then she sees me, and she says how lucky he is to have such a sister in-law – and then she sees you.

She stumbles over the next few words, embraces Nick and leaves the room.

After the final applaud, someone announces that there's coffee and biscuits offered in the lounge. Anna mumbles something and goes to Nick's side. The party breaks up. The room empties but for us.

Alone in the room, you are still in your seat, rigid, staring at the space where Yasmeen stood. In the last week, you haven't reacted to anything, but this time, it's your turn to be stunned by a ghost.

'I met her when I brought Nick here.'

'She's like Nick, a junkie?'

'Well, she had a lot of problems...but she's putting the past behind her. I heard Yasmeen's story. In fact I've been to your "safe place" in Hounslow – yes, Marc, I've met Sam. I read your notes – the one the social workers collected on you. It's not everything, I'm sure, but...hey, I've even spoken to the next girl. The one in San Francisco who thinks you're flying in from a training course in New York tomorrow. I get the feeling this week isn't turning out quite how you planned, is it?'

I'm just about to leave when Yasmeen pushes past me into the room. She stands in front of you, smirking.

'Just don't forget your promise. This time, you do it right.'

Her eyes are fixed and intense on your face. She looks at me and walks away.

thursday morning

There was only the dregs of night left after we'd returned from Oxford, not that we would have slept much anyway. Now, as the sky tips towards morning, draining out the colour, we lie on the bed, neither of us having bothered to undress properly. Like that first morning you came back, a week ago, we do not speak. Anything said would brutalise the first layer of membranes sealing us together. Even the slightest touch is too tender. And now the cold splash of reality. Our last day.

Chantal and Gerry are having a pre-breakfast row upstairs. My sister is waking with Nick, the first morning of their newly-minted lives and in a week or so, Anna will have her fourth baby. Later today, I'll have to say yes or no to the offer of my new post at another hospital. And you are waiting to hear if we will begin living our lives together again.

You stop the alarm before it goes off. You hook me in the crux of your arm, draw my head to your lips and kiss the top of it. I could wake up every morning like this. With you.

'Coffee!' you say, as if you've discovered the solution to everlasting life, or at least to us. You jump out of bed – then fall back theatrically. The little show makes me laugh because the tension is just so high we'd do anything not to plug into it. And you're trying to make this easy for me. It's not like you haven't been here before, but I'm just a novice.

I'm thinking of Anna and Nick. We were at their house last night when he returned home. The kids chanted their daddy's name, attacked his bag in search of presents while Anna made hot chocolate for them and kept repeating that daddy was back. But none of them knew who he was anymore or what family he was returning to. For now they are slowly beginning to remove the bandages, pulling out the stitches, assessing what there is to work with.

I roll up your sleeve to look at my name on your arm. Nothing can take me back to that night, you in that tiny hospital bed, showing me the tattoo you'd had done, signing me over as the architect of your future.

'I learnt more about you when you were away than when we were married. That's not the right way around, Marc. But I now understand why you left me. It was all you'd known.'

'I want to change.'

'I know. But maybe, one shouldn't start at the end –'

'It's not the end, it doesn't have to be...' You speak into my hair.

'What happened to that coffee?'

When we'd left the treatment centre, the first port of call was my parents' home to collect the children. Anna got out of the car first, then Nick. I followed. When my mother saw the fourth person in the back of the car, she said, 'Kate, not him. Not him. I don't want him in our house.'

You didn't need to hear her, you appreciated the sentiment. You sat until we returned.

My mother showed remarkable restraint not asking about you as she bundled up the children's things and tried not to stare at Nick who was smoking in the garden, flicking ash over the rose buds. Daddy wasn't there, apparently he 'needed to finish something off in the lab'. My dad will take a long while to absorb the information about Nick, let alone your return.

But then as we loaded up the car and arranged the sleepy children wrapped in their pyjamas, my mother rushed from the house up to the car window where you sat.

She banged on the window and shouted, 'How could you do this! How could you do this to my girl?'

You stared back at her. She opened the car door and looked at you.

'First you leave her – leave her without a word – then you come back! You are selfish! Selfish and cruel. Don't ever think you can come to our house again – never! And I speak for my husband. Never! You are...scum!'

She slammed the car door shut in your face and ran back into the house.

Anna held the cowering children as Nick and I stood opened mouthed. None of us had even heard my mother raise her voice before.

Nick helped Anna back into the car, propped Bruno on her knees, shoved another children beside her and shoe-horned himself in. He pulled the back door closed. I jumped in, turned the ignition key as the headlights lit up the camellia that'd been planted the day I was born. You moved to the front passenger seat with Ellie sitting on your lap. I started to reverse, relieved that I could avoid looking at you. I kissed the top of Ellie's head as she looked out the window then back at you.

'Scum', she repeated against the window, an oval of steam against the glass. 'Scum.'

I rest the side of my face against your back, my arms around you as you pour the coffee. I can hear your heart, deep inside you; your good heart, breaking against mine.

'I need the morning free, sort things out.'

'Sure.'

You escaped on boats, airplanes and strangers' cars, and today I revert to my default settings, 'sorting things out'.

'Where will you be this afternoon?'

'At Sam's. I said I'd look after Hervé this afternoon, she's got something.'

It's the first time you speak these names out loud. And look, it wasn't difficult?

'I'll come find you there then, eh?'

'Yes, if that's what you want.'

When I return from the bathroom, you are dressed and about to leave. I kiss your cheek, one side, and then other.

'Bye.'

'A tout à l'heure.'

You hold my hand. It's a grip that sometimes I give to patients, an earnest "I'll take care of everything" clasp. We can never promise that to anyone, but doesn't it feel good to try?

Moving around the empty flat after you'd left, I shift things from one place to another, wipe surfaces, empty the bin. I'm not changing anything, I'm not making a difference - with all the expectation that'd been built around this seventh day, I would have thought I'd have something to do apart from plumping up cushions and brushing my teeth.

I open all the windows. The sun has broken out of winter and is charging over London. Everything's in colour. The tops of the roofs steam, birds swoop by busy on missions, music plays from inside cars. It's all going on regardless, and I didn't know it'd be beautiful today.

I have a shower, enjoy how easy and freeing it is to dry my hair now it's short, a few rubs and done. I scan the line of beauty products on the window shelf. These are my things, and they will be here, when maybe you will not.

You preside over all my thoughts, waiting to find out what you will do with your forever. Meanwhile, I'm going out to cash in on the beautiful day, maybe buy a *Grazia* magazine which I haven't done for years, take a little walk, separate the night from the day.

It's bright, clear enough to see the studs on the branches where new leaves will sprout. People appear from cracks and crevices, without hats and scarves but colourful jumpers and surprised buoyancy. They are sitting outside cafes in sunglasses, chatting and laughing loudly, looking around for more people to join them, trying to reassure themselves that it's not completely insane to be sitting outside at the beginning of March - because, in truth, it's freezing out there.

You said once that this is when you mark the New Year, in Spring, when the cycle of nature re-sets its clock; not in January, dead of winter, when half the living world disappears in hibernation.

With a few groceries and the magazine which I'll probably never have time to read, I return to the building. There's an open van outside and two removal men lifting Tom's sofa into it.

I move fast to his flat where a young emaciated woman is standing in his living room with a clip board talking on three telephones at once.

'Where's Tom?'

'Um. Uh. Um...'

She puts up a hand to me to stop me talking as she takes instructions from someone on the phone: 'Okay. Thanks. Ciao.'

She turns off one of her phones, looks at me and remembers hearing something about having to give people older than you respect – or at least an answer.

'Where's Tom?'

'New York.'

'Where are you taking his stuff?'

'New York.'

'New York? For good?'

'Yes.'

She decides to decorate her answers with more than two words, said clearly for the hard of hearing and slow in understanding – just another really annoying thing she has to do as part of her job.

'Tom's moving to New York. This is going on the market.'

'I saw him a few days ago, he didn't say anything.'

She shrugs her shoulders. One of her phones starts ringing.

Tom's flat is heartless without his television on, his boyish smile and constant chatter. I miss him. I regret the way everything turned out between us, that I could have been so naive as to think just taking from someone could be simple.

I'll write Tom an email in the next few days. Obviously I need to know if he's also going to sell my flat, but more than that, it's important to say good bye.

I walk up the stairs and into the home we bought together, although probably not that much is left of the original flat we first saw. When the insurance money covered the flood damage, I bought new furniture, put in new little halogen lights and replaced the old Victorian sash windows – even the outlook is different – and it's not even our home any more. Yet we say people never change.

My intercom buzzes.

I let whoever it is in, assuming it's part of Tom's removal party.

I'm looking into my fridge, about to take out some cheese when I see Frances standing in front of me in the kitchen.

'You knew!'

She has an expression on her face I've never seen before: fury.

'You, you knew all along!'

'Knew what?'

'Bloody everything is bloody what!'

'Frances – I –'

'No. No! I've just been speaking with Michael Simmons. Michael Simmons – a private detective. We get together every once in a while to talk about cases. Your name came up and he said he'd worked for you. In 2004! You asked him to investigate Marc, the man you were engaged to. And he gave you this!'

She throws a large manila package on the table. The table wobbles, my magazine slips off the side.

I know what's in the material.

Yes, I knew.

'I wasn't going to marry a man I knew nothing about.'

'No. No, you wouldn't. Always two steps ahead of everybody else, aren't you?'

'Hardly!'

'You can stop playing the innocent with me.'

'I'm not playing anything.'

'No? No. For the last year I've been traipsing around chasing a phantom for you, and all the while, you were aware of his identity – aware about his mother, the baby he left in the hospital, the newspaper clipping about him is in there. Mr Simmons – Michael to you – told you everything and yet you married him anyway. Married him - knowing all that – knowing he was probably going to do the same – knowing there was a child growing up somewhere with no idea where his dad was – and you – you knew!'

'Frances. I came to you to find my husband when he left. It was you who approached me to find out about him. Okay, I could have given you that information but...you turned up other things...'

'Oh I don't think so – Michael Simmons was in fact more thorough – I should give you a refund. You could have used him again but no, no! You...you...took pleasure – relished – making a complete fool out of me! I've been wasting your time and you – Doctor - have seriously been wasting mine!'

She breaks from my stare and looks at the envelope again.

'You are made for each other.'

I hear her bumping down the stairs, the calls for the removal men to 'look out love!' and feel the sweep of the front door as she slams it shut.

Birds tweet, kids shout across the road, buses hoot, it all sounds clearer through a cloudless sky.

Yes, I knew it all. And the night before you left, I told you, I knew it all.

Like I said to Frances, I wasn't going to marry a man who claimed to have no past. You must have come from somewhere. Michael Simmons had been a friend of Dave's from University, he'd gone to prison in his third year for some internet fraud scam – quite a scandal at the time - and a few years after, I'd heard through the grapevine that he'd set himself as security expert. It wasn't hard to trace him and ask him to do a background check on my fiancé.

We'd met in a hotel inside Victoria Station and he passed on what he'd found out about you. I had our wedding invitations in my bag, ready from the printers. My mother was coming up the following day to help me pick a wedding dress. You and I had signed the papers that morning for the flat we were going to buy and live in after we married.

After we'd married.

When Michael left I ordered a double brandy at the grimy hotel bar.

I looked through the folder he'd given me.

I never wanted to make a fool of Frances. But when I first read about you, I was shocked, and there's something about a shock that makes you want to re-live it over and over again. Every time she uncovered details about you, it brought me back to that tobacco smelling, dimly-lit hotel lounge and the time I saw the man I was to marry for who he really was.

He'd been thorough, as Frances said, it was all there. Your birth certificate: Father Unknown, your mother's arrests, hospitalisation for depression, drugs, overdoses and finally her death. Your childhood spent in care, itinerant work spells and finally, your reason for being at the hospital the day we met. A son.

I finished my drink. Leaving Victoria Station I dropped the dossier in a bin. It was then I made my decision.

After making a few phone calls to the hospital, it's time.

I know where to find you.

The first time I'd seen the house in Hounslow it had seemed so grotty, banal and nothing to do with you. But I know this late morning, it's everything to do with you. This is where you have a home. This is where your son lives.

Walking up to the front door, I hear shouts and laughter. A family are in the garden playing football and by the sounds of Sam's cries, I guess she's in goal.

I ring the doorbell, stand outside, asking myself, will they let me in?

Sam comes to the door after the second ring, she stands in front of me, red and laughing.

'Katherine,' she says, catching her breath. 'Sorry, we were...nice day, innit?'

She stands to the side and gestures for me to pass. They were expecting me.

Through the kitchen slide-doors, I see you lying on top of Harvey, grappling for the ball. He has your laugh. You are curled around each other. When you look up to see me, you stop tussling, let him go. You jump up and walk over to me. I speak first.

'He has your eyes.'

'He has a better strike,' you say.

Harvey runs over, looks up at us.

'I met you before!'

You take my hand and kiss it.

'This is my wife.'

'Wife? I didn't know you had a wife!'

You squeeze my hand, the doctor-knows-best grip.

'I do. Katherine, this is Hervé, or Harvey.'

The boy laughs, 'Herrrrrvé!'

You laugh with him.

Sam jogs up with a little girl in her arms, knocks the ball out of Harvey's hand, he chases after her. You shake your head at them and lead me into the kitchen.

'Tea or...there's beer.'

'Beer sounds good.'

I follow you to the kitchen. You don't hesitate over where to find the glasses or the bottle opener, and I realise this is the first time I have ever been invited over to your place.

We stand opposite each other, you with one hand in your pocket, the other holding the bottle of beer up to your chest.

'So this is what you tried so hard to keep from me?'

'I'm not ashamed of Harvey, Yasmeen or Sam or anyone...just myself. I wanted to protect you from the big mess I made of their love, and most of all, your love. I don't think I've succeeded to impress you much this week. I dreamed I would show you how much I love you and need to be with you, I missed you every day I was away and then when I saw what I'd done to you...I wondered if I'd just made you suffer more, been just as selfish. I thought being away I'd learnt a lot, but then, maybe nothing.'

'I learnt this week that love is all about mess.'

'Yes, me too. But this time I want to stay in it, be the man to deserve it, to make you happier than we've ever been – together. If you want that too...'

'I do want that too. It's what I always wanted.'

Before I touch you, I have to ask, 'Marc, the woman in San Francisco...'

'She's a friend, I promise. There's been no one else but you. No other woman. You are my wife.'

We put our beers down and hold each other so tightly.

And you are back.

We break apart when Yasmeen walks through the door carrying a tray of food.

'Allez tout le monde – sorry I'm late ! Come on, *à table ! Hervé !* Hi Sam.'

Sam and Harvey run through the living room to help her with the food she's carrying. They go through together into the garden. Another little boy a few years younger than Harvey waddles out.

'Brownies!' shouts Harvey and the boy jumping up to see them. Yasmeen slaps his hand down, says something fast in French. Disgruntled, he pulls up a chair.

Sam shouts over to us, 'Marc, don't forget the salad dressing!'

'It's coming!' you call out as you start pulling bottles out of cupboards.

'Because of you I forgot all about the *vinaigrette!*' you say to me. 'You go on *cherie,* I won't be a minute.'

I walk back into the garden while Yasmeen is loading food onto the children's plates.

'Katherine,' she says, kissing both my cheeks. 'Marc said you were coming here today. I'm really happy to see you. I'm sorry for yesterday. I was a bitch to you both but it was a shock, *hein?*'

'I can imagine. Sorry – I should have warned you, but I didn't know you'd be there.'

'Excuse me, who's the winner of hide and seek?' Harvey asks me while loading some quiche into his mouth.

'I don't know, who's the winner of hide and seek?'

'The skeleton in the cupboard!'

Yasmeen and I laugh. She starts filling up my plate.

'Did Nick get back alright?'

'Yes, it was a bit rocky with my parents but he seemed pleased to get home.'

She shakes her hands in the air, her bracelets rattle and she has an endearing giggle, 'All these skeletons! But I liked him, and your sister too. We plan to have lunch when I get back. I leave for Paris tonight, Fashion Week's coming up and I have a show to prepare. I just came to say goodbye to Hervé.'

The toddler asks Sam for more juice, she takes her cup to refill it. It's just Yasmeen, the kids and I around the table. She kisses the crown of Harvey's head.

'He's a really lovely boy. I bet you're very proud of him.'

'I am, really proud. I've done nothing else to be pleased with in my life...but him. He's very happy here – and he loves Marc. It's a little crazy, these *familles recomposés* but...it's modern life, eh?'

'Marc and I...I think we're going to try and patch things up.'

I don't think she understands the expression but she knows what I'm saying. I add, 'You probably think I'm really stupid but...'

'I think you're brave – and to be brave, you have to be a little stupid. Hervé? *Attends!* Katherine...' She drops her head, breathes in and says, 'It's probably not important but...I wanted to confess something. I lied to you when I said that when I saw Marc again, three years ago, we...had...'- she lowers her voice – 'sex... It wasn't true. It wasn't like that. We had a dramatic moment – after all those years – as you can imagine - but, in the end, he made me a promise. He said he would accept Hervé, share him with me and be a father. We brought Hervé here and for some time he visited and did things with him, and then he disappeared again. That's why I was so angry with him and I directed it at you. It was unfair. And I'm sorry.'

I look back at the house, the home where you found refuge all those years ago.

'I really do understand. I'm not proud of things I've done either...I just want you to know, I will do everything I can to make sure Harvey has a good father and...stepmother.'

'I know you will. And when Hervé is with me in Paris, you must both come and visit.'

That's the promise you made to Yasmeen, to take her child, your child, and give her back the life she'd not been able to have while she was looking after him alone and juggling her hectic career. This is where you started working out your repentance – and that night before you left, it was I who threatened to tear down the amends you were trying to make.

The night before you left. That dinner party. We were tired from work, we wanted more than anything to be alone in front of the TV and I made us go out. I didn't have time for your protests, I didn't really listen to you when you said you wanted us to be together that night, that you had something to tell me. I thought if it was important, it could wait.

And Anthony was there. I saw you watching us while we talked of hospitals and his connection with my father, and I could tell you didn't like it. Seeing you a little jealous was touching, but what you saw was that your wife chose this sort of night, rather than being with you. Of course, you'd only just been with Yasmeen, met your son, made a home for him with Sam who was the only person who knew about your childhood and your secrets, that night you must have despaired ever reconciling those two worlds.

Later in the taxi home, you said something you knew would hurt. You said that that man, Anthony, was the sort of man I should have married. And when I couldn't contradict you, it must have wounded you even deeper.

I sit in the garden with Sam, her children and Yasmeen as Harvey talks about the football game we're going to play later now we almost have a full team. Sam ladles out the salad.

'Marc! Get a move on with that dressing!'

There's no answer from the kitchen. She calls again, 'Marc!'

We look to each other.

'Marc?'

'Ma-aarc?' calls out Harvey.

Sam gets up and goes into the house. A cloud passes over the sun.

Yasmeen and I put our knives and forks down. The little girl starts to cry. Sam comes out again.

'He's gone.'

The night before you left, I knew ours was a holiday romance, and we were dying, we were terminal, Marc. I married you because I wanted to pretend to myself that we could make it, but we couldn't have done. Not as I was then. Before you left, we were already moving apart, expanding into the void, put simply, our marriage was decomposing. You were suffering in front of me, but I overlooked the most obvious symptoms.

And it was then I said you could never be a father, a husband. I said that you were just like your mother, incapable of responsibility. I saw the shock in your eyes, realising that I had always known about you and I said, yes, I should have married someone like

Anthony, and had a home like Gina's and a husband like Sally's Paul. I told you that I had made a mistake marrying you and that I should never have gone through with it after I learnt what you really were.

Once again, you've slipped out of our lives. It's what you've done before, why would you do otherwise? But what you said fifteen minutes before is still loud in my head.

Yasmeen lights a cigarette. Sam holds Harvey tight against her. Neither woman can face looking at me.

The food's getting cold. Untouched.

I have to look at me, now, instead of always looking at you, and I see someone who's been weak and stupid and arrogant. It's often the case that a doctor can try everything in their power to help someone get better, but it's just not enough, the miracle doesn't happen and we just have to let go. I thought I could love you better but I was wrong.

The front door slams.

The kitchen door slides open and you appear, carrying a bottle and a handful of spare change.

'You were out of white wine vinegar. What?...What?' you ask taking a seat next to me. 'Katherine – you thought I'd gone?'

Do you remember the time when I let you watch me operate on someone's heart? I'd seen you in your kitchen working, and you came to watch me do what I do. Half way through, one of the juniors had to lead you out of theatre. It wasn't like when I watched you make *Cabonnades Flamande*, it made you sick and faint, it does that to most people. When I came out to find you having a cigarette outside the hospital, white and tremulous, I apologised for exposing you to something so bloody, so violent and terrifying. It's probably best when we don't know what goes on inside. You looked at me and you said, it wasn't the blood, Katherine, it was the smell. People really stink.

I'd forgotten to warn you that. Bodies cut open, they stink.

You gave me a choice. Seven days ago you returned. You entered my home, a stranger with his own door key. You came into my bed and gave me a week.

Yasmeen fills our glasses with wine and raises hers.

'*Santé!*'

We chink our glasses and drink to 'health'.

Today, a week after you've returned, we have to turn away, continue to live with whatever diagnosis we have. We have to close it all up, keep going, for the sake of our recovery, for the sake of the stench.

From the author:

Seven Days to Tell You in fact took me seven years to tell you, writing late into the night after work and early morning before the school run. I'd like to thank everyone who encouraged me, above all Deborah Paxford, Alex Adamson, Cecilia Garcia-Peñalosa, Pamela Screve, Jamie and Tanya Ivey, the MA Creative Writing class of 2010 at Manchester Metropolitan University and my tutor Paul Magrs; the Arvon Foundation and Sarah Hall for an unforgettable week in August 2005. Thanks to my editor, Yvonne Barlow of Bookline and Thinker, who brought this book to life and to all the reading groups who participated in the Hookline Novel Competition. Finally, Jon Bryant, my harshest critic, best friend and still the funniest man I've ever met. Never forgetting my children, Bluebell and Edison, whose constant interruption while writing this has always been worthwhile.

Ruby Soames was born in London – too late for the sixties, too early for the punk era. She studied Literature and Theology at Bristol University before teaching English in secondary schools.
Ruby now lives in the South of France with her two children, journalist husband and a non-allergic dog, Elvis.
She lectures on Comparative Education at the Institute for American Universities in Aix-en-Provence. This is her first novel.

For more information about the author, please visit:
www.rubysoames.com

Lightning Source UK Ltd.
Milton Keynes UK
UKOW03f1923111013

218944UK00016B/810/P